Praise for
Letter Perfect, by N.H. Avenue

"A good, suspenseful cop story…the type of book that you find yourself half way through before you put it down for the night."

—*Desert Outlook*

"Distinctive."

—*The Queens Courier*

FOR PETE'S SAKE

FOR PETE'S SAKE

N.H. Avenue

iUniverse, Inc.
New York Lincoln Shanghai

For Pete's Sake

iUniverse, Inc.

For information address:
iUniverse, Inc.
2021 Pine Lake Road, Suite 100
Lincoln, NE 68512
www.iuniverse.com

ISBN: 0-595-30665-9

Printed in the United States of America

Dedicated to the thousands taken from us
September 11, 2001

To my grandmother, Ruth,
who left us shortly thereafter

And to my son Matthew,
born a few months later,
who helped me recapture my sense of wonder

Acknowledgements

The author wishes to thank the people who helped, in their own way, to make this project possible: My dearest Lisa, for just about everything; Joan, Claire, Gabriela, Merry and Danni, for creative insight; Sue Grafton, for being brutally honest; Jeremy Quince, for fuzz therapy; David Abolafia, for letting me borrow a character or two; Dorothy York and North American Precis Syndicate; George Steinbrenner, for keeping things interesting; my monthly poker game; and for inspiration, in no particular order, Brad and Debbie Firestone, Tim Dacosta, Joe Kohut, Sandy Levine, Isaac Kumer, Peter Haley, Peter Manekas, Robert Phillips, Michael Boruch, Eagle Glazer, Shannon Bender, Hope Adler, Andrea Almonacid, Kathleen Carey, Randy Greenspan and Tom Kelly.

PROLOGUE

▼

"Have you ever seen *The Shawshank Redemption*?" Wacky Jacky asked near the end of our session.

"No," I said off-handedly, "men's prison flicks aren't my thing."

John Sandusky looked at me, and I at him, and for a brief instant he ceased being a police psychologist and I was no longer the crackpot du jour. We shared a smile and a bit of a laugh, like two old friends revisiting a private joke—the first light-hearted moment either one of us had experienced in more than a month.

It was a bad time for New York. Anthrax was in the air and in the mail, our armed forces were bombing the hell out of some cavernous crag of a country in southwestern Asia, the Yankees had just lost the World Series and everywhere you looked there were ominous reminders of the events of September 11—and the spirit of the city that had collapsed along with the World Trade Center.

The first few weeks after the attacks, the police and fire departments did everything humanly possible—occasionally reaching super-human capacity—to pull hope from the wreckage at Ground Zero. "New York's Finest" and "New York's Bravest" were no longer nicknames, but badges of honor we did our damnedest to live up to. Too many of us died trying. An even dozen, as far as I could figure, from the personal Rolodex in my mind. Three cops, eight firefighters and a family friend who worked at Cantor Fitzgerald.

In those first few weeks, I did everything I could think of—for the most part, it was the uniformed officers who were in charge of keeping the peace, at Ground Zero and around the city—from fielding phone calls and compiling lists of the dead to pitching in at Yankee and Shea Stadiums, sorting supplies and packing them together for the crews who worked their way through the rubble. We handled food, personal hygiene products, pain relievers, tissues—even booties for the body-sniffing dogs. It was all part of an outpouring of kindness from businesses and individuals, a case where the result was truly greater than the sum of its parts.

"The reason I asked about the movie," Wacky Jacky added, "was that it contains some useful advice that I think applies to you, Amanda. Sometime near the end of the flick, Morgan Freeman has to make a decision. He has to decide whether he's going to honor a promise he made years earlier, and head down a path that could change his life forever. Or he could do nothing and spend the rest of his days in the squalor of a halfway house."

"I'm not sure how that applies," I said.

"Just before he leaves his bare little room and gets on a bus for parts unknown, he says to himself, 'Get busy living, or get busy dying.'"

And that was it. Much easier said than done, of course, but it was a quick recap of the mental state I found myself in, the professional impotence which left me unable to do my job. I had had sessions with Wacky Jacky before, to contend with a panic attack and other emotional issues, but this was different. Something inside of me had died along with the thousands who'd perished two months earlier, that little part of my being which kept me keeping on, which made me give a damn about anything. Juxtaposed with the horrors I'd seen, first-hand and replayed continuously on TV for days afterward, could anything else even begin to matter?

I knew then it would take more than an overworked police shrink to pull me from my funk, to free me from the shackles of malaise. Little did I realize that I would find my salvation in the eyes of a 7-year-old boy.

CHAPTER 1

▼

Strangely, the whole thing started with a different kind of explosion, one that hit much closer to home. The apartment next door, in fact.

Prior to my being blown up, my 30th birthday had started about as well as could be expected. A November rain pitter-pattered against my window, a soft drumroll that underscored the despair that enveloped the metropolis. The annual appearance of cardboard and crepe-paper turkeys—not to mention early Christmas decorations—always makes me feel like damaged goods, no closer to finding that someone special, yet closer still to becoming worm food.

I was in the middle of making an Everything Omelet, one of my mother's tricks for stretching the scraps taking up room in the fridge, when the phone rang. Given that it was just before 7 a.m., there was only one person it could be.

"Yeeesss?" I cackled, picking up the kitchen extension. "Who eez, please?"

"Please, Amanda, I've never even been to Eastern Europe. You sound like I had a torrid affair with Bela Lugosi."

"Does Dad know?"

"It'd only be fair. I think he's screwing Melody Rapp, anyhow."

Some people might be aghast at the notion of one of their parents having an affair. Others might be disturbed by the casualness of the accusation. For me, it was just another conversation with my mother. Sex was never a taboo in our house when I was growing up; my folks didn't try to hide their lovemaking from their only child. Instead, it was always an open topic of discussion—"Better to learn about it now," my father would say, "than try to muddle through when there's someone else in the room." When I came out, it was their openness, their willingness to accept me as I was, that helped guide me through the rough patches. In fact, I think they took that news easier than when I said I'd enrolled in the police academy.

"Dare I ask who Melody Rapp is?" In the background, I could hear my father make an out-of-breath comment as he huffed and puffed on the treadmill.

"She's a plastic surgery victim who moved into 4A. We met her at the Harris' New Year's party."

Compared to the soap opera in my mother's mind, my omelet suddenly seemed a lot less tantalizing. "You've inhaled too many bread fumes, Mom. Dad's not that subtle."

"It's not him, it's her. I think those botox injections are turning her into Lady Chatterly or something."

"Really?"

"It's written all over her squeegeed face."

I slid my eggs out of the pan and onto a plate, shuttling it to the table before grabbing the orange juice from the fridge. All the kitchen maneuvers left me tangled in the long phone cord, and I needed to limbo out to keep from strangling myself. "Is that why you called, Mom, to fill me in on Dad's extramarital affairs?"

"I am _not_ sleeping with Melody Rapp," he hissed, his voice crackling over their speaker phone. "Besides, she's probably a lousy lay. That's why her husband left her."

Sometimes talking with my parents was like playing arbiter between Dr. Ruth and Dr. Drew. "Can we get on with this? My eggs are getting cold."

"Do you believe this, Cal? Our daughter turns 30 and she starts getting snippy."

Snippy, she says. Day hasn't even begun to break and the sarcasm's already in full swing.

"Er, Mom…"

"All right, all right." If the song that followed wasn't the most out-of-key rendition of "Happy Birthday" ever performed, it could at least have shared space on the trophy shelf. My father's failure to stop training for the imminent New York City marathon didn't help matters, taking his wheezy baritone to dog-whistle pitch during the final line. If you ever meet my parents, by all means have my mother bake something. Ask my father to listen to your heart. And if God's in a good mood, you won't have to hear them sing. Ever. I had pretty much gotten used to the celebrational cacophony, but I'm sure that it drives the neighborhood cats into a mating frenzy.

"You two been practicing?" I asked once the last note had been butchered.

"There it is again, Cal. Snippy. You might want to leave that attitude at home, young lady. Criminals are already in a bad mood. They don't need some snippy police detective to come along and tell them what's what."

I would have kept up the snappy repartee, but my eggs were rapidly becoming inedible. The pastry chef on the other end of the line would understand. "Sure thing, Mom. Bye, Dad. Tell Mrs. Rapp I said hello."

"That's <u>not</u> funny."

"Life is a souffle, Mom. Lighten up."

It was advice I could have used myself; I still wasn't sure if I'd ever be able to make it back to the precinct. Even before September 11, I'd been seeing Wacky Jacky, trying to sort through the rummage sale in my head and heart, chaos that had led to, and been punctuated by, a panic attack. I don't claim to know how the thousands who worked in Towers One and Two felt when the passenger planes tore through, but I suspect those moments of personal terror came close. Back then, after nearly botching an investigation by letting my feelings get the best of me, I'd been given a temporary suspension by my lieutenant, during which time I'd practically taken up residence in Wacky Jacky's office. Even then, it still wasn't easy getting back on the job. My partner's new relationship was blossoming while I was still cooking dinner for one. It's not as though I'm not happy for Randy and Diane, but I could feel my eyes turning green.

Having finally gotten my parents off the phone, I made a quick dash to retrieve the newspaper before sitting down to my morning repast. I opened the apartment door just in time to see my neighbor, Charlotte Kilmer, sending her 7-year-old son Pete down the hall to the elevators, presumably to school.

"Morning," she said, her voice a mixture of worry and relief.

"Morning. Pete seems to have grown every time I see him."

"He's at that age now, where he's asserting his independence. He doesn't want me to walk him to school anymore. Only little kids need their mommies to go with them."

"That's sweet," I said.

"May be," she replied, turning toward the sound of a microwave beeping in her apartment, "but they're the last words a mommy wants to hear."

She was gone before I could come up with a response. Good thing, too, since I'm still not sure where kids belong in the overstuffed case file of Amanda Ross. I went back to join my eggs at the dining room table, dawdling with the newspaper. At one point, I thought I heard something in the hall and looked over toward the door, but there was no knock, no doorbell, no conversation, so I let it go. As it was, I quickly realized that the Monday paper is a paltry excuse for a periodical; I was washing the newsprint smudges from my hands by 9 a.m.

I had nothing planned for the day, surprise, surprise, so the hours until I had to be at New York Institute of Technology that evening loomed large. Work was out—I wasn't ready to be a cop again—leaving me with large, gaping holes in my schedule (not to mention my state of mind). It wasn't as if I was a tourist who could spend all day long oohing and aahing at the architecture. Then again, I'd never done it before...

Twenty minutes later I was showered and dressed in a complete outsider ensemble: jeans, sneakers, Yankees cap and an "I Love NY" sweatshirt I rescued from the bottom of a drawer. I considered bringing a camera, but didn't expect much of a view from any observation deck. Besides, playing tourist in your home city is one thing; making a permanent record of such silliness is quite another. I considered checking out Madame Tussaud's, maybe the planetarium. In a more innocent time, lunch on top of the World Trade Center would have been the order of the day.

I got out the door just in time to catch Charlotte returning from a run. She was clad in soggy sweats, part physical exertion and part autumn misery. I admired her determination to stick to a workout regimen even when the weather was uncooperative. Made me feel like even more of a slug.

"Good run?" I asked.

"The rain stopped a little while ago, but I'm soaked to the bone," she said between pants. She was a decent-looking woman, a few years older and a few inches shorter than me, with black hair cropped close. Somewhat fuller across the bust and butt, too, but in reasonably good shape. "Let me reheat some coffee, then we'll talk."

"Sure," I said. Tourism could wait. With the hours I normally worked, it was difficult to get to know people. Charlotte and Pete had moved in about 18 months earlier, and we'd barely shared more than a casual "hello." The past few weeks, however, had given us a chance to get better acquainted. She was a reader for a literary agency, going over manuscripts at home and offering her opinions as to which held promise.

"How're you doing this morning?" she called over her shoulder, peeling off clothing as she made her way into her kitchen.

I edged inside, peeking around the corner to continue the conversation. Her apartment was at a right angle to mine, with a mirror-image layout. The entry-way was filled with drawings and paintings from a child's hand. "Dunno yet.

Father Time just dropped in, and I haven't figured out if he's a welcome house-guest."

"Today's your birthday?" she asked, poking her head back in. "Why didn't you say something? I would have cleared my schedule, and we could have done some girl stuff around the city."

"I was planning on a little sightseeing myself. Maybe step inside a few of those buildings I pass by every day."

I heard her give a knowing chuckle as she poured a cup of coffee, popped open the microwave and slammed the door shut. She pushed a button, the appliance beeping in response. And as soon the motor started, there was a deafening explosion. The shock of the blast threw me back into the doorframe, hard. My head made solid contact with wood. As I slumped down to the floor, I thought I saw blood wash over my eyes. Then everything went black.

C H A P T E R   2

▼

"Ngf?"

I was ripped back into the conscious world as quickly as I'd slipped out of it, the smelling salt awakening my senses. I opened my eyes, initially taking in a walleye view of the apartment before a man in a suit settled into my hazy field of vision.

"Can you hear me okay?"

Though I could make out what he was saying, there was a buzz behind each word, like a bad phone connection. "What's going on?" I asked. "Bomb squad? Fire department?"

"Whoa," he said, crouching down to my level. "Let's not get ahead of ourselves. You've had quite a shock and you better take it easy. What's your name?"

"Amanda Ross. I'm a detective with the 11th squad. I live next door."

"Good to know you, Amanda," he said, offering his hand. "Jason Perelli with the 20th." He was about my age, bald to the crown, his remaining brown hair swathing an eternal baby face. He was dressed in an off-the-rack, blue two-piece, with a white shirt and striped tie, but the gold-rimmed glasses made him look more accountant than cop. "You want to tell me what happened here?"

Charlotte.

"Where's Charlotte?" I asked, trying to stand, my voice straining desperately. "Is she okay?"

Perelli stood, and assisted in my effort to do so. I was a little woozy, but my legs held firm. "She never stood a chance. She couldn't have been more than a foot away when the thing went off."

Dear God.

"What about her son? Is he all right? Does he know?"

"We'll have an officer go over to his school, try and get in touch with the father."

There was an impressive lump on the back of my head, but all the residual maladies seemed to be going away. "Father's in the wind, far as I know."

"They'll have an emergency contact on file at the school. Meanwhile, you should probably go to the hospital and get yourself checked out. We can get a full statement later. No sense in your rushing back to work."

"She's on vacation, but by the looks of things, she's not very good at it." My partner appeared in the doorway and shook hands with Perelli. "Randy Ulrich with the one-one."

"Jason Perelli. I take it you know Detective Ross."

"I'm the partner she abandoned for her week of R&R. I recognized the address from the dispatch and hauled ass over here." As usual, Randy was covering *my* ass, slyly omitting the real reason for my being home in the middle of a Monday morning.

"You'll make sure she does the smart thing here?"

"I haven't been too successful at that in the past, but she doesn't look like she's in any shape to put up a fight."

Even pretending to put up a fight would have taken too much of an effort. As the adrenaline drained out of my system, my limbs turned to stone, the weight of the world making it difficult to move. My gaze was fixed on one of Pete's creations, a crayon drawing of a woman pushing a little boy on a swing. It was titled, "Mommy and Me."

This time what washed over my eyes were tears. Randy knew better than to say anything. He slowly walked me out of the apartment and downstairs, allowing me the company of my misery.

Outside, it was November in the worst way, an eviscerating wind ripping through me with each step toward our police sedan. Randy helped me into the passenger seat and belted me in. I'd faced my own death in the past, but now an explosion had turned me into a blubbering idiot. I barely heard Randy get into the car, hardly acknowledged the traffic as we crawled along toward the hospital. My hold on reality, something I'd been trying so hard to regain over the past few months, had just been blown to smithereens.

Like most institutes of higher medicine, Roosevelt Hospital has a dignified and detached air, as if all the scrubs-wearing personnel have somewhere else to be, someone else to see, some other life to save. Doctors and nurses and patients were passing every which way as Randy tried to sort out my paperwork. I gave him my insurance card and he filled in all the forms. In one regard, it was nice to be tended to, since this "vacation" was already off to a shitty start. In another, Randy's efforts merely pointed up my vulnerability and my knack for getting myself beat up. The bones may not have broken, but the spirit definitely needed a splint.

"You have any family history of kidney disease?" Randy asked as he flipped the form over.

"No."

"Liver disease?"

"No."

"High blood pressure?"

Given what I'd been through, mine was probably at astronomical levels, but I didn't inherit that from anyone. "No."

"I'm assuming you'd tell me if you *did* have a family history of something." Randy and I had been partners for nearly two years and our relationship had pretty much been drawn along specific lines. He was the people person and I was the loose cannon. He was in line for his gold detective shield, and he'd get it if I didn't mess it up for him. Two years younger than me, he's broad shouldered and fit, with brownish-gray hair and crystal blue eyes that hint of Caribbean waters. He handed in the forms and waited with me.

"I feel so bad for that little boy," I said. "What's going to happen to him?"

"If he's got some family, then they'll step up. No one's gonna abandon a kid like that under these circumstances. Even if he winds up in the system, the phone's gonna be ringing off the hook with people wanting to take him in."

For one crazy moment, I felt I could be one of them.

Who are you kidding? You can barely take care of yourself.

"Still," Randy continued, "he's going to be in for a lot of lonely hours 'til he understands what happened."

"Yeah."

Randy could see that I was still on edge. He shifted in the plastic chair until he could come up with a safer subject. "Speaking of lonely hours, did you hear Mitch Black is performing in town this weekend?"

That was a name I hadn't heard in a while. Mitch Black was a Grammy-winning singer-songwriter who had been all over the pop charts—his last single, "Lonely Hours," was a haunting ballad that hit number one. But then he disappeared, musically speaking. Not a note of new material had been produced for nearly five years. "Really?"

"Couple of shows at The Bottom Line. You know, benefits for the WTC Fund. Diane's dying to see him. You interested?"

Another time, another place, those words might have been music to my ears, pun possibly intended. But right there, in the emergency room, barely 90 minutes after feeling Charlotte die, Mitch Black's melancholy threatened to hit too close to home. "Pass."

"Tickets go on sale this afternoon, so if you change your mind..."

I shot him a tired look and killed another topic of conversation. At that point, a nurse called my name and escorted the two of us into the ER proper. She was a slip of a thing, barely five feet tall and 90 pounds at the most. She had long blonde hair and wore thick glasses, her head resting on a non-existent figure. The only parts of her that smacked of an X chromosome were her locks and her nametag—Kathleen. She took my vitals, including temperature (normal), pulse (slightly elevated) and blood pressure (ditto), then asked the always dangerous question, "Why are you here?"

Randy might have had a more delicate way of phrasing it, but I didn't see any point to that. "I got blown up."

It is said that emergency room personnel have seen and heard it all. From self-mutilation to murder attempts, from sex games gone horribly wrong to klutzes too stupid to live, there are no original injuries or ailments as far as they're concerned. But then, Kathleen might have been a rookie. Lord knows, she didn't look to be more than 12. "You what?"

"There was an explosion," Randy corrected, "and she was in the path of the shockwave."

"I hit my head," I added, suddenly feeling like a 12 year old myself.

"Show me." She had to climb up onto the examining table with me in order to get a decent vantage point. She looked, but thankfully didn't touch, then scrawled a few notes on my chart before sticking the dismount. "The doctor will be right with you, Ms. Ross."

"That's Detective Ross, actually," I said, trying to exact a modicum of authority, but Kathleen was already on her way to her next triage. I looked around the ER, which was crowded but not overly so.

Good to be a Monday morning wreck instead of a Saturday night special.

There were sounds of pain, with medical professionals speaking in placating tones. Across the way, a child cried and an old woman babbled incoherently to herself. The flimsy hospital curtains did very little to keep anyone's private life private. After a few minutes of listening to the masses, we were approached by someone who truly looked like he belonged there. He was tall and thin, with a shaggy fringe of white hair around a smooth pate. His eyes were sunken behind a hooked nose, and I immediately thought of Sam the Eagle from "The Muppet Show."

"Detective Ross, I'm Dr. Calamari."

"Dr. Calam—," I said, stifling a laugh. I could tell Randy thought it was funny, too, for he glanced around for somewhere to bury his face. "You're kidding, right?"

He fixed me with a sub-zero stare. "Do I look like I'm kidding?" Glancing down at my chart, he continued, "Any squid jokes you've got, I've heard them already, so keep them to yourself. Otherwise, I just may have to recant the Hippocratic Oath. Any questions?"

We shook our heads. "Good. You," he said, pointing at Randy. "Husband?"

"Friend and partner."

"Blow up one cop, get two off the street," he muttered disapprovingly. "Unless you want to know Detective Ross more intimately than you'd ever imagined, I suggest you take your leave."

From then on, I knew Squidman and I would get along fine.

CHAPTER 3

▼

"It's not your case, Amanda. Stay away from it."

That was Randy's parting shot before he left me in the capable tentacles of Dr. Calamari. Mere mention of Jason Perelli's name had put my partner on the defensive, another salvo in his ongoing attempt to keep me from crossing a line, from scratching in the wrong litter box, and killing my career in a single shot.

The good doctor took his time with me, asking me to describe the events that led to my presence in the ER. His commentary was brusque, officious—he could probably have used a refresher course in bedside manner—but he was knowledgeable and thorough. His main concern was the threat of a concussion, and for that he checked my pupils and made sure my eyes were tracking properly. He also had me squeeze his hand, touch my finger to my nose and cross my legs for a reflex test. He scribbled on my chart for a while, then draped his stethoscope around his neck. "After the explosion, did you lose consciousness?"

"I think so."

"Any bleeding?" He began probing the lump on the back of my head, gently pressing it and feeling the area around, which still felt raw.

"Not that I'm aware of."

"Effect on your eyesight?"

"Things were a little blurry at first, but it's fine now."

"Irritability?"

"No more than usual."

"Headache?"

"Before you started asking the questions…or after?" He hit me with another chilling glance; he didn't have the time or patience to deal with a smartass. "Yeah, I guess. Why? What's your concern?"

"Any idea what a subdural hematoma is?"

"No, but it sounds bad."

"Getting whacked on the head, as you have, can cause blood to collect in the space between the inner and outer membranes covering the brain. The blood then collects into a mass that presses on the brain, potentially damaging the tissue and leading to a loss of brain function. If it's an acute case, symptoms will appear within about 24 hours. Fortunately, you've got a pretty thick skull…and given that your sense of humor appears to be intact, you're probably safe. But I'd like to keep you overnight for observation, run a CT scan to make sure."

You wish. I'm already getting my head examined.

I started to slide down off the table. "I'm on vacation. No fun being sick when no one's gonna notice I'm not there."

He put his hand on my wrist. "This is the kind of thing that can lead to permanent brain damage, Amanda. Seizures, memory loss, bleeding on the brain. Not something you want to take lightly."

"If I have any problems, I'll come back. I'll be sure to ask for you."

"You won't necessarily make it back," he said, his voice free of sarcasm. Those words, coming just as I was finding my footing, nearly sent me reeling. I bumped into an EKG or some such device, giving the hospital's prophet of doom yet another tick on his scorecard. "Against medical advice" is the term they use for people who check out contrary to doctor's orders but, as usual, I was taking leave of good judgment and common sense as well. The doctor made a few more notes on my chart, realizing that it was pointless to try and keep me there. "I'll have the nurse get you an ice pack for your head. You have someone to look after you?"

I was about to make up a story about a maiden aunt who lived on the East Side when a familiar silhouette appeared on the other side of the curtain. "I'll take her home."

The doctor whisked the partition around on its track, revealing the figure of Andrew Devane, a crime beat reporter on one of New York's finer tabloids. He was dressed in a navy button-down shirt and charcoal slacks, with a heavy black windbreaker protecting him against the elements.

"You a relative?" asked Dr. Calamari.

"Dutch uncle," he said.

The doctor looked over at me, and I didn't object. "She's all yours. No aspirin, no alcohol, no caffeine for the next 24 hours. And if anything happens—and I mean *anything*—you get her back here immediately. Understand?"

Devane clicked his heels together, with a stiff-arm salute. "*Ja wöhl.*"

Calamari was not amused. "Sign here," he said to me.

And with that, I was a free woman. Sort of. Devane didn't say anything as we made our way out of the emergency room, out of the hospital, to the visitors parking lot. I just followed him to the silver Honda that served as his means of transport and mobile office, and got in the passenger side. In the days of New Age, touchy-feely talk, one might have said that Andy Devane and I have "issues." We dated for a while in college, right up until I came clean about my sexual orientation. Being honest with him meant being honest with myself, and unfortunately, he got caught in the crossfire. I came out of the closet on the same night he was about to take our relationship to "the next level," and it laid a corrupt foundation for whatever kind of friendship would follow.

"What are you doing here?" I asked.

"Hello to you, too," he replied, letting the engine idle.

"Skip the pleasantries. Am I a story all of a sudden?"

"You're always a story, Amanda. It's a question of whether that story's worth printing. In this case, I've got a single mother killed by her microwave and an off-duty cop wounded in the blast. That kind of thing sells papers, kid."

When I'm the lead investigator on a case, when I'm the primary source, I have some control of how much information Andy and his ilk are able to glom. Here, I was the innocent bystander.

No, Charlotte was the innocent bystander.

"You mind stopping by the 20th? Might as well give Perelli my statement now, get it over with."

"On my way."

I hadn't seen Andy in several months, and it looked as though writing about the worst parts of the human condition had decimated his spirit, and his body had no choice but to follow. He'd lost weight, his face gone from flush to gaunt. The hands with which he'd once held me dearly were callused and red, as if he'd tried to wring some great truth from the horrible misdeeds of others. Who knows how many ghosts he'd seen, or how many more he could bear to witness. I'd loved Andy Devane once, or something close to it, and somewhere on the way to forgiveness we'd both gotten lost. Which is probably why we keep running into each other, and why I continue to treat him like a tagalong kid brother.

"You going to tell me what happened, or am I going to have to read it from Perelli's report once you're gone?"

"I make a lousy witness, Andy. Charlotte came back from her run and went into the kitchen to nuke a cup of coffee. I was standing in the entryway. Boom. Charlotte's dead, I'm knocked cold, end of story. I come to and my fellow officers are already at hand."

"You see her die?"

"No, and I can't believe you'd—"

"Then how'd you know she was dead?"

The sonuvabitch was making me think, and that was making my head hurt; the ice pack wasn't helping. "Perelli told me."

"Not very good policework on his part, if you ask me," he said as he slowed in the vicinity of the 20th Precinct. "For all he knows, you could have planted the device, knowing its blast radius. Set yourself up as an accidental casualty. And he goes and tells you the bomb hit its target. Not only does that let you know you accomplished your objective, but it also takes away the element of surprise."

"But I'm a cop."

"He doesn't know that. You produce ID or anything when you woke up? Even if you did, you think your being a cop disqualifies you from being a suspect?"

Being questioned was frustrating in light of the morning's events, but his observation was spot on. Classic Devane. "You're right," I said, slumping in my seat. "I also don't have an alibi for the two hours leading up to the explosion."

"So? Bomb could have been planted two *months* before."

"No, that would've meant using a timer. No way of knowing for sure she'd be there when it went off. The blast came immediately after she fired up the microwave. Even a remote control couldn't guarantee results."

Andy pulled into a parking lot and took a ticket from the booth attendant. "What makes the preceding two hours important?"

"She used the microwave. At about 7:15, I was out in the hall, talking with her, and I heard it go off. Right after she sent Pete to school."

He glided into a space, threw the car into Park and reached around to retrieve a canvas briefcase from the back seat. "Attention to detail. You always had that, Amanda. You're a better witness than you think."

Somewhere deep inside, I still liked hearing him say my name. There was a wistfulness in his voice that belied the brashness with which he carried himself on the mean streets of the crime beat. Andy Devane had been my first and only "boyfriend," and as such will always hold a special place in this broken-down heart of mine.

"Thanks, Andy." I got out of the car and started to walk away, but I hesitated, slowly turning back to the vehicle. I rapped on the window, which slid open halfway. "Take care of yourself," I said.

"I'd offer you the same advice if I believed you'd take it." The window slid back up and he pulled away, leaving me in the precinct parking lot. It seemed odd to me that I'd never come by the 20th or gotten to know any of the cops who make up my neighborhood watch. Making my presence felt downtown, so that the residents might feel safer and more comfortable in approaching me, was part of my civic duty. But there was no reason the door shouldn't swing the other way with my brothers and sisters in arms.

If the 20th Precinct represented the modern police station, then my own house was something out of "The Flintstones." Every desk had a computer and, even more impressive, each officer appeared to be fluent in the high-tech hieroglyphics that always left me scratching my head. Still, the 11th was on the fast track for modernization, and that was exactly why I'd signed up for the computer course at NYIT.

A couple of patrolmen were huddled near the PAA's desk, and it wasn't until they broke up that the civilian aide noticed me standing there. She looked to be in her early 30s, with a bad complexion and blondish-gray hair sculpted around a pudgy face. She was not well-packaged in how she carried her weight, but she appeared competent, courteous and professional. "May I help you?"

"I'm here to see Jason Perelli."

"Regarding?"

"I need to give him a statement, about the explosion this morning."

"Oh, you must be Detective Ross," she said, her voice taking on a doting tone. "How are you doing?"

"Better than expected," interrupted Perelli as he approached us. "I didn't think you'd be able to make it by today."

"Might as well," I replied with a delicate shrug. "Nothing else to do but go home and be a victim."

"Can I get you anything?" the PAA asked. "Coffee?"

"I'd take a bullet for some, but my doctor's got other plans."

"All right, but if there's anything I can do, don't hesitate to ask. My name's Mimsy."

"Thanks," Perelli and I said in unison, before turning tail and strolling over to his desk. When we were out of earshot, I asked him. "Mimsy?"

"Believe it," he said, using his tie to clean off his glasses. "It's not short for anything, either. If you ask her, she'll talk your ear off, starting with 'Jabberwocky.'"

I remembered the poem from a long-ago English class, but didn't feel the need to get into a discussion with the precinct's den mother. "Some other time," I remarked, taking a seat facing him. "My recollection of this morning is a lot of Swiss cheese, so let me just tell you what I know, then you can try filling the holes."

He took out a steno pad and pen. "Shoot."

I went over the events as best I could, complete with the embroidery that Devane and I had come up with on the way over. Of course, I skipped Andy's comments about Perelli blowing the initial interrogation. I don't know whether it was an emotional disconnect or my brain's feeble attempt to process data it found hard to swallow, but none of the words seemed right, nothing I said coming close to describing what actually happened. Exclamation points attached themselves to trivial details, while important points dribbled out of my mouth without embellishment.

The lights are on, but the bulbs are dim.

"That's a good point about the two-hour window," Perelli said when I was done blabbering. "It certainly gives us a place to start, see if anyone saw someone hanging around this morning. You get a lot of traffic through your building?"

"It's not Penn Station, if that's what you mean. It's not that big a place, but it's got the usual…tenants, delivery people, utility guys…"

"I didn't see a doorman when we were there before. Are there any security cameras?"

"Not at the rent I'm paying."

After that, the conversation got away from police business, taking a tangent into the subject of Manhattan real estate, followed by talk about the neighborhood. It was the same kind of chitchat I might have made in my own precinct.

You have to walk the walk in order to talk the talk.

After a while, we wrapped things up and I promised to get back in touch if I thought of anything else. I declined Perelli's offer of a ride home, opting instead to see if my legs still worked—unlike most of the rest of me.

It was only a few blocks back to my apartment. I had an uneasy feeling in my gut, but I couldn't be sure if it was anxiety, sadness or hunger. I'd lost a friend and my home had been invaded by someone who'd set out to take her life. Suddenly my haven, the one place I'd been able to retreat to, was no longer safe. In just six hours I'd gone from the road to recovery to the most desolate stretch of highway in mind—and my birthday breakfast omelet seemed like it'd been six *days* earlier. My heart and soul were starving, but my stomach was making the noise.

I got off the elevator and trooped down the hall. There was a lone technician processing Charlotte's apartment, taking measurements and making notes behind a barrier of yellow tape. My door was open a crack. Had I left it open? I couldn't remember.

I slowly eased the door open and slid inside, keeping my body low, trying to prepare myself for any kind of confrontation. I hugged the wall, trying to get a sense of whether there was someone else in the apartment with me. It wasn't more than 30 seconds, but I knew I wasn't alone. I felt around for some kind of weapon; the only thing I could come up with was a fanny pack. I wrapped the strap around my wrist, ready to whip it in the face of...

"Hey, Betsy, how ya doin'?"

It's a good thing I hadn't been carrying my Glock when I left my apartment that morning. It would have been out of the holster and in my hand when I got my first glimpse of the intruder. Every tabloid in the nation would have wondered how Mitch Black, reclusive rock singer, had gotten into my apartment. And no one on earth would ever have known the real reason I'd shot him dead.

But I've *always* hated that nickname.

CHAPTER 4

— ▼ —

I hadn't seen him in almost ten years, not since he'd gone from playing small clubs in Colorado to platinum albums and sold-out tours. I'd bought his CDs, caught his talk-show appearances, but I'd never buried the image of an open guitar case littered with singles and change. Back then, while I was still trying to find myself in college, Mitch Black's music was comfort food, and I could be sure of a regular helping every Thursday night at The Iron Works.

"Hate to say it, Betsy," he said, surveying my sorry state, "but you look like shit."

"I just got out of the hospital," I snarked, "and you'll be heading there in an ambulance if you call me that again."

"You were in the hospital?"

Nicknames aside, Mitchell James Black had been a dear friend way back when. We'd spent long hours after his sets, talking about dreams and everything after. He was my living example of one of those fantasies that had crept its way into the real world. Yet even now, the worry in his voice was not just a pleasantry; his first live shows in five years were coming up and I was all he seemed to be concerned about.

"Yeah," I said, moving in for a hug. He's good at those.

"What happened?"

I invited him to sit with me on the futon and told the story again—the fourth time in four hours. He was still so easy to talk to, I might have seen him last Thursday, rather than a decade ago. "In short, I got blowed up real good."

He smiled—the sensitive smile that graced two million copies of his second album, *Get Real*. Of the six he'd recorded, that was the one where he'd let his guard down. It showed in the music, the lyrics and the album cover. "You haven't changed."

"A little worse for the wear, perhaps, but I'll survive. What about you, Mr. Rock-and-Roll Star? How's the good life treating you?"

"Can't complain," he said. I wasn't convinced, but I let it pass.

"Thought you might have hit a rough patch…resorted to breaking into people's homes. But next time, you might want to pick someone with stuff worth stealing."

"Always the pauper," he said, running his hand along the futon cover. It was definitely in need of some stitchery. "Good thing you know how to win a bar bet."

"How *did* you get in here? I didn't think I'd left the door open."

"I may not have recorded anything in five years, but this mug's still famous enough to cop a favor from a building super—especially one with a teenage daughter who's a fan."

He was right; he still looked the same—narrow face, goatee and a mane of light brown hair that ended around his shoulder blades. He was slender, a few years older than me, a tick under six feet tall. In my college days, he could have had his choice of coeds, but he never took advantage. I'd sometimes joked that I was pimping for him, bringing my dorm-mates down to hear him play, only to have them fall instantly in love with him.

What made Mitch different from other musicians I'd known—such as his drummer, J.T.—was that he never seemed to get caught up in the trappings of fame. Critics weren't always kind to him, but they never accused him of selling out or following a trend. He was a singer-songwriter, pure and simple, who made music because he didn't know how to live any other way.

Then why did he stop?

Mitch stretched, his back arching and his heels digging into the carpet. "God, it seems like forever since I was in New York, but it really wasn't that long ago. Sometime late last year, I think, when I was doing the cross-country thing."

"The cross-country thing? What does *that* mean? You've hit every nook and cranny in America, every place that's got a concert hall."

"Let me ask you something," he said, putting his hand on my shoulder. "Have you ever been up to the observation deck of the Empire State Building?"

"I was going to. Today, really I was," I replied, indicating my sweatshirt.

"You spent four years going to college in Colorado. Did you ever once see the Grand Canyon, or go up Pike's Peak?"

"The Grand Canyon is in Arizona," I protested.

"There's so much of this country to see, and most of us never even take the time to look around. Sure, I played all 50 states, and God knows how many cities and towns, but that's no way to take in the sights. Can you imagine trying to do Washington, D.C. four hours at a time, with maybe three trips in two years?"

I was finally starting to get his point. "You couldn't even make it through the Smithsonian in that kind of time."

"Right. And everything changes…well, not everything. Mount Rushmore was pretty much the same each time I saw it. But I was sick of living on a schedule hammered out by lawyers and agents. Tour for nine months, two months off, three months writing and recording a new album, then start over again. When *Wonderland* came out, that was the end of my contract, and I didn't sign another one. Granted, Vertical Records has been very good to me, and I promised I'd call them first if I ever go back into the studio, but I needed a break. So I took one."

My stomach rumbled again. "Speaking of breaks, I really need to eat something. You want some lunch?"

He stood and delicately helped me up. "I'm still kind of strung out from my flight, but I could really go for a kosher pickle."

"I just might be able to oblige," I said, heading for the kitchen. "I haven't been shopping for a while, but I like to keep a supply of pickles on hand for all my pregnant friends."

Mitch tagged along, hopping up on the counter while I rooted in the fridge. I extracted some bread, mustard, salami that still smelled remotely like it should, a brick of cheddar (ditto), a jar of kosher dills and a bottle of ginger ale. He poured the drinks while I made sandwiches, which we then carried into the dining room. As we ate, Mitch told me about some of the more interesting sights he'd found within our borders, from roadside attractions to national monuments, from amusement parks to wide open spaces that we cityfolk could barely imagine.

"I must say I'm relieved. When you pulled a disappearing act, I was afraid something was really wrong. Like the songwriting well had run dry."

I'm not quite sure what it was, but his manner changed. It was a slight dimming of his smile, a downward glance, but I felt as if I'd just called one of his personal demons by name. "What is it?"

He let out a long, slow, rumbling sigh that might have made an interesting percussion track, then stood up and paced back and forth behind his chair. In almost comic fashion, he started to speak two or three times, each time opening with a forceful hand gesture, but then receding into reconsideration. On the fourth take, he managed to put it together. "There are really two reasons I came to see you, and not just because I happen to be in New York. First off, I need your help."

"Why, what's up?" I asked genially, thinking he might need a restaurant recommendation or directions to The Strand.

"I think my life may be in danger."

Whoa!

"Come again?"

He picked up his lunch dishes and carried them into the kitchen, with me tailing along behind, hoping the problem wasn't as serious as it sounded. "Everything I told you about needing a break, and wanting to see the country is true, but that's not why I stopped recording. I guess that's what I've been telling myself for the last five years, but truth be told, I'm just too damn scared."

We both put our dishes in the sink and I rested my head on his shoulder. "What happened?"

He let out another sigh. "I was doing a radio call-in show in Chicago. At least, that's where I was in the studio. But the whole thing was syndicated, so it was heard all around the country. 'Lonely Hours' had been out a couple of weeks and it was starting to climb up the charts, so a lot of people were calling to find out the story behind the song."

"I'm with you so far."

"It took me years to write that song. You remember Beth? I think she and I started seeing each other when you were still coming to see me play." I smiled at the thought of my halcyon days, and led Mitch back into the living room for him to continue his story. "We had a good thing going, but she had a hard time when I started going out on the road. Unfortunately, it's just one of those things that happen; she knew when she took up with me that I was a musician and that to make a living I'd have to get out and perform. She might have been able to accept it in her head, but she needed something more in her heart."

"She cheated on you?"

His body seemed to sink into the futon with his confession. "Yeah. Twice, actually. I forgave her the first one, but the second, when some guy answered the phone at *our* apartment, I just lost it. She was it. The one. The woman I lived for. So, as I'm wont to do, I vented…through my music. But there was too much raw emotion there. I got about halfway through the song and I just stopped. I couldn't finish it. So I found other ways to numb the pain. Drinking, sex, parties. Anything to get my mind off her."

"You wrote 'Just Short of Paradise' for her, didn't you?"

"Good guess," he said with a soft smile. "That's why I always saved that one for the encore, so I could get the hell off the stage before I broke down. I mean, that was my first big hit, so it's not as if I could just drop it from the set list. But playing it live…man, that was tough. In any case, 'Lonely Hours' sat unfinished for years. I'd go back and look at it in my notebook every so often, but no matter what, the ending just wasn't in me. But a couple of years later, I had an encounter in Phoenix. Something I can't really describe. Some*one* I can't really describe— it's a long story. But that one night, it gave me a fresh perspective, some kind of positive to dig up from the ashes of what went before. And I was able to finish the song."

I had to get up and walk around. I felt stiff all over, my muscles suffering repercussions from the blast. "Okay, but what does that have to do with the call-in show?"

"Oh, right, well, there I am in the studio, and they go to some guy named Gordon on line three. He accuses me, on the air, of stealing his song. Claimed he wrote 'Lonely Hours,' or at least a major portion of it."

"Anything like that ever happen before?"

"Unfortunately, yes," he said, ruefully shaking his head. "It's the nature of the beast. You're famous, and people see you as a cash cow. Anyone can sue anybody for anything, regardless of whether the case has any merit—and half the time they win, or at least come away with something in an out-of-court settlement. According to my label, I get hit with two or three of these nuisance suits a year, so I didn't think anything of this guy Gordon. But before the DJ could cut him off, he says that I ruined his life, stole his ticket to the big time. And that he'd get even."

"Did he sue?"

"It might have been easier if he had. At least when you file legal papers, you have to cough up a full name and address. But this guy Gordon, he's remained almost invisible. A phantom menace. Sending me threatening letters, a CD cover riddled with bullet holes, a tape of my music overdubbed with screams, a 'Mitch Must Die' T-shirt. And, naturally, the police won't step in until the guy actually *does* something."

It hurt to see him so worked up, more so that it had caused him to give up his music. "Why do you give this guy so much credit?" I asked, gently massaging his shoulder. "He may be a whack job with an axe to grind, but very few of them ever have the balls to act."

He looked at me with a frigid stare that made me regret opening my mouth. "This one's got the balls. He's also got the means. The last live show I played, five years ago in Raleigh, he rigged one of the pyro pots. I don't know how he did it, but instead of shooting up sparks, the thing exploded—and I was right in front of it. A piece of metal skewered me just below my left shoulder blade and I collapsed right there on stage. I almost died."

"My God," I said. "How come I never heard about this?"

"Vertical's PR people played it down. Said there was some faulty wiring and that I'd sustained some minor injuries. It was the last date on the tour, so there were no shows to cancel. I had emergency surgery, and was also checked out by a neurosurgeon to make sure I didn't lose sensation in my arm. I was in the hospital for a couple of weeks—under an assumed name, of course. The crew had the equipment checked out, and even though the pot looked like it had been tampered with, they couldn't say for sure that the explosion *wasn't* an accident."

"That's not very comforting."

"Exactly. So I was all set to go home and regroup when a card arrives at the hospital. No one knows I'm there, supposedly, but this card shows up. The front of it showed a mushroom cloud and the inside was pretty direct: 'Sorry you didn't go out with a bang. Play another note and I'll be sure you will.'"

He and I looked at each other for a long time. Not that long ago, I'd been in his position, about to be thrown in front of a subway train. Sure, police work has its moments of terror, but it's not personal—the punks and skells never shoot at you, but rather what you represent. In the Columbus Circle station, I knew my attacker, and he'd wanted me dead. Those terrifying seconds, when I fully believed that the cement platform, the soda cans and gum wrappers between the rails—and worst, Frank Spencer's face—were the last things I'd ever see, were a nightmare unlike anything I'd ever experienced.

Now imagine living with that fear for five years.

C H A P T E R 5

▼

From public fan and closet friend, I'd suddenly been drawn into Mitch Black's spotlight. His request was simple: he wanted me to shadow him, to be the bodyguard that no one noticed, and hopefully get to Gordon before Gordon got to him.

"Hopefully, Gordon won't make an appearance. It has been five years, after all."

"Why me?" I asked, just before he dashed off to a *Rolling Stone* interview and photo shoot.

"You're someone I can trust. You knew me before I was anything and made be believe I was something." He let out another seismic sigh. "Whoever this Gordon is, he's gotten close to me, knows too much, and I've *got* people looking out for me. He couldn't have done that without at least a little help. He's touched someone on the inside, so I have to get someone on the outside."

"Lucky for you I'm taking a leave of absence. My lieutenant frowns on that sort of thing." I regretted saying it almost immediately.

"Look, if it's too much to ask..." He turned to go.

"No, of course," I said. "Mitch, I'm just a little gun shy about getting out on the street. But I'm yours. Wherever you need. Whenever."

"Thanks," he said, managing a weak smile. He looked at his watch. "I've got to run, but I'll be in touch."

He was almost out the door before I remembered something. "Hey."

"What?"

"What's the second reason?"

"Hm?"

I gave him my best winsome, groupie glance. "Don't play coy with me, Mr. Black. You said there were two reasons you came to see me."

"Boy, make a few hit records and even the lesbians come a-calling." We both laughed—a rich, therapeutic laugh. Something both of us needed. He pulled an envelope out of his pocket and gave it to me. "Happy birthday." He gave me a quick kiss on the cheek, and then was gone.

I couldn't believe he remembered; I actually stood there by my apartment door for what must have been five minutes before I opened the envelope. It contained a card from the Far Side collection. The cartoon showed pictures of a highly wrinkled old man and a similarly grizzled canine, with youthful versions playing outside in the yard, and the caption: "Portrait of Dorian Gray and his dog." Inside was a handwritten message—"I'd never guess you were a year older, and certainly not ten"—and four tickets to that Saturday's concert at The Bottom Line.

Sometimes we do things that go against any sense of rhyme, reason or logic. My pregnant pause at the door had assured that Mitch would be well on his way to *Rolling Stone*, but still I bolted out into the hall and up to the window that gave me an easterly view down 61st Street, toward Broadway. I couldn't see him, of course, yet there I was, pawing at the glass like a pound puppy. Perhaps I wanted to follow him around because he reminded me of a more innocent time, one when my heart and my head were still in working order. A bygone era where all I needed was a Saturday night, a cold beer and a Mitch Black tune, and life would be just about perfect. And on the occasions I had a little female companionship, the Cheshire Cat would have been envious of my smile.

This reverie was interrupted by the appearance of a woman getting off the elevator at my floor. I didn't recognize her and, given her disoriented stare, she didn't look as if she belonged. She was dressed in a loose-fitting black top and slacks, with long, straight black hair. Her roundish face was obscured by large, Elton John glasses with tinted frames. "Can I help you?"

She looked at me, then down at a scrap of paper in her hand. "I'm, uh, looking for Charlotte Kilmer's apartment."

"And you are?"

"Her sister-in-law, Janice."

"I'm Amanda," I said, offering my hand. "I live next door. Would that make you her husband's sister or her brother's wife?"

"The second one," she replied, though she was uncomfortable with the conversation. "My husband, John, Charlotte's brother, he would have come himself but he's a total wreck right now. I just came by to get a few of Pete's things."

Be glad somebody's looking out for him.

"He going to be staying with you?" I walked back toward my apartment, indicating that Janice should follow.

"For a while, anyway. Truth be told, we don't really have the room for him. We've got a little two-bedroom house out in Queens, and with two kids of our own, it's going to be tight. We couldn't take him on any kind of long-term basis."

"Oh," I said, my voice a little colder than it could have been. Janice picked up on it.

"Hey," she said, jamming a pale finger in my face, "I don't know who you think you are, but don't you start judging me. Where I come from, family is family and we look out for our own. If there was some way to make it work, we would. Besides, he's *got* a father."

I leaned against my doorframe. "Nobody knows where he is."

"That's why we're taking Pete…for now. Until the police can figure out where the guy is."

"And what if he's dead?"

The finger snapped back in place like a switchblade. "Don't start getting all social worker on me. Charlotte and I didn't always get along, but that has nothing to do with this. We're barely making ends meet with two kids. Taking Pete in wouldn't be good for him, and it sure wouldn't be good for us."

You're losing her.

I took a breath and tried a new tack. "How'd you hear about the accident?"

She scrunched up her eyes at me. "I wouldn't call an exploding microwave an accident. But some cop reached John at work, uh, Perelli. When John called me, I could barely understand what he was saying. All I made out was that Charlotte was dead and that we'd be looking after Pete for a while. So I called Perelli to find out what the heck was going on. Once I got all the details, I figured I should come over here and pick up a few of his things. Perelli said it would be okay, and that I might run into a Detective Ross."

"That would be me."

"*You're* Detective Ross?" She did a double-take as she surveyed my battered appearance. "What happened to you?"

"Let's just say that Charlotte had company when she died."

That gave her pause. "You were there? I mean," she looked over at the yellow police tape that criss-crossed her sister-in-law's door, "here?"

"Yeah."

It was if the news had struck her mute, for she stared at me a few seconds then quietly reached into her purse and found the key to Charlotte's apartment. I was pretty sure that the police hadn't locked it before they left, but I didn't bother to point that out. Janice seemed slightly dazed as she pushed opened the door and ducked under the tape, not even noticing me as I followed her in. She barely gave the kitchen a second glance, instead heading right for Pete's bedroom. I, however, was startled by the scene. The microwave had been removed, presumably to be further examined by the bomb squad, but its path of destruction was pretty clear.

The backsplash showed a distinct scorching pattern from the heat of the blast, as well as a light brown splatter, which I assumed to be Charlotte's coffee. Because the microwave had been wedged in beneath the cabinets and pressed fairly close to the back wall, the shrapnel had had no place to go except forward. There was a sizable blood stain on the floor, and a descending spray down the front of the fridge, following Charlotte's trajectory as she fell. Like mine, the kitchen was pretty small so, even if she'd known about the bomb, it would have been impossible to get out of the way.

I found Janice in Pete's bedroom, collecting items into a duffel bag. She'd already set aside a sleeping bag and pajamas, and was putting together several days' worth of clothing. I was happy to see her also pick up a few personal items—a plush dinosaur, toy cars, a few Pokemon cards—that might give Pete a little peace of mind as he headed into an unknown future. She looked around to see if she'd missed anything before her gaze settled on me.

"Did you ever meet Charlotte's ex?" I asked.

"You asking as a friend or a detective?"

"More as a friend. I'm concerned about Pete, so I'm trying to get a picture of the invisible man."

Janice shrugged. "I only met him a couple of times. Their wedding, our wedding. I think there was a Christmas get-together, but he's been out of the picture for more than four years. He seemed like a decent enough guy, and he treated Charlotte fine, but he always seemed to be somewhere else. A little absent-minded. 'Lost in thought,' as my father would say. He never said all that much, unless it was about technology. Vic was kind of a computer nerd, so listening to him was like going to a lecture at M.I.T."

"Vic what?"

"Renzo. Charlotte took her name back after they split."

"And since the divorce, he's been a total no-show?"

"In a sense. According to John, the guy always pays his alimony on time, but he doesn't send monthly checks. He deposits the money straight into Charlotte's checking account."

"Making it all the more difficult to keep track of him. No postmarks, no cancelled checks. We could probably look into which branch takes each of the deposits, unless he's got some kind of electronic transfer set up."

"That's *your* department, Detective," she said, sounding perturbed. "But if you find the guy, hey, great. I don't think John needs his sister's kid around, reminding him that she got blown to bits." She shouldered the duffel, tucked the sleeping bag under her arm and left without another word.

I was tempted to follow her, find out what was behind the attitude, but it was getting late and I wanted to be over at NYIT by 6:45. Fortunately, the college's main building is at the end of my block, so I could be there in minutes. At least Janice gave me a couple of leads on the husband, starting with a name. Of course, I was going to pass all of this information on to Jason Perelli, but I had one thread I needed to pull on my own.

James Finley lives in the apartment above me. I consider him my best friend, but also my personal geek. He's a consultant who keeps ridiculous hours and spends most of his time in front of either a monitor or a Scrabble board. If he's not upgrading some company's mainframe or defragging whatever it is that you defrag, he's running a couple of weekly Scrabble clubs or participating in weekend money tournaments. Perhaps most importantly, he's my sounding board when I have trouble getting my mind around a case; talking to him helps me put things in perspective.

I went upstairs in hopes of talking to him about Vic Renzo, seeing if the computer world was small enough that two of its shining stars might cross orbits every now and again. Unfortunately, he wasn't home, so my technological astronomy lesson would have to wait. As it was, I was about to make my own entrance into that world and, with it, hopefully eradicate one of my most irrational fears.

One down, how many more to go?

CHAPTER 6

▼

I don't drive, so the New York City subways are generally my travel method of choice. However, when I need to get to the other side of Central Park, I don't have much choice but to walk. It would take at least three subways to get across town; for the most part, the geniuses at the MTA concentrated on the up-and-down form of commuting, and didn't really address the side-to-side.

Oh, sure, there are crosstown buses, but like cars they are subject to Manhattan's unpredictable traffic conditions, which at any time might be dictated by accidents, road construction, cab drivers, potholes, protest rallies, well-meaning but ill-advised traffic cops, rain, snow and other phenomena that fail to sway letter carriers but somehow manage to keep the flow of above-ground vehicles at a constant crawl.

These distance dilemmas are the main reason I chose to take my computer course at NYIT instead of another, perhaps more prestigious, institute of higher learning. Or you could just call me lazy, saying that I chose the path of least mileage; it wouldn't be entirely untrue.

Perversely, at that moment in time, there was another benefit. Should I have chosen that particular occasion to drop dead from my subdural hematoma, I might be happened upon by a good Samaritan that wouldn't mistake me for a homeless person choosing to snooze on 61st Street. Then again, as Mitch had so eloquently pointed out, my mode of dress might, in fact, lead one to the conclusion that I was bound for the nearest shelter and soup kitchen. If I were to kick the bucket on the subway, however, I'd probably ride around for days before someone complained that a corpse was taking up too many seats.

I arrived at New York Tech just fine, thank you, and managed to find the computer lab without too much trouble. As I surveyed the room, I realized just how much of a freak I was. Virtually everyone in the class was at least 20 years older, part of a separate generation that predated the digital age. Personally, I had no excuse, somehow skating by for all my years without really getting to know the difference between a Mac and a PC. I brightened a little when I saw a man about my age poke his head in, but he was looking for the calligraphy class down the hall.

The instructor turned out to be *younger* than me—a grad student in her late 20s. She was thin, almost painfully so, with short brown hair brushed and layered toward the back. She wore an off-white T-shirt from some wildlife sanctuary, tan slacks and sneakers.

"Hi," she said in a voice that projected both confidence and friendliness, as she patrolled the front of the room. "If everyone's here, why don't we just get started? My name is Jean Ackerman and I'm in the computer science department here at New York Dreck. I'm not the 'Miss Ackerman' type, so feel free to call me Jeannie. This is Basic Computing, and I'm going to be spending the next eight weeks showing you all that computers don't bite and, no matter what you do to them, they won't blow up, either."

The class laughed, myself included. Those were both facts I knew to be true, but that didn't stop most desktop machines from giving me the willies.

"Let's begin by going around the room and introducing ourselves. Go ahead and give your name, what you hope to get out of this class…and any other personal information you care to share."

The first person to speak up was a woman on the far side of 60. She was compact and maternal, with a gentle face and silvery blonde hair cut close to the scalp. "My name is Anne, and I'm here because my kids gave me a computer for my birthday. One's out in Oregon, one's in Pennsylvania and one's not too far away in Connecticut, and between the three of them I've got a growing passel of grandkids that I'd like to keep in touch with. Last time I saw the youngest, he's just 4, he asked me, 'What's your e-mail address, Gram?' His folks have all these pictures they've scanned, that they'd like to send me. Well, I'd like to surprise them one of these days, send them a picture of *me*."

There was a small burst of applause, with Jeannie giving a welcoming nod. "By the time you're done here, Anne, you'll not only have your own e-mail address but your own Web site, so you can post your itinerary when you go visiting. Sound good?"

The class nodded, part in appreciation, part in awe of the power that would soon be theirs. The various people had different reasons for diving into the pool of technology. One man was an Oakland Raiders fan and wanted to be able to get the sports news from California. A woman who was just re-entering the workforce thought she'd have better job prospects if she were computer literate. Another woman had taken up bookbinding as a hobby and thought she might make a business of it, so she wanted to set up shop online. There was a writer who thought it was about time he stopped relying on an old Smith-Corona, and the crossword puzzle addict who wanted to access *The New York Times'* archives. Hearing their stories did me some good, and with each of them, Jeannie had an additional explanation of what we'd learn, what we'd be able to do, that would go beyond our initial expectations.

"And you?" she said, looking in my direction. "What brings you to my humble class?"

Showtime.

"My feet, but only because I couldn't get a cab." The joke elicited a mild chuckle; Jeannie rolled her eyes. She'd probably heard it before. "Actually, I'm here to get over a totally irrational fear of the damn things. I don't know why I have such a problem with computers, since they've been around for most of my life, but I just never took to them. Sometimes I feel like a duck who can't swim. Besides the fact that my department is moving into the 21st century and getting all hooked up, so I should probably get with the program."

"What kind of work do you do?"

"I'm a detective with the 11th Precinct."

I had prepared myself to be laughed out of the class. What kind of cop can stare down criminals but cowers in fear at the sight of a CPU? What happened next, though, was something I hadn't expected: a spontaneous standing ovation. I certainly didn't feel like a hero, but New York was a city still in need of some. 9/11 had touched everyone who lived here, and all of us had heard the stories of absolute selflessness and valor. To the people in that classroom, I was the flesh-and-blood embodiment of all the good that had come in response to the horror. So many others deserved it more, but were no longer around to receive the praise.

Jeannie came over to the station where I was sitting and stood right by me. "It's an honor to have you in our class, er…"

"Amanda."

"Welcome, Amanda." She gave me a smile, a soft and easy parting of the lips, that I found incredibly alluring. It might have been nothing more than heroine worship, and it was gone in an instant as she turned toward the blackboard, but it bore further investigation.

The rest of the class was spent on familiarizing ourselves with the desktop environment, the various icons that made up the Windows background. We learned how to get a directory of files, how to launch Microsoft Word, how to open and save a document, and how to access e-mail. She also set up an e-mail account for each of us, and when we checked messages, we found a syllabus and a homework assignment for the following week: Bring in a picture of yourself to scan.

By that time it was almost 9:30, and people were getting antsy and restless, with the scraping of chairs and shuffling of papers. Jeannie quieted everybody down and announced, "Good class, everyone. We got a lot accomplished. If you have access to a computer, be sure to practice what we've learned, and I'll see you next week. Now, if anyone would care to join me, I'm going up the street for a drink. This is one teacher who likes to socialize. First round's on me."

There was a genial murmuring, but it looked as though no one was going to take her up on the offer. Not that surprising, since most normal people have families to get home to or jobs to get up for.

Not so for students or freaks.

"I'm with you," I said, after the rest of the class had cleared out.

"I was hoping you'd say that," she replied with a smile, shrugging into a chunky red winter coat.

The other Continuing Ed courses let out at around the same time, so there was a large hubbub in the hall. One group was determined to take the elevator, but the rest of us were perfectly content to take the stairs. We spilled out onto Broadway and the crowd dispersed, leaving a small bunch of stragglers.

"Which way?" I asked.

"Houlihan's is right nearby."

Two blocks, in fact. It's a chain restaurant/bar that usually gets lumped in with all the Applebees and T.G.I.Friday's and Ruby Tuesdays out there, but it's a little more upscale than that. Still, most of the finger food on the menu—which was all I might have had the stomach for—was deep-fried in enough grease to put even a pig in the market for Lipitor. The clientele was mostly made up of college students, most of them jammed into the bar area for the week's edition of "Monday Night Football." I was half-tempted to pull out my badge and check IDs, just for fun.

"Why don't you get a table and I'll get the drinks," she called out above the throng. "What'll you have?"

"Ginger ale," I called back, my taste buds crying out for something a little more potent. I grabbed a table in the dining area, which was just as well. The bar looked to be fetid with cigarette smoke; the five-dollar-a-pack sticker price hadn't done much to make the city to go cold turkey.

Jeannie spotted me from across the room and waited, drinks in hand, for an opening in the flow of bodies to scoot in my direction. She placed the two schooner glasses down, then shed her coat over the back of her chair before sitting down. As soon as she met my eye, the look returned.

"What?" I asked defensively.

"Ginger ale. What's up with *that*? No, wait, let me guess…12 step."

"No."

"You're still on duty."

"Uh-uh."

"Cold medication."

"Blunt force head trauma."

After a moment or two of ton-of-bricks stupor, she shook off the absurdity of my response. "You want to run that by me again?"

How shall I put this?

"Pick up the paper tomorrow morning and you'll probably find a story about a woman who was killed when her microwave exploded as she was reheating a cup of coffee. What said story may or may not mention is that the woman, Charlotte Kilmer, was not the only casualty of this particular appliance bombing. Also injured in the blast was a certain female detective with the New York Police Department, who happened to live next door and was paying a visit when the explosion occurred."

Jeannie sat motionless, her beer frozen in mid-sip. She eyed me suspiciously, then put her glass down. She appeared to be grasping for something to say, and when words didn't come, she snatched up her glass again and took a big slug. "Please tell me you're kidding."

I raised my ginger ale in a mock toast. "Happy birthday to me," I said, then swallowed a few gulps.

"I can't imagine…my God, you must have been scared out of your mind."

"I wasn't conscious long enough to be scared. I hit my head and was down for the count. That's the reason I'm not drinking with you tonight. My doctor told me to lay off caffeine and alcohol, at least until my brain figures out how badly it's hurt."

We sat in silence for what must have been five minutes before she leaned over and whispered to me, "Is it really your birthday?"

"Not one I'll care to remember, but yes."

She pulled her chair around so she was sitting next to me, and pressed in further, her warm breath tickling my cheek and neck. "I think I've got something that could give this day a happy ending," she said, sliding her hand toward my inner thigh.

Not the most subtle come-on, but effective. I felt myself going flush, in my face and between my legs.

CHAPTER 7

▼

Jumping into bed with Jeannie wouldn't have been the dumbest thing I'd ever done—yet it probably wouldn't look too good on a Mensa application, either. Lord knows, she had the goods to make me quiver and, now that she'd offered herself up as a birthday present, I couldn't wait to see her unwrapped. In my mind, the teacher-seduces-student scenario fell somewhere between a porn film fantasy and a *New York Post* headline.

I took her hand gently in mine, softly caressing her palm, and whispered back, "Not tonight, I have a hematoma."

Out loud it sounded just as ridiculous as it had in my head, but Jeannie took it in stride. "That bad, huh?"

"The doctor wanted to do more tests, find out if I've got something seriously wrong. But I'm a little too thick-headed, both literally and figuratively, to sit for something like that. I should be fine, but I need to take it easy. Otherwise, I might drop dead in the throes of passion."

"Oh, wow," she said, leaning back. "I've gotten the dead fish before, but that's usually at the *end* of a relationship."

I'd only known her for a couple of hours, but Jeannie Ackerman was saying all the right things, working her way into my heart. Given time, I could see her taking up residence there. She was smart and funny, I liked the way she looked and the way she looked at me. Perhaps most importantly, she was understanding; she'd thrown a full-throttle pass, only to have it batted away, and she was still there with me.

We talked for a little while longer as we finished our drinks, she explaining how she'd become enamored of computers, me reiterating how I couldn't stand the sight of them. We talked about music—she said I should check out India.Arie, and I convinced her to give Chicago another chance, especially the older stuff.

We left together, huddling on the sidewalk against the evening's chill. She gestured that she'd be heading north, that she shared an apartment with three roommates. I pointed southwest, back toward the college, and she nodded. Then, without provocation—and without resistance—she took my face in her hands and kissed me. Our lips melded, our tongues touched and my knees melted; I had to grab onto her for support, which, I suppose, was the point.

"Consider that a sneak preview," she said, still cradling me.

I recovered my balance enough, and wrapped my hands around her arms. "I had to arrest the last woman who tried to get me into bed." I'm not sure why I said that, or even why it was significant—was I defending my defense mechanisms?—but Jeannie had already clued into the fact that I was going to be a challenge. She didn't seem to have a problem with that.

"Okay, Detective, I'll be on my best behavior." She smiled, that same smile I'd been smitten with earlier, clasped my hands, then let me go, and started walking toward home. There was something mischievous in her voice, and I liked it. I stared after her for a little bit, then made my short trek home. I hadn't eaten dinner, but I wasn't hungry. I was bone tired, and barely made it in the door before my body called it quits for the night. It took me every last ounce of energy to get undressed, brush my teeth, pull on a T-shirt and hit Play on the CD player. After my face hit the pillow, I was gone almost instantaneously.

I woke up far too early—in the sense that it was still morning. The events of the previous day and evening had left me brain-tired, and the notion of a week-long coma struck me as strangely appealing. Unfortunately, my body refused to cooperate, intermittently interrupting my attempts to wring a few more hours out of a night long since passed. An itch here, a twitching hair there, a kink in my back, a cramp in my neck. I was unconsciously undermining my own sloth campaign.

I finally threw off the covers at around 10:30, got up and went into the bathroom to inspect the damage. There weren't any alien tumors or bloody blotches across my face, just a sizable wen at the back of my head. I was conscious, standing erect, lucid and, thanks to the nimble fingers of a certain sultry brunette, perhaps even a bit giddy.

Amanda 1, hematoma zip.

I padded into the kitchen, poured myself a big bowl of Smart Start and drowned it in skim milk. After two or three spoonfuls, I proclaimed myself capable of carrying on a human conversation. But I decided to test the theory first, giving Jason Perelli a ring. I caught him at his desk, and offered up the Cliff's Notes version of my encounter with Janice Kilmer. He listened carefully, taking a special interest in the information I'd gotten on Charlotte's ex, Vic Renzo. Perelli hadn't had any luck in locating him, but believed the electronic support payments were a good place to start. I also parroted Janice's disinterest in looking after Pete, hoping to light a fire under my fellow officer, that he might pull a responsible father out of thin air.

"How are you doing otherwise?" he asked. "You okay?"

"No internal bleeding," I said, then, after a pause, "that I know of. Of course, if my doctor'd had his druthers, I'd be Exhibit A in this morning's grand rounds at the hospital. All I got was a whack on the head—something my partner's been wanting to do for years."

"You sound better than you did yesterday, I'll say that."

"Detective, heal thyself."

"Sure thing, Hippocrates," he said with a laugh. "I better get started tracing these money transfers. Give me a holler if you need anything."

What I need and what I can have are two different things.

"Will do." I hung up the phone and it rang back almost instantly. I let it ring a second time, thinking it was a line check or some phone company hiccup, but when it rang a third time, I picked up. "Hello."

"Amanda?"

Mitch was calling on a cell phone, and the windy static made it difficult to hear. "Mitch?" I yelled.

"Sorry to give you such short notice, but I was just reminded that I have to make an appearance this afternoon. Can you be there?"

"Where?"

"Tower Records, down on Fourth."

"What time?"

"The publicity material says from 4 to 6."

I took a little time before answering, realizing that if I said yes, and was in fact up to the task, I might actually be capable of getting back to my real job.

One for the money, two for the show…

"Amanda?"

"Yeah?"

"We've got a terrible connection. I just wanted to make sure I hadn't lost you."

"No, I'm still here…and don't worry…I'll be there at Tower."

"Maybe no one will show up, then we can knock off early and go get an egg cream."

"Somehow I doubt that, Mr. Rock Star, though I may take you up on the egg cream. Where are you now?"

"I'm at Ground Zero," he said, and for the first time in the conversation, I was able to discern the sorrow in his voice. "I can't believe what I'm seeing. It's unlike any war zone I could possibly imagine. My God, some of this stuff is still burning...and it's been almost two months."

"Yeah," I said, and I could feel the muscles in my face and neck tighten. My eyes were blinking rapidly, and my throat felt very dry. "I gotta go."

"See you at four."

I didn't answer him; I was in tears before I could even hang up the phone. I wasn't sure what was happening to me—I was being flooded with feelings of doubt, fear, sadness, self-loathing, and my knees felt like they were going to buckle under the weight of the world. I slumped down to the floor, the cold tile prickling my bare skin. By this time I was bawling uncontrollably, crumbling against the counter and wishing I had something—or someone—to hold onto.

You've never even been down there.

"Come on, Amanda," I sobbed after a few minutes of wallowing. "Get a hold of yourself."

I scooched up against the wall, reaching for the phone and dialing a number I'd called far too often—so much so that I'd programmed it into my speed dial.

"Hello," came a voice much too crackly to be real. "You have reached the office line of John Sandusky, police psychologist. I'll be out of the office all day Monday and Tuesday. If this is an emergency..."

"Shit," I said, standing up and banging down the receiver in one motion. The bout with Ultimate Suffering had subsided some, enough for me to realize that I couldn't possibly function in this cold, cruel world if I was going to fall to pieces every time I was reminded of September 11. I swallowed whatever self-pity hadn't already spilled out onto my T-shirt and the floor, and resolved to start taking myself—and Wacky Jacky's advice—more seriously. Besides, I had another reason to stand up for myself: Jeannie had been the aggressor the night before, and I couldn't let her go on thinking I was ready to be someone's bitch.

I showered and got dressed, pulling on a baggy polo shirt, jeans and sneakers. I'd had it in mind to do some food shopping—to my recollection, the cupboards were almost entirely bare—but that didn't seem nearly as important as doing something that would get me out of this prolonged funk. I snagged the apartment keys and bounded—well, walked—upstairs to see if James was home.

To meet James, you might think he'd gotten his wardrobe from a Devo video. He's always got on these sleeveless shirts and parachute pants that went out of style more than a decade ago. He's tall and thin, with salt-and-pepper hair and a sort of nasally monotone to his voice. He knows everything about computers, and he's responsible for my Moody Blues attachment. He also happens to be gay, which has kept all those Harry-met-Sally feelings from interfering with our friendship. It also means that I don't have to worry about him stealing my girl-friends.

James came to the door wearing a black sleeveless shirt and pants with vertical black-and-gray stripes. He also had on glasses with a slight tint—he always wears thick lenses, as he's incredibly farsighted—but lately he's taken to protecting his eyes from monitor glare and something he calls "computer vision syndrome."

He hugged me, gently, right there in his doorway. "I am *so* sorry. I know you and Charlotte were close—or getting there. I would have popped down to see you, but I got in pretty late and didn't know what kind of shape you'd be in. From the way they described it on the news, I'm not sure how you're not still in the hospital."

I pulled back. "It was on the news?"

"Yeah. Channel 5 had a small piece on it. I'm not sure about the others. You coming in?"

"Yeah," I said, and followed him into Mission Control—the apartment contains more computer equipment than the lab at NYIT, and I'm sure it's capable of much bigger things. "Did the story mention anyone by name?"

We sat at one of the square game tables that account for much of his remaining furniture. "Just Charlotte," he said. "They reported that a neighbor had been injured in the explosion, and that police were looking into it. They also mentioned that Charlotte had a 7-year-old son. Where is he?"

"Staying with Charlotte's brother and sister-in-law, but only until they can find someone else to take him."

"What about the father?"

"That's what I came up here to talk to you about. Charlotte's ex was a computer guy named Vic Renzo. You ever heard of him?"

James scrunched up his face and stared at me; I might as well have told him that Charlotte had been wed to a flying moose. "Charlotte was married to Vic Renzo?"

"Yeah, why? You know him?"

He smacked his lips, as though he were trying to work up a taste for the words. "Vic was always sort of strange bird, so I can't imagine anyone actually being married to him."

"How so?"

He interlaced his fingers and leaned forward as he spoke. "The best way I could describe him would be to say that he was manic-depressive, but all anyone ever saw was the manic stuff. He was always jazzed about whatever he was working on, was always sure his latest project would be the one that would turn him into the next Peter Norton."

I didn't know who that was, but he sounded like a big deal. "Did he have the goods to pull that off?"

"Yes and no. He was like a brilliant writer who lacked creativity. He could never come up with the ideas on his own, but once he got the ball, he'd run pretty far with it."

"When was the last time you saw him?"

"Probably a convention of some sort, maybe 18 months ago."

"What was he working on then?"

"He'd gotten himself juiced on encryption, trying to come up with the ultimate kind of encoder."

"Any kind of success?" I asked.

"Not that I've heard of. If he had come up with something, it'd have shown up in *PC* or *Wired* or online somewhere. When information travels at the speed of light, secrets—even trade secrets—don't stay that way very long."

It didn't seem like there was anything there, any reason to think that Vic Renzo's work would have any bearing on what had happened, but there was one last bit of Woodward and Bernstein. "Is there any money in that kind of work?"

"Oh, sure, provided you patent and protect the new technology, but remember, matey," he adopted a Jolly Roger accent, "there are pirates everywhere. Unless you create the paradigm for the industry, your ideas will be plundered until you're no longer worth paying royalties to. That's why so many innovations are brought out under the auspices of the big computer companies."

"They can afford to safeguard their wares."

"And they can afford to pay their programmers. If the artist starves to death, he's not much good to anyone, is he?"

"No, I guess not."

James squirmed a bit in his chair, which usually meant that a lecture was coming—about my work habits, about my clothes (like he's one to talk!), about something that I'm doing to deepen the creases in his brow. "What did the doc-tor say?"

Bingo.

"He's an old worrywart like you."

"Amanda, they said on the news that the bomber used some serious hardware. The explosion was meant to kill. And you were part of the blast pattern. You *sure* you're all right?"

"I'm *fine*, James. Really I am. A little bump on the head is all. Now get back to work; I've got some food shopping to do."

He walked me to the door anyway. He was handling me with kid gloves, and sometimes they hurt worse than a rabbit punch.

I didn't have time to stew over it, fortunately, as my 5'6" birthday present was waiting just outside my apartment.

CHAPTER 8

▼

"Hey, you," she said, as if I'd just returned from the bathroom, rather than sliding through 12 hours and a million daydreams. She was as vital as I'd remembered her, wearing a lined denim jacket over a faded denim shirt and jeans.

"Hey," I replied, momentarily forgetting that she was paying *me* the visit. I rocked on my heels, keeping my distance and keeping my cool, waiting for something—anything—to happen. We weren't quite prizefighters in the ring, but we were sizing each other up, wary of the left hook.

After a minute, she nodded toward the police tape. "That where…?"
"Yeah."

More silence and awkward glances. It was if the hallway had turned to quicksand, and we might sink through the floor if either one of us moved.

"Look, this is silly," I said, only after realizing I was already sinking. "Why don't you come in and we'll…talk."

"Actually," she said, pulling her hands out of her pockets, "I came by to see if you were free for lunch."

"Well, yes and no." I took out my keys and unlocked the door. "I have the time, and I'd be happy to do lunch, but I *really* have to get some groceries. Otherwise I'm in more danger from malnourishment than blood on the brain. If you want, come with me to Fairway and we'll grab a couple of sandwiches in the café upstairs. You okay with that?" I pushed in.

"Sure," she said, following.

"Let me just grab a coat and my limousine and we're ready to go." I left her in the entryway, figuring I'd give her the tour later on, when I could *really* show her everything.

"Your what?" she called after me.

I retrieved my wallet from the bedroom and returned, pulling aside the curtain in front of the hall closet. I extracted a collapsible white shopping cart along with my leather jacket. "My limousine. That's what my grandmother always called these things."

She was truly befuddled by this. "Aren't you supposed to *ride* in a limousine?"

"Uh-huh," I said, checking the locks and scooting her out the door. "And in this case, the groceries ride."

Fortunately, Jeannie knew better than to argue with my brand of logic. We took the elevator down and stepped outside into a day that had shaken off its November misery. It was still cool, but it was bright and breezy, the kind of weather that was made for the Yankees and Mets, as opposed to whatever football teams were claiming to be from New York that week. We rounded the corner of 61st Street, heading uptown on Columbus Avenue.

"By the way," I asked, as Jeannie stopped to pet a dachshund that was quick-stepping away from its owner, "how did you find me? I'm not in the phone book."

Without looking up from her new canine companion, she said, "You're talking to a computer geek with access to the campus mainframe. You signed up for a class, complete with your name, address and favorite song."

Well, duh. Some detective you are.

"It's something I probably should have done a long time ago, but I always figured that my brain wasn't wired for the digital age."

"User-friendly equipment can only go so far," she remarked, giving her short-legged friend a final scratch on the ears. "You have to be a little amiable yourself."

"I can be amiable," I said as we continued up Columbus, ultimately merging into Broadway.

"I certainly hope so. I don't want any curmudgeons in my class...or in my bed."

There it was again, the sexual frankness I found so appealing. Yet it was also frightening, for it was forcing me to take stock and make a decision—one I wasn't sure I was ready to make. Could casual sex be a sort of foreplay for something more substantial? I'd tried it before, with questionable results. Sure, there was Chris, who started out as a party favor and stuck around for nearly two years, but she was the exception rather than the rule. Still, Jeannie had already managed to push some of the right buttons, and in the process reminded me that all my parts were still in working order.

"Only if you leave crumbs," I said.

"Well, there's this thing I do with pretzels, but hey, it's your loss."

I was in the process of crossing 68th Street when she dropped her little pretzel nugget on me, and it froze me in my tracks. She turned and quickly pulled me out of traffic; I fell into her arms and we got ourselves tangled with each other, the limousine and half a dozen dogs on leashes, all being walked by a single young man. He was tall, in his early 20s, with long, black hair tied back in a ponytail. He wore a baggy, long-sleeve T-shirt, jeans, sneakers and thick glasses with plastic frames and lenses. His four-legged charges included a pair of ginger poodles, a Lab mix, a schnauzer, some kind of terrier and a mutt who looked like he'd been stitched together from the scraps of a quilting bee. I don't know if the dogs found my clumsiness amusing, but both Jeannie and the young man had a good laugh at my expense.

"Sorry about that," Jeannie said to him, lifting one of the poodles to get her free from the wheels of my shopping cart. The schnauzer wrapped himself around my legs, then tried to take off after a stray plastic bag. Fortunately, his leash would only let him go so far. Otherwise he might have dragged me back into the street.

"I normally don't take this many at a time," said the dog walker. "But the poodles are new. Fortunately, everyone seems to get along."

We sorted out the rest of the leashes, legs and limousine, and left the furry flotilla to head eastbound while we continued north. It was one of those cutesy New York moments, embarrassing at the time, but well worth repeating at a later date. Jeannie leaned in close to me as we walked, partially to snuggle but, I was sure, also to make sure I didn't do any more damage to myself or the dogs of New York.

The next six blocks passed without incident, and we made it to Fairway in one piece. For people who live in my section of Manhattan, there is no substitute for groceries—produce in particular. Most Gotham residents get their everyday foodstuff from the little markets and delis that can be found on nearly every street, or one of the chain stores like Food Emporium, but for a double-barrel shopping attack, Fairway is the place to stock up. Its slogan is "Like No Other Market," and I'd have to agree.

It covers most of a city block, with two levels of delicacies to choose from. Out front is an amazing selection of fruits and vegetables, with everything from cucumbers to lychee nuts, and that's just the beginning.

"Wow," Jeannie said, agape at the enormity of the place. "I didn't think there were places like this in the city. I mean, there are these big supermarkets and such upstate, but everything's different here. Smaller places and more of 'em."

"Upstate where?" I asked, grabbing a package of bean sprouts.

"I grew up in Albany, and was looking to get away when I applied for my undergrad, so I wound up in Plattsburgh."

"Cold up there, isn't it?"

She shivered just thinking about it. "You have no idea. Not a lot of snow, but wind and temperatures like you wouldn't believe. And depressing, my God. A few years ago, when the Canadian dollar started to fall, everything seemed like it was going under. The air force base had closed down, and they were in the process of turning it into some kind of international trade facility. It was all over the local paper but I never quite understood what was going on."

"Well, you were an outsider in the city. In your own little world there on campus, without a lot of opportunity to interact with the locals. It's the same all over. Towns need the colleges because of the money they pump into the economy, but how often do you see anyone—short of a landlord renting off-campus housing—actually getting to know some of the students?"

"Still, after four years of that, I was looking for someplace a little more friendly."

Friendly? You walked into a regular lovefest, sister.

We continued talking as I loaded my cart: eggs, chicken, cereal, milk, fresh pasta, two different kinds of sauce, cold cuts, tuna, mustard, cheese, a few cans of soup, a shepherd's pie. I added rice noodles, sauce and peanuts, figuring I'd cook up a batch of Pad Thai—for Jeannie or some other occasion.

We combed all the aisles, making sure there wasn't some great surprise hidden among the flatbreads and hot sauces. I kept suggesting that Jeannie pick up something if it struck her fancy, but she demurred, saying that she'd bring her roommates the next time; the corner market had quickly lost all of its appeal. We toted everything up to the register so I could pay for it all, but just as I was about to swipe by ATM card, Jeannie said she had one thing to add. She mischievously plunked a bag of pretzels down on the conveyor belt, and as they slid up toward the cashier, an odd smirk crept onto my face.

Oh, yes, she would be mine.

The café, upstairs at Fairway, has gained something of a reputation, for two different reasons. First, the bill of fare includes some of the most amazing pancakes. Second, the café is a common meeting spot for the power brokers of Hollywood East. Many a TV movie has been discussed and packaged over poached salmon or the vegetable plate.

There are about 30 tables-for-two, sometimes pushed together to accommodate larger parties, and a counter area that adds another half-dozen seats. Fresh pastries are displayed on a bakery stand, through which the waitstaff would travel, to and from the kitchen. The tables and chairs were silver and black, harkening back to the art deco times of F. Scott Fitzgerald, with the personnel dressed accordingly. We sat at a table by the window, and I tucked the limousine in behind my chair. I didn't think we'd be so long that my perishables would start turning into science experiments.

We spent a minute or two glancing at the menu before a young woman came by to take our order. She had an unseasonably dark tan, which only worked because of her streaky bronzed hair, cascading down in long wisps. Her round face was accented by gold, wire-frame glasses, with squarish lenses covering light-brown eyes. "What can I get you?"

I gestured to Jeannie, who opted for the smoked salmon cream cheese with scallion on pumpernickel, and a Coke to drink. I chose the grilled Cajun chicken on rye, with my usual ginger ale. As our waitress cleared the menus and disappeared into the kitchen, I noticed Jeannie pull a little white packet from her pocket.

"Lactaid," she said, catching my look.

"You're lactose intolerant?"

"Yeah," she replied with a shrug. "That's part of why I'm so thin. So many of the things I could eat to put on weight—milkshakes, cheese, ice cream—just don't agree with me. Even a lot of the weight-gain supplements have milk products in them."

"But you just ordered cream cheese."

"That's what the pills are for. They usually work, and when they don't, I pay the consequences. Some things are worth it, though."

"I guess," is what I said, though in reality I couldn't imagine what it must be like, having to avoid so many foods because your body hits the panic button. However, her explanation did allay one of my fears, that there was some more serious reason for her appearance.

Our sandwiches arrived, and we devoured them with gusto, each bite more scrumptious than the last. This wasn't exactly a date, but I started to give Jeannie the condensed version of my life story: how I'd grown up in the city and gone to school in Colorado, how I'd come to join the police academy, how my parents were the worst singers on the planet. She listened closely, smiling at the right moments, making me glad that I hadn't had much opportunity to rehearse my patter. Sincerity, complete with stammers and thought derailments, is usually the natural winner.

It was one of those meetings that I didn't want to end, with everything from her gentle laugh to the way she licked cream cheese from her fingers embedding itself in my mind. Unfortunately, a glance at my watch reminded me that I had someplace else to be. I flagged down the waitress for our check.

"Did I say something wrong?" Jeannie seemed hurt by my abrupt change in attitude, from twitterpated to time-sensitive.

I took her hands in mind. "Not at all. I promised a friend that…well…"

How do you explain this one?

We split the bill as I looked for a reasonable explanation for my sudden need to depart. I was still hemming and hawing and Jeannie helped me carry the grocery-laden limousine down the stairs and out onto Broadway.

"Remember how I told you I went to school out in Colorado?"

"Yeah."

"Well, there was this guy who used to sing at a bar off campus, and I guess you could say I was one of his earliest fans. Also one of his biggest."

We were moving south, back toward my apartment, but Jeannie walked slowly, and I could see her trying to puzzle out what my tale had to do with her, or with anything else.

"He's going to be down at Tower Records in a couple of hours, signing albums and such."

"And you want to get his autograph?"

Not exactly.

CHAPTER 9

▼

The mere mention of Mitch Black's name was enough to stop Jeannie in *her* tracks. For someone who hadn't played a note in five years, he had certainly left a song in numerous hearts.

"You're kidding, right? *The* Mitch Black?"

"Well, I didn't ask him for ID or anything, but he looks the way I remembered him."

"Wait a minute, you saw him?"

"He was in my apartment when I got back from the hospital yesterday afternoon."

"Omigod!"

We were unloading groceries in my kitchen while I quickly told of my lasting friendship with Mitch; subway service can be a bit sporadic at mid-afternoon, before rush hour gets underway, so I wanted to be sure I left myself enough time to get down to West 4th.

"And you've kept in touch all this time?"

"On and off. It's been a while since we've actually been in the same room, but there's been the occasional phone call, the postcard from Japan or Stockholm or wherever he was playing." I placed the peanuts and rice noodles in the pantry, along with the tuna and soup. Jeannie's pretzels I left on the counter; who knew when they might come in handy. "We're not as close as we were then, but I'll say this, he remembered my birthday. I can't say the same about any of the other men I spent yesterday with."

"No birthday kiss from Dr. Calamari?" she said teasingly.

"I can kinda forgive Andy—I'm not sure where his mind's been lately, but I figured my partner would have at least said 'boo.'"

"From what you told me, he's a little scatterbrained, too, with a lovely lady in his life." Jeannie stacked the plastic containers of pasta sauce in the fridge, next to the eggs and my supply of ginger ale, and tossed the cold cuts and cheese in the meat drawer. I stashed the shepherd's pie in the freezer, gently making sure she stayed hunched over, that she wouldn't whack herself on the overhead door.

The perfect accessory for today's couple: matching head injuries.

In truth, I felt odd discussing Mitch with her because I wasn't able to divulge the real reason for his visit, and the need for me to head downtown. Mitch hadn't exactly sworn me to secrecy regarding his request, but I wouldn't be much good as an incognito bodyguard if I started telling everybody about it.

"You free for dinner tomorrow night?" I asked as a means of changing the subject. "I figure maybe I'll do a little cooking, have a couple of people over."

"Showing me off already?" She grabbed a handful of pastel-colored M&M's from the jar on my counter. Easter was long since gone, but the candy lives on thanks to my aunt Emmy, my father's sister, who's a sales rep for M&M/Mars and keeps me supplied with the chocolate overruns. In college it had been a great way to meet people, leaving my door open with the jar in plain sight. Fortunately, I've never been addicted to the stuff, so I can keep it around without bingeing. I'm sure my skin is thankful for the self-control.

"I don't know if Randy was able to get tickets for any of the concerts, but I figure I'll blow his mind with these." I held up my birthday present. "And from what he said, Diane will be thrilled."

"You're a good person, Amanda," Jeannie said, giving me a quick kiss on the cheek. "I'll see you tomorrow night, around what, 7?"

"Come by earlier if you want to help."

She laughed. "I don't think you want my help. I can't even microwave popcorn."

"Then you can set the table. Besides, I'm kind of a tyrant in the kitchen. Someone starts lifting pot lids, or telling me how *they'd* do it, I start throwing things."

"Boy, I never knew cooking could be a contact sport. There's probably a cable TV show in there somewhere."

I didn't want her to leave, but I shooed her out the door before my loins took over whatever sense of reason I had left.

The trip downtown was relatively short and uneventful. I'd barely taken any time to get myself together, so I half-expected to see Jeannie on the street as I walked over to Broadway and down to Columbus Circle. Then I remembered that she'd said she lived north of me, and I was going south. I quickly navigated the huge subway station, going down to the platform to catch the A train. Across the way, another train had just departed, and the wind hit me a moment later, like the wake of a passing boat. Some months ago, I'd nearly died in this very terminal, where a psycho cop named Frank Spencer had tried to throw me to the tracks. Spencer had been stalking a young woman named Pamela Taylor, and I got to know her while investigating her brother's murder. What Spencer hadn't been willing to accept was that Pamela preferred girls to goons. He'd seen me as a threat, and opted to take me out. Only a leftover act of God saved me, and Spencer was the one who became acquainted with the third rail and the underside of a C train.

Mitch's hope of making a quick exit from this publicity stop was probably dashed at around 1 p.m., when the first eager fans got online in front of Tower Records. By the time I got there, about 3:45, the crowd stretched around the block. Not just teenagers, but people my own age and older. Many of them held CDs—one heavyset man in a flannel shirt and leather vest had a whole stack of them—but there were a few who'd managed to rustle up vinyl for the occasion. The LPs had to have come from dust-covered collections, or were recent rescues from one of the city's many used record shops.

I skirted the pair of dreamy-eyed tarts who headed the queue and entered the store. I wasn't sure how I should play it, but I presumed to hide in plain sight unless another action was called for. It'd been so long since I'd done any real police work that I was off my game, staring back at my rookie self: a clueless kid who didn't even know which side of the uniform to pin her badge. I felt like a kid at the edge of the Central Park pool; even though I knew cannonballing was the right thing to do, but that didn't make the water any less cold.

A scrawny, nametagged clerk was setting up a table and chair for Mitch, and though I couldn't read the plastic badge, Pierce wouldn't have been an inappropriate name for the guy. Nose and eyebrow rings were the most obvious pieces of metal, followed by the dozen or so studs that filled his ears.

Going through the metal detector at airports must be a trip.

Coordinating the proceedings was an African-American woman who looked to be barely 19, but her voice and position of authority bumped her up to my age or so. Her hair was unnaturally straight and stiff, held behind with a scrunchy. She wore a turquoise sleeveless top, with a purple bra strip sticking out on her left shoulder; her skirt showed an underwater scene playing across the aquamarine expanse below her knees. The Pin Cushion referred to her as "Laqueesha."

The section in which I'd planted myself wasn't particularly enthralling: rap and hip-hop. I knew somewhere nearby I'd find the soul-singing India.Arie album that Jeannie had recommended, but flipping my way through the N.W.A., Jay-Z and Public Enemy gave me the best view of the signing table…and the best shot should I need to take it. The Glock felt warm and tingly in its holster, like a long-lost limb I'd had grafted back on. Whereas once it felt comfortable in the nock under my arm, it now rested oddly against my breast, a lump that would—were I not such a stubborn fool—probably be biopsied away for good.

Mitch came in shortly after 4, dressed pretty much the way he'd been the day before. He was escorted in by Laqueesha and another woman, a few years older than him. She was smartly dressed in a khaki blouse and slacks, her not-quite-Asian face framed by well-coiffed, short black hair. She carried a cell phone, but didn't seem to have a real reason for being there; she contemplated Mitch as one might a bowling trophy before a big tournament, while Laqueesha did all the talking. My guess: record company rep.

Once he got past his initial shock at the number of people who still wanted a piece of him, Mitch picked up the publicity thing right where he left it, five years earlier. He was charming and funny, attentive to the people's words without letting them puff up his ego or turn him into anything but the humble guy I've always known. He took his time in answering questions, and never said word one about the number of items people wanted him to sign, or the unusual nature of some of the requests. One of the tarts at the front of the line even wanted him to sign her bra—while she was wearing it. He handled this particular boob job with the help of a fabric pen she produced; I could only imagine the end result if he'd tackled—and bled through—her D cup with one of the permanent markers the store had supplied. It certainly would have made for an interesting conversation the next time she did a strip tease for her boyfriend. A Scripto'd breast was probably a pretty big offense on the cheating scale—lower than a Lewinsky, yet higher than a handshake or a kiss on the cheek.

While Mr. Black handled the procession with diplomacy, tact and professional courtesy, the same could not be said for some of the people on line. About 45 minutes into the signing session, a heavyset woman in a clear raincoat over a gingham halter-and-shorts set pushed through to the front, barking about how much time it was taking. It didn't seem to matter that she was spewing right in front of the man himself.

"Do you have any idea how long it took me to haul my ass down here just to get a stinking autograph," she bellowed at Laqueesha, the lady in khaki, Pierce, me and the lions in front of the New York Public Library. "Three stinkin' buses and two goddamn subways just to stand in a line of frickin' kids who don't even know what music is."

Laqueesha was apoplectic, and in-store security was trying desperately to get the woman to calm down, without actually laying a hand on her. I considered arresting her for disturbing the peace and any other offense I could think of: bad taste, for one. She continued to rant and rave, but Mitch stood up calmly and approached her, waiting for a break in the tirade to deliver a palpable hit. It was a long time in coming, but even the blue whale has to come up for air every so often.

"Excuse me," he said, gently tapping her on the shoulder.

"What do you want?" she barked before she'd turned around, oblivious to just who had interrupted her.

"I just wanted to say I think you're right." He flashed his interview smile to the line of patient people, just to let them in on the joke.

"It's about time. I've got things to do."

"Isn't that special?" Mitch said. I don't know if he meant to add a Church Lady sneer to his voice, but that's the way I heard it. "And special people deserve special consideration. In fact, we should all be lining up to get *your* autograph."

He escorted her over to his table, continuing his tribute while gradually getting louder, to be sure that it had the desired effect. "Why don't you sit down here, take my seat. You've got plenty of markers there, so you just go ahead."

Her bubble burst, she sat. Mitch turned to the 20-ish couple who were at the front of the line and added, "I hope you don't mind, but I've waited a long time to meet her."

They smiled back at him, happy to have front row seats—well, floor—for this particular jousting match.

Mitch returned to the table, shuffling his feet as a shy child might approach a department-store Santa. "I wish I'd brought something for you to sign, but for the life of me, I can't recall exactly what you did to merit the spotlight. Me, I've only recorded six albums and won a couple of Grammys, but you. What were your accomplishments again? Oh, yes, that's right. Taking the bus. Riding the bus. And being a general pain in the ass."

He might have gone on trash-talking the woman, but Mitch *was* on a clock, and *did* have people he really wanted to spend time with. She was so embarrassed that she slinked away on her own, anyway, right into the company of in-store security, who quickly escorted her out. That's when something occurred to me:

For someone who'd supposedly come to get Mitch Black's autograph, she seemed to have little or no clue who he actually was.

Gordon.

I kept my eyes on the signing table, as Mitch got back to work, giving each CD and record a personal touch, but I moved around, darting my field of vision, trying to take in any possible threats. Over in the Metal section, the skinhead in a dirty T-shirt and fatigue pants looked like a good candidate, but he seemed more interested in the track listing of the Slayer CD he'd found than the proceedings on our side of the store. I combed the line as nonchalantly as I could, searching for a long coat, jittery behavior, furtive glances up at Mitch—anything that might be indicative of harmful intent. In such a public place, though, even factoring in the cross-section of Mitch's appeal, someone who fit the profile I'd formed of Gordon would be seriously out of place. Maybe the gingham-clad twit was a distraction, but more likely just a clueless broad, there to get a signature for her daughter or niece. Had she even bothered to look at the CD she'd been holding, she might have realized who she was talking to, and had an amazing story to tell.

The next hour passed without incident, but the lineup of people, and Mitch's dedication to his fans—especially given the time he'd wasted, dealing with the aforementioned distraction—caused the session to run over, with Mitch keeping his writer's cramp in check until it was nearly 6:30. By then, the throng had petered out, and even Laqueesha was checking her watch. Ironically, at that time I was approached by a beefy guy in a black Tower Records shirt.

"Ma'am, I'm going to have to ask you to leave the store."

I was stunned. "Um, why?"

"You're loitering, ma'am. You've been here for nearly three hours without making a purchase."

Well, when you put it that *way.*

I didn't want to leave Mitch, but I didn't want to blow my cover, either. I started to go with the security guy, but suddenly the woman in khaki came to my rescue.

"Mr. Black would like her to stay."

I was tempted to stick my tongue out at the man in black, but I felt kind of sorry for him. It's not that he was bad-looking, but his face seemed sculpted into a perpetual scowl; with the puckered lips and the deep creases around his mouth, he didn't even seem capable of smiling.

See what happens when you don't listen to your mother? You made that face and it stayed that way.

I tailed the record company rep back to where Mitch was sitting, still marveling at her reference to "Mr. Black." In all the years I'd known him, I'd never heard anyone refer to him in such a formal manner. To me, he would always be Mitch, the troubadour trying to make himself heard over a noisy bar.

"Having fun yet?" he asked as we approached.

"Oh, sure," I replied sarcastically. "I found a few Outkast and De La Soul discs to put on my Christmas list."

"Hey, don't knock it 'til you've heard it. Those guys make some pretty good music."

"I guess…though I don't plan on paying a visit to Stankonia anytime soon. You free for that egg cream now?"

"Sorry, Sondra just reminded me that Vertical's throwing a cocktail party over in midtown," he said, indicating the woman that I'd been following. "I really need to put in an appearance."

We shook hands briefly, with her filling in the last name Fisher to complete Mitch's semi-introduction. She then left us alone to continue our conversation.

"Is that what she does, remind you of social engagements?" I asked

He stood up and stretched; that folding chair couldn't have been all that comfortable, certainly not while hunched over a table for two-and-a-half hours. "That's part of it. She's my personal liaison with the record company. She makes sure I've got everything I need while I'm out shilling my stuff."

"Keep the moneymaker happy, that sort of thing?"

"I'm sure that's what they say in the boardroom, but I've never quite felt the need for it. I mean, I can get my own bottled water."

"Hey, if they want to pay you the big bucks *and* coddle you at the same time, why complain?"

He looked hurt by my comment. "I'm not that guy, Amanda."

I put my hand on his arm, letting him know that he never had to explain himself to me. "I know."

"Sorry about the egg cream," he said, casting his gaze downward.

"It's okay." Suddenly, I had a brainstorm. "You free for dinner tomorrow night?"

"I'll have to check with Sondra, but I don't think there's anything scheduled. After all, this weekend is the first time I'll be playing for a while, so they don't want to tire me out. Besides, I try not to overbook myself when I'm here in town. There's always more city to explore."

Sadly, a little less these days.

"So, I'll see you at my place around 7?"

"Sure…is it okay if I bring someone?"

That surprised me. I figured he'd have mentioned a special someone. "Of course. Just don't forget the seltzer."

"You bet," he said, quickly checking back to make sure he hadn't forgotten anything before moving to join Sondra for their exit.

CHAPTER 10

▼

On the subway ride home, I started thinking about Pete, and what kind of nightmare he must be living in. Any city kid, under different circumstances, might relish the opportunity to spend a little time with his cousins in Queens. As great as Manhattan can be, there's something to be said for the outer boroughs, where there's less population and greater room for expansion. As a result, there's more parks, more bike trails, bigger schoolyards and, despite the mayor's best efforts during his last days in office, something that our little island may never have: sports stadiums.

I hadn't told Perelli, or even Andy Devane, my own personal hunch about Charlotte Kilmer's death, especially because I could see from their point of view how reliable the intuition of a broken-down, half-crazy cop must seem. But the explosion had been almost personal—set up to kill one person and one person only. Even if Pete, or someone like myself, had been in the kitchen with Charlotte, chances are he or she would have survived. Whoever had rigged the microwave had done so with an agenda: the boy lives, but Charlotte has to die. Hopefully, my fellow officer had stumbled onto this same line of thinking; it was a dirty place my thoughts had wandered off to, and my head was starting to throb.

I was a soup of emotions by the time I let myself into my apartment at around 7:30. Part of me was glad that I'd been able to do Mitch a solid turn, but my psyche was left standing in the cold November rain. I was contemplating how I might nourish myself—either physically or spiritually; it didn't much matter at that point—when the phone rang. I grabbed the handset in the kitchen and stretched my way into the dining room, where I could settle in for a friendly chat.

"Hello?"

"Hey there, partner." As good as it was to hear Randy's voice, his cautionary tone made me feel a little too much like a bedraggled puppy in the pound. "How're you feeling?"

"Bit of a headache, but I don't think I'll be keeling over anytime soon. How's things down at the station?"

"You know, same shit, different day. No homicides coming down the pike, which I suppose is a good thing."

"Great," I said. "Clean up the city so there's no need for me to come back to work."

Back to work. I couldn't believe how appealing—and how frightening—those words sounded. The 11th Precinct was so far gone from my conscious thought that it was a childhood trip to Disneyland, the background in a long-ago snapshot. Helping out Mitch was a step in the right direction. I could feel it.

"I don't think that's something you have to worry about, kid. The war still rages on…I just…never thought you'd be one of the casualties."

I knew just what he meant. From the time I'd enrolled in the academy until the mini-breakdown I'd had two weeks earlier, I'd never once questioned my decision about being a cop. In part, being on the sidelines was like scratching at a phantom limb, wanting to feel something that just wasn't there anymore. Wacky Jacky and I had talked about coming through this on the other side, but what if there was no other side? What if I survived the destruction only to step out into a barren wasteland, naked and alone?

"You still there?"

I had let the phone slip down to my chest, and I wondered if Randy could hear the rapid beating of my heart. "Sure. Just zoned out for a second."

"Did I catch you at a bad time?"

"No, I'm okay. Staring into the fridge and hoping something'll invite me over for dinner."

"Diane's got a little candlelit thing planned. Otherwise I'd swing by and we could grab a bite."

"Please. The last thing I want to be is guest of honor at a pity party." Diane Maxwell had been a witness in a murder investigation Randy and I had handled not quite a year ago. She was everything someone could want in a girl from Ipanema—tall, tan, young *and* lovely—but she came with baggage, of the four-wheeled variety. A drunk-driving accident, for which she was completely at fault, had left her a paraplegic—enough to scare away most of the wolves who would otherwise be howling at her door. Randy had seen something special in her, a beauty that wasn't full of herself, and threw the police manual out the window in favor of a romantic overture. There was no whirlwind, but a steady, gentle breeze that kept them moving forward into the stuff that dreams are made on.

"Well, if there's anything I can do…"

"Stop right there. I am your *partner*, Randy, not your charge, and I am not going to be made into an invalid, imaginary or otherwise."

I could hear him whistle on the other end of the line. "And I thought that doctor was cranky. You could teach him a thing or two about surliness."

"Wacky Jacky will be back in the office tomorrow, and I'll ask him for a pharmaceutical pick-me-up. Fair enough?"

"Amanda, I'm not suggesting you pack up and move to Prozac Nation, but do talk with him. When a dumptruck unloads that much debris on someone, it's easy to get buried."

"You've been spending too much time in the self-help section," I said, exasperated by his doggedness. "Try moving over to fiction or, should the divine Ms. Maxwell be willing, romance. Besides, if you keep yakking with me, those candles you mentioned will be guttering before they've had a chance to work their magic."

There was a slight hesitation. "A pair of Mitch Black tickets and the candles would pale compared to the real fireworks. But they were snapped up before I could even get over to The Bottom Line."

"Oh, come on, she's not holding that over your head, is she?"

"Of course not, but I know she's disappointed. The last time he came through town, she was still recovering from the accident. From what she told me, her boyfriend ended up going with someone else. And with the lights out at the rehab center, she couldn't even listen to the post-concert rock block on the radio. It would have meant a helluva lot to her."

Not nearly as much as what I had up my sleeve.

"Well, I'm sorry to hear about that. She's a good kid, Randy."

"You don't have to tell me that."

"I know. Look, I'm having a couple of people over tomorrow night. I'm cooking Thai, and I'd like the two of you to come."

"You sure you're up for preparing a dinner party?"

I had to bite my tongue to keep from cursing him and his platitudes. "You're incorrigible."

"And you're impossible. See you tomorrow night."

"Around 6:45."

I hung up the phone, pleased with myself for orchestrating my little meet-and-greet, complete with jaw-dropping special guest. But before I could do anything more for the following night's meal, I had to first contend with my immediate hunger. That started with a pot of water, brought to a boil on the stove. While that was heating, I rinsed off lettuce and tore myself a salad, topped with croutons, fakin' bits and Thousand Island dressing. I'm not sure what Emily Post would have thought of eating one course while preparing another, but table manners and etiquette have a tendency to crumble when there's no one around to shoo your elbows off the table.

I cooked up a double portion of penne, leaving half in the strainer to be burped into Tupperware for a subsequent meal. The rest I dumped onto a plate, covering the steaming pasta with a layer of fresh tomato-and-basil sauce from Fairway. I'd have preferred the pink vodka sauce, but I could just hear Dr. Calamari admonishing me about alcohol. Besides, I wasn't quite ready to be a "Death By Pasta" headline in the *Post*. While I ate, I sifted through the day's mail: cable bill, two pre-approved credit card applications, a trial subscription offer from *The Advocate* and a sports memorabilia catalog. Even though this particular periodical was meant for my neighbor downstairs, I took my time flipping through it. If I had a dog, I could definitely see myself dressing it in the Denver Broncos sweater.

After I finished eating, I put away the leftover penne, washed out my dishes and set them in the drain rack. I then put in a quick call to Wacky Jacky's voice mail, letting him know I'd be paying him a visit in the morning. I considered stopping upstairs to see James, but I didn't want to make too much of a nuisance of myself; I'd only just bothered him about Vic Renzo that morning. I might have given Jeannie a call, but I'd somehow managed to skate through the last 24 hours without getting her phone number. That left me back where I started.

You need to either get a real life, or more friends to populate the current one.

Maybe it was the fact that I hadn't had a cup of coffee in nearly 36 hours, or that I was running around Manhattan with a time bomb in my brain, but I hit a wall at around 9:30—just as I was getting into *Vertigo* on one of the classic movie stations—and the wall hit back. Even dragging myself from the living room to the bathroom became a chore, my toothbrush heavy as a shotput. I left a trail of clothes from the sink to the bed, barely stopping long enough to pull on my nightshirt. I turned on the CD player and wormed under the covers.

Perhaps in the morning, I will have metamorphosed into a beautiful butterfly.

When I got up to go to the bathroom at 3:30, I was still a caterpillar. Likewise at 8:45, when daylight insisted on waking the dead.

I got out of bed and spent about an hour playing chambermaid—scrubbing, sweeping, dusting, vacuuming, picking up and otherwise erasing the evidence of my recent slovenliness. My apartment, fortunately, isn't that big—sizable by New York standards, but not what you'd call spacious. Given my scattershot schedule and irregular cleaning habits, the place often looks to be on the verge of complete disarray. But I always manage to step in and eradicate the dust bunnies before they start building their own warren.

By the time I was finished, the apartment looked spiffy and I was convinced that fumes from the cleaning chemicals were the only reason that Merry Maids could still call themselves that. If I had to clean like that every day, several times a day, truth in advertising laws would force me to rename the business to something unprintable in the family yellow pages. Meanwhile, I'd worked up enough of a sweat to merit tossing my nightshirt in the laundry, rather than wringing another night's wear from it.

I showered, loofah'd, shampooed, conditioned and even blew dry, emerging from the bathroom with my hair looking fabulous, my skin looking fabulous and the rest of me ready to vomit if I used that word again. So I pulled on some undies, black jeans, a lightweight gray blouse and a loose-fitting black sweater; if the day was uneventful, I wouldn't have to change for dinner. I finished the rest of my morning routine—cereal, juice, vitamin and a quick skim of the paper—before trying to get a foothold in the Cliffs of Insanity.

James answered the door with a bundle of folded clothes in one hand and a cordless phone tucked up against the side of his face. "No, first class is fine. Honey, I'm not the one paying for the ticket. You could sit me on the pilot's lap for all I care. Just get me to Logan today." I followed him back to the bedroom, where he dropped the pants and shirts in a wheeled suitcase and paced.

"Idiots," he said to me, turning his head away from the mouthpiece. "Enough money to buy a state-of-the-art mainframe and server, but not enough brains to properly train someone to get them up and running again after a crash."

I scrunched up my face in disapproval, hoping to convey that even *I* wouldn't do something *that* stupid.

"Yes, that's right. Logan International Airport in Boston. JFK or LaGuardia. Doesn't matter." He rolled his eyes, then put an imaginary gun to his head. I didn't have to hear what the ticketing agent on the other end of the line was saying. All the anxiety in James' face drained away the moment he had a flight number. "American Airlines, JFK, 4:40 p.m. Perfect. Just perfect. The name is Finley. F-I-N-L-E-Y. First name, James."

I rocked on my heels while he continued packing and gave the rest of his personal information, including the credit card he used for business expenses. When he finished, he terminated the connection and tossed the phone on the bed. This wasn't the first time he'd been called out of town at the last minute, but I gathered the arrangements usually weren't so exasperating.

"You're flying?" I asked anxiously. "Doesn't that make you a little nervous? You know, with all that's been going on?"

I think James intended to scoff at my concern, but what came out of his throat sounded more like he was hacking up a hairball. "Darling, we're watching bell bottoms and platform shoes make a comeback. Death couldn't be any worse."

I was surprised by his cavalier attitude, but he quickly followed up his remark with, "I'm not going to live my life in fear."

"I hope this client is worth it."

"I'm happy to take their money, but I'd just as soon they got their heads out of their respective asses."

"Why you? Isn't there someone local who can help?"

"Of course there is, but I configured the whole system for them, and they don't trust anybody else with their baby. With the amount of information they store on their server, and I'm sure they don't back it up as often as they should, I can't really blame them. If there was some kind of disaster and they lost everything, it's unfathomable how much it would cost to replace it."

"Not that you'd ever let that happen."

He stopped, smiled and zipped up his suitcase. "Not on your life, sister. Now, I know you didn't come by to hear me bitch. Not looking like that."

"You like?" I asked with a girlish twirl.

"You bet. For such a ragamuffin, you clean up real good."

"You're sweet," I said, giving him a buss on the cheek.

"Now stop that," he replied, pushing me away. "I've got a good dudgeon going and I don't want to waste it. So…" He shook out his shoulders and put on a cranky face. "What do you want?"

"I was wondering if you could do a Web search for me. I know you're busy, but this really can't wait until my next class."

He perched on the edge of the bed and shoved the suitcase aside so I could sit next to him. "That's right. You finally took the plunge into the digital world. How'd it go?"

"The class was fine," I replied with a sheepish grin. "The instructor's even better."

"Amanda!" he said with mock shock. Then, with a conspiratorial tone, "That explains the get-up…but aren't you a little old to be the teacher's pet?"

"You've got to be kidding. I'm the only one in the class who isn't collecting Social Security."

"What do you expect? You're a freak. Most people your age are, if not literate, at the very least have *some* facility with computers."

"Better late than never, right?"

"Right. Now tell me about this teacher of yours."

I stood up, trying to coax him into the living room. "Can I do it while you do the search? You've got a flight to make and I really need you to do this."

"Come, grasshopper," he said, leading the way. "What do you need me to find?"

"Vic Renzo."

With the amount he shook his head back and forth, you'd have thought James was watching the final match of the U.S. Open. "What?" I asked. "Needle in a haystack?"

As he settled in front of one of his keyboards, he shook me off again. "More like a needle in a needle factory. Someone like that, with all the pies he's gotten his fingers into, is going to be all over the Web."

"It's probably a futile endeavor, but I've got to find something—anything—that'll give me a place to start."

"Suit yourself." I still get the terms "Web browser" and "search engine" mixed up, but James called up one of them, and in the data field entered the words "Vic" and "Renzo," with a plus sign in between. This, he explained, would make sure it only found sites that included both terms, rather than one or the other. He clicked the mouse on "Submit" and sat back in his chair. The search took less than a second, but the results couldn't have surprised James more.

The screen was filled with links to numerous Web sites, with what he called "keywords" under each one. But under none of the site names were the two names connected. Most were lists of names—a high school's recent graduating class, authors of a literary anthology, an intramural soccer team—all with someone with the first name "Vic" and a different person with the last name "Renzo."

"That's impossible."

"How do you mean?" I asked, leaning in closer.

"The likelihood of someone having a zero Web presence, especially someone in the computer industry, is just infinitesimal."

"How come?"

"Because *everything* is on the Internet. Take someone like yourself, who has nothing to do with computers. If I were to do a search for you online, I'd get at least a dozen hits. Not only would I probably find another Amanda Ross, but I'd come up with newspaper archives, your police academy graduation photo, the program from a play you did in college. They say idle hands do the devil's work. Well, the Internet is full of such things. People who have nothing better to do than make useless information available to anyone with a computer. Try it next time you're in class. Or, if you're so hot for teacher, ask her to show you how. Type in your own name and see what it comes up with."

I didn't quite grasp what James was saying. "You mean Vic Renzo isn't on there anywhere?"

"These days, virtually everybody is on the Web, even newborn babies thanks to birth announcements. If you're nowhere online, then you don't exist. Or you don't want to be found."

I ran my hands down my face and shook my head in frustration. "From all I've heard about Vic Renzo, either one is possible."

CHAPTER 11

▼

It wasn't my case, and I wasn't *really* investigating anything, but I still felt as though I were on an express bus to Nowhere…without a transfer.

Even though we both had other places to be, James gave me the chance to gush about Jeannie. Inside, though, it felt like a premature celebration, as if I were sneaking a peek at a gift on Christmas Eve rather than Christmas morning. "Now all we have to do is find someone for you and all will be right with the world."

"Sure thing, Pollyanna," James said with a lovelorn smile. "Sorry I can't make your little shindig tonight, but I'll be sure to have a lobster to mark the occasion."

"But I'm cooking Thai food."

"You protest too much. Besides, there *are* lobsters in Thailand. Now scoot. We've both got things to do."

As much as I'd have liked James to be there for dinner, it was probably for the best. I only have service for six.

In taking the subway downtown to the 11th Precinct, I tried to imagine myself heading in for a shift, ready to hit the streets again for a full day's work. Granted, there was no rush-hour crowd on the A train, but it nonetheless felt just about right. I skirted the squad room on my way in—I wasn't avoiding the people in it, per se, but how they'd respond to my presence. I figured it to be about 50–50: sticky sweet sentiments and encouragement on one hand, the cold shoulder as One Who Couldn't Hack It on the other. Maybe 60–40; I already knew where Randy stood.

Unlike the psychiatrists' offices I'd seen on TV, Wacky Jacky and the NYPD didn't do much to protect the privacy and anonymity of the loose screws in the house. Yes, he was in a lightly trafficked corridor, but if anyone saw you there, everyone quickly assumed that your deck was missing a few cards.

Yeah, but cops start out with only 48 or so...49, tops.

Through our sessions, John Sandusky had become my confidant, my confessor and my metronome. He always has the right words to keep my personal cuckoo clock from popping a spring.

I found him seated at his desk, his shirt sleeves rolled up, a bagel and the *Daily News* in front of him, bluegrass music softly twanging from his tape deck. He looks like a tenured professor, someone who'd lecture on literature, or shape young minds with his Socratic theories. But with his penchant for $2 ties and $7 haircuts, he'd never crack the Ivy League.

"How're you doing, Amanda?" he asked without getting up.

"Like I jumped out of a plane three minutes ago and I'm just now reaching for a parachute."

He hesitated before gesturing toward the recliner that took up far too much of his cluttered office. "Have a seat. I got back late last night. Otherwise, I'd have called to check in."

"Where were you?"

"Homecoming," he said, hooking his thumb in the direction of a Syracuse Orangemen pennant. "The wife and I decided to make a long weekend of it, catch whatever foliage was left on the trees."

"I never pegged you as a football fan."

"Marie is the football *fan*," he corrected. "I am the football *fanatic*. Ex-players usually are."

I blinked twice and stared in at him. He was broad-shouldered, but with something of a paunch and slight stoop he'd acquired in his trip over the hill of 50. But if you knocked off 30 years and 30 pounds, I could see him butting heads. "What position?"

"Tight end and special teams, mostly. Scored a few touchdowns, blocked a few kicks. Nothing too remarkable. Why, you a fan of the game?"

"Well, you won't see me in any cheerleader uniform, if that's what you're asking, but yes, I enjoy watching it every so often." I wasn't sure how I felt about the flicker of fantasy that danced across his eyes—especially since I found myself consciously crossing my arms to cover my pom-poms. After an awkward silence, I spoke up. "I think you just crossed some kind of line, and there weren't any referees around to signal that you were out of bounds."

"Wow," he said, shaking his head. "Didn't realize I was that transparent. Well, you're right, it was completely unprofessional for me to think about you in that way. I'm sorry if I made you uncomfortable."

Trust never comes easily for me, particularly with me, so I couldn't see the point in making a federal case out of the matter. There was no way I was going to start over with another shrink. "Apology accepted."

After all, he is the weaker sex.

I proceeded to tell him about the explosion, about Mitch and Jeannie, about Charlotte and Pete, about the tears I'd shed over Ground Zero and the fears I had regarding James' flight to Boston. As always, Wacky Jacky listened, asking just enough questions to draw out my words, my emotions.

"It's interesting what you said when you came in," he offered, flipping back the written-upon pages of his yellow legal pad. "You're doing much better than you were a few weeks ago."

"Flabbergasted" is as good a word as any to describe how I took his diagnosis. "How can you say that? It's like my mind has given over to complete chaos. Everything's going so fast that I can't even process."

"Amanda, you gave your mind over to chaos long before I met you. It's who you are. That rapid-fire brain of yours is part of what makes you a good detective." He used his foot to lean himself back in his chair, his hands resting on his lap. "You mentioned jumping out of a plane. That was you. Maybe it predates the panic attack, but when it came to your work, you never used to worry about parachutes or safety nets. It was gung-ho-and-God-help-me all the way. Now, though, there's some caution in your step."

"I've lost my edge," I said, pouncing on his words.

"Life isn't a whetstone, Amanda. We all grow duller with time—and there's nothing wrong with that. But your choice of verbs is what strikes me. You said that you were 'reaching' for a parachute. That implies that, deep down, you believe that there *is* a parachute—something to slow you down, to break your fall. You've got your own self-preservation in mind, but you're still willing to take the risk."

I found that a little hard to believe, seeing as how I'd just been James' agony aunt, but I kept my mouth shut.

"What would have worried me is if you'd said you were 'grasping' or 'fumbling.' To me, that says you yourself don't believe you've got any kind of security, that you're floundering, trying to find some kind of purchase."

Without realizing it, I'd given him the password to my subconscious. "So you think this bit of bodyguard duty is a good idea?"

"Not if it gets you killed," he said matter-of-factly. "We've already lost too many good people. But as far as prep work for a return to active duty, you've stumbled onto better therapy than I could ever prescribe."

Maybe all I'd needed was confirmation. I left Wacky Jacky's office feeling better than I had since before Tower One came down. And the better part of the day still lay ahead.

The 2 train was a few blocks away, but better served my purposes for the return trip, as I stayed on, bypassing Columbus Circle in favor of the 72nd Street terminal. I hadn't been planning on quite so much company when I'd shopped with Jeannie, so an encore excursion to Fairway was in order—namely to double up on a few items: chicken, noodles, sauce. I also grabbed a jar of spicy peanut sauce, wooden skewers and a small box of teabags. I was counting on my guests to mind their manners and contribute to the vittles so I wouldn't have to deal with dessert or drinks.

The afternoon air was cool and pleasant, with a light breeze fluttering the few leaves that hung on the occasional tree. It was almost 2:00 when I began the walk home, and I deemed a snack to be in order. It was too late for lunch and too long until dinner, especially if I wanted to "scint" that evening. If I go too long between feedings, I'm apt to become rude, crude and socially unacceptable.

I'm not sure how long Gray's Papaya has been in business, but it seems like forever, with its gaudy yellow signs and prominent corner location. It suited me just fine, being conveniently located between points A and B, supplying me with an opportunity to mini-feast on "The Best Damn Frankfurter I Ever Ate" and a papaya smoothie. Among the establishment's many slogans were a number touting the fruit's restorative properties, some going so far as to make the papaya sound like a megavitamin that had been plumped with water from the Fountain of Youth.

If I drink enough of it, do I get the invisible jet and the bulletproof bracelets?

Gray's Papaya is a walk-through business, with doors opening out onto both 72nd Street and Amsterdam Avenue and no seats in sight. I ate at the counter, sharing the dining space with a short, 50ish man with dark brown hair, pale jeans and a dirty white T-shirt. He wore a blue-on-blue Yankees cap and a ring with enough keys to open every office in the Empire State Building. He said nothing to me, nor I to him, both of us too involved in our gluttony to worry about social graces. We did, however, share a moment—call it a mutual food orgasm, complete with grunts and groans of sheer ecstasy.

The light on my answering machine was blinking when I got home. I stashed the groceries and took a breath, fully expecting one or more members of my dinner party to be canceling. Instead, it was another sort of gathering—one I'd completely forgotten about.

"Hi, Detective Ross, um, Amanda, this is Janice Kilmer, Charlotte's sister-in-law. I don't really know how close you were or anything, but I thought you might want to know about the funeral. It's tomorrow morning at 10:30…"

She proceeded to leave the address of the church, which was just a few blocks away, and the interment, which would be out in Queens. I wondered if she'd told Jason Perelli or, if he was a thorough investigator, if he'd gotten the information on his own. As for me, I was on the fence about going, my relationship with Charlotte cut short while we were still on the outskirts of friendship. The fact that I was doing a bit of freelance snooping made me curious about who might show, but I also wanted to see how Pete was doing. The laws of nature generally dictate that we bury our parents, but it is usually with thicker skins and harder hearts shielding us from the shock of raw emotion. At 7, would Pete be more affected by the mourning mass or by seeing his mother in a box? I never saw Charlotte after the explosion, but an open-casket service was probably out of the question.

I saved the message and set myself to some of the prep work for the evening meal. First, I filled a vase with water. Then I grabbed a handful of skewers and dunked in a dozen, leaving them to soak. Next, I took out a couple of chicken breasts and cut them into chunks, using the dull side of the knife to slide the pieces into a bowl, which I covered and stowed in the refrigerator. Then I took two more breasts and sliced them into thin strips, which I threaded onto the skewers. With a glaze brush, I slopped the kebabs with peanut sauce. I spread them out on a plate and laid a sheet of plastic wrap on top, popping the dish into the fridge so the meat could marinate. Lastly, I spread a couple of handfuls of peanuts on the cutting board and crushed them with a rolling pin. I also took out a large pot, my George Foreman grill and my electric wok—a Christmas gift from my mother, of course—my implements of destruction for the night.

Had it not been for my dolled-up 'do, which had held up pretty well over the course of the day, I might have taken a nap at that point. But bed head was supposed to be the *post*-date happening, wasn't it? Instead, I took another look at the Scrabble "cheat sheet" James had given me. It contained all the two-letter words, including such peculiar combos as AI and OE; all the three-letter words, from AAH to ZOO; and a number of other lists. I was specifically trying to get down the U-less Q words. QAT and QAID were pretty easy to remember, and QWERTY was permanently etched in my brain from my high-school typing class, but the rest of them: Would I ever use QANAT in a conversation, or have a need for SHEQALIM anywhere but on an El Al flight? TRANQ I could see, but what the heck is a QINDARKA?

I had segued onto the vowel dumps, and was trying to sort out the order of letters in AUREI and URAEI when the doorbell rang. It wasn't quite 6:30 and Jeannie was standing in the hall wearing a tan sweater set, plus slacks with narrow, black-and-tan vertical stripes. She smelled good—her perfume carried just a hint of autumn—and looked even better. She wore no jewelry other than a simple pair of gold ball earrings, and carried a white bakery box tied with string. I ached to touch her, to feel her, so much so that all my other bumps and bruises couldn't possibly compete. Her presence was my elixir, and her smile should have been classified as a controlled substance—I was already a junkie.

"Missed you today," she said warmly, stepping close and brushing her cheek against mine.

I put my hands on her hips and held her tight, not wanting to let go. "Me, too."

"Careful," she said, pulling away slightly and holding out the bakery box. "You might want to put this somewhere safe."

Tonight, my dear, nowhere is safe.

"Come on in," I said, retreating into the entryway. "You're the first to arrive."

"I'm guessing that's not an accident."

"Perceptive. I like that. You'd make a good detective." I put the bakery box on top of the fridge, out of harm's way until the six of us devoured it.

"I hope you like apple crumb."

"Not to worry. With the gang I'm expecting tonight, any dessert is an endangered species." In recent months, Randy, having reached his diet goal, had allowed himself a little more leeway in his food choices. He still worked out regularly, though, as part of his concerted effort to keep those 43 pounds he'd lost from finding him again. "I've got to put the water up and dust off my chef's apron, so why don't you set the table?"

"That I can do…if you show me where the dishes are."

"Cabinet over the sink," I said, pointing. She pulled out plates while I ran water into the pot and plugged in the Foreman. "I don't know if anybody's bringing wine, so you might want to put out multiple glasses. No goblet for me, remember."

Jeannie poked her head back into the kitchen. "Oh, yeah, I almost forgot. How's your noggin?"

"Tougher to crack than a coconut, but fragile just the same."

"The swelling gone down at all?"

"Sure, but a phrenologist would have a field day with me."

She hit me with a puzzled stare. "I'm not even gonna...oh, wait a minute...is that the person who predicts your future by reading the bumps on your head?"

A formidable adversary.

"That's the one."

"I think that came up in an anatomy class I took my sophomore year. Funny how we remember things like that."

Her sophomore year. In that moment, I realized just how young she was—25, maybe 26—a couple of Congressional terms younger than me. It felt a little odd, as all my previous partners had been my age or older. The difference between Jeannie and me was bound to affect conversation—we'd essentially grown up on different TV shows, different music, different toys—and I was just old enough to recall the leftovers of the Vietnam era. Was it a gap that we could cross? Maybe she could help me regain some of my long-lost youthful idealism.

Randy and Diane arrived a few minutes after I had my wrinkly realization. I hadn't spent much time with Diane—in the year or so she and Randy had been together, this was the first time she had been to my apartment. I also hadn't considered the fact that my apartment building wasn't all that wheelchair friendly; Randy probably had his work cut out for him getting his lady up my front stoop.

"Good to see you, partner," I said as he wheeled Diane through the front door. She was dressed quite fashionably, as she had been every other time I'd seen her, in a black sleeveless top and skirt. Her ensemble was completed by delicate black studs in her ears. "You too, Diane."

I did a quick round of introductions, catching an approving nod from Randy. He'd only been witness to a few of my affairs, but he knew my taste in women—it wasn't that different from his own. Diane gently took Jeannie's hand as they said their hellos, then, almost as an afterthought, passed along a pair of wine bottles. "One red, one white," Diane said. "We didn't know what Amanda was cooking."

"Yeah, she's always full of surprises," Randy chimed in.

"Come on," I said, relieving Jeannie of the bottles, "let's not turn this soiree into a fire hazard. The living room awaits."

The three of them proceeded on their own as I made a detour to put the bottles out on the table. "Can I pour anyone a drink?"

"I'll take a white," Randy called.

"Make that two," Jeannie said.

"Diane?"

"Um, something non-alcoholic if you've got it."

I assumed this was because of her accident, but I wasn't about to press the point. "Ginger ale okay?"

"Sure."

"A girl after my own heart. Randy, can you open the wine?"

"You got it." He got up and produced a Swiss Army knife, flipping out the corkscrew. Meanwhile, I gathered a pair of tumblers from the table and brought them into the kitchen. As I was pouring ginger ale for Diane and myself, I heard Randy ask, "So, Amanda, I see six place settings. Who else is coming?"

As if on cue, the doorbell rang, saving me from having to answer the question.

Let the games begin.

CHAPTER 12

▼

They didn't faint when Mitch came into the living room, but the expressions on their faces were absolutely priceless. Diane actually appeared to be on the verge of tears, whereas Jeannie had to grab the arm of the couch to keep from heading into a full swoon.

"You're…you're…" Randy stammered.

"Everyone," I said, sidling up behind Mitch and resting my elbow on his shoulder. "I'd like you to meet Mitch."

"Well, we know who he is," Randy responded, catching his breath, "but the bigger question is—"

"What am I doing here?" Mitch finished, putting his arm around me. "Well, the simple fact is, I couldn't come to New York and not stop in to see…" He looked at me. "What was your name again?"

Randy, Diane and Jeannie laughed, and I was glad to see there wouldn't be too much tension to the evening. Mitch sat in my old wingback chair, facing them. Each took turns with introductions—Jeannie referred to herself as my "computer teacher and friend"—desperately working to stopper the gush of questions and compliments; the corks were bound to pop sooner or later.

I brought Mitch a glass of red wine and sat down on the arm of the chair. "I thought you were bringing a date."

"I did," he replied casually. "Last I saw him, he was hitting on someone in the lobby."

"J.T.?" It made sense, though I was still somewhat surprised. "I half expected you to bring Sondra."

He took a sip of his wine. "*That* is a strictly professional relationship. She works for the record company," he said to the others to bring them up to speed. "She'll probably be stopping by later and, unfortunately, that will be my cue to leave."

"She's coming here? How come?"

"She wants to make sure I actually leave. I'm doing the morning talk shows tomorrow and I have to be 'fresh.' That's her word."

I went into the kitchen, leaving Mitch to hold his own in the conversation, and found the water boiling. I opened both packages of rice noodles and dumped them in. Then I retrieved my chicken skewers and placed them on the Foreman, closing the lid to a satisfying sizzle. I was in the process of spooning the remaining peanut sauce into a dipping bowl when I felt a hand on my ass, the touch too rough to be Jeannie.

"I know you need both hands to play," I said with an exhale, "so you've got about two seconds to reverse course. Otherwise, the only stick you'll be holding is a traction bar."

J.T. took a step back so I could turn and face him. "Same old Amanda. How're you doing?"

"My ass is just fine, thank you, as is the rest of me. And talk about same-old, same-old, you've been pawing at me for what, 12 years? Has it ever gotten you *anywhere?*"

"Hey, at least I'm consistent." A quick putdown featuring hobgoblins and little minds was on the tip of my tongue when the interloper committed cardinal sin number two, sniffing the air and asking, "So, what's cooking?"

"Get…out…of…my…kitchen," I growled. When he didn't move, I ended up chasing him toward the living room with a whisk (it was the closest thing I could grab). In his flight, he nearly collided with Mitch, who was bringing me my drink. The accident avoided, I took a bit to collect myself. "Mitch, how many guys in your band?"

"Five, not including the backup singers."

"Then get this dog on a leash, now, or you'll be a quartet Friday night, with one member missing and presumed *neutered.*"

Mitch snapped his fingers and pointed to the floor. "Heel!"

J.T. glanced over at his three-person audience and barked, then bounded to Mitch's side, squatted down and panted. They carried the canine routine even further, with Mitch scratching J.T. behind the ears and J.T. shaking his leg with pleasure.

As much as I like to think of myself as having been present at the start of Mitch's music career, J.T. McGinnis was around even earlier. He and Mitch were buddies from high school, and Mitch had rescued him from the dead-end hell of overnight bank security when he'd set out on his singer-songwriter path. In the music world, J.T. was known for two things: his mastery of the drums and his insatiable appetite for women. The former had developed over time, starting from when he and Mitch were just a two-piece ensemble—guitar and voice backed by a simple snare and cymbal. The latter seemed almost inborn—he was probably groping cute cousins and aunts while still in poopy pants. His sexploits occasionally landed him in the pages of the nation's finer tabloids—twice on the cover—and Mitch's guilt by association was just enough tarnish to keep rock fans from writing him off as a squeaky-clean square. It'd been a dozen years and J.T. was still trying to get me to play for the other team.

What always surprised me about J.T.'s debauchery was that he never lacked willing partners—despite a pronounced lack of charisma. He had an okay face, surrounded by longish brown hair going prematurely gray. His upper body was developed from years of bashing the skins, and he had the thick, muscular legs of a wrestler, but the two parts didn't quite meet; he was sort of squishy around the middle. His offstage wardrobe consisted of concert tees, Hawaiian shirts and jeans. Tonight, in deference to the cooler weather, he topped a *Wonderland* tour shirt with a blue-and-black plaid flannel. How he'd become such a successful lothario was as much a mystery as his first name. There are even members of his family who claim to be in the dark about that one. I'm sure the supermarket rags would pay a lot more for that information than for yet another paparazzi shot of his half-naked bod.

I took the pot off the stove and dumped the noodles in a colander, running cold water over them and letting them drain. Next, I plugged in the wok and, while it was heating, removed the skewers from the grill. After arranging them on a serving plate—dipping bowl in the center—I brought the makeshift satay out to my guests. Mitch was still in the wingback, Randy sat on one side of the couch, holding Diane's hand. Jeannie was on the other side of the couch, while J.T. circled the group, in the midst of what sounded like a raucous tale of life on the road. He swigged from a beer bottle, and I noticed two six-packs perched on the dining room table; J.T. must have brought them in just prior to launching his sneak attack on my posterior.

Before I could make my way back to the kitchen, Jeannie let loose the first salvo of culinary kudos.

"This is great, Amanda."

"Really tasty."

"Reminds me of a Thai place we went to a few weeks ago," added Randy.

"What do you call this again?" J.T. asked.

"Instant satay," I explained as I scootched into the kitchen. "There'll be more shortly."

I knew the main course wouldn't take long to prepare, but I still wanted to keep their palates tantalized. With the rest of the skewers cooking, I got out four eggs, which I cracked and beat in a small bowl. I poured oil into the wok, then scrambled the eggs, which took less than two minutes. When the eggs had reached the right consistency, I slid them out of the wok and into their original bowl.

Having reached full heat, the Foreman didn't need long to cook the second round of satay. I grabbed the skewers and brought them out, pausing just long enough to dip one for myself. The peanut sauce was strong and flavorful, but not overpowering. Experiment number one was definitely a success.

I splashed a bit more oil into the wok and stir-fried the chicken I'd cut up earlier. Then I added the rice noodles and two full jars of Pad Thai sauce, stirring until everything was well-coated. Next came the bean sprouts and peanuts, followed at last by the eggs, which I chopped with my wooden spatula. I mixed everything vigorously so the noodles wouldn't burn, but I had to be careful not to slop over—the quadruple batch I had prepared was about as much as I could cook at one time.

"Get it while it's hot," I called, unplugging the wok and bringing it to the table. "Rather unceremonious, I realize, but it's serve yourself."

Randy wheeled Diane over to the table and took the chair next to her. I sat at one end, with Jeannie on my left and Mitch opposite—J.T. sat between them, his gaze flicking back and forth between the food in front of him and the female forms around him.

"Man," he said, "I haven't been surrounded by this many beautiful women since…when was the last time we were on tour?"

Mitch laughed. "Don't tell me you reformed your horndog ways just because we weren't playing out every night."

"Reformed? Never," he replied, scooping out a heap of Pad Thai with the rubber-coated spoon I'd supplied. "More like downsizing. After all, we session schlubs don't have quite the exposure, or the appeal, of our live, in-your-face alter egos."

I could tell Randy was just itching to drive home a diss, especially with the way J.T. was eyeing Diane, but he held his tongue—and both their plates—as he served.

"What do you mean?" Jeannie asked after a brief silence. "About being a session schlub."

"Well, darling, since my meal ticket opted to take an extended hiatus from recording and touring, I've had to find other gigs to fill my time. So Vertical rents me out, so to speak, and I end up playing on other people's projects."

"And then what?"

"And then I move on to the next paycheck. Most established acts have a standard touring lineup, but they sometimes bring in extra musicians for the recording sessions. In my case, they usually have me in for a guest spot, to add a little star quality to the deal. It's often for up-and-coming bands that might not otherwise get much airplay. But stick my name on it, or even better, Mitch's, and you instantly up the record's credibility."

"You ever get jealous," Randy asked, "always being in the background? Supporting the star but not sharing the spotlight?"

J.T. shook off whatever effrontery was cocked and loaded behind the question, and gave Mitch a chuck on the shoulder. "Jealous of what? I make more money than I ever dreamed, I've got fans all over the world and I get more puss—" He fumbled, looking around at the three members of the XX club, whose stares quickly turned to glares. "Ah, perks, than you could possibly imagine."

He took a big slug of beer before continuing. "Besides, when you get right down to it, I owe this guy everything. Sure, I got on board before he was a bandwagon—when he was just a hatchback trying to scrape together enough gas to get to the next town. It's been an amazing ride, but Mitch has always been in the driver's seat. And I'm perfectly fine with that. I can just sit back and watch the scenery."

"But don't you ever get lonely?"

Mitch fielded that one. "This circus life we lead is murder on relationships. In so many ways, what we do is all-consuming, from our time to our hearts and minds, that there's not always a whole lot left over to give someone. And that's not really fair to that other person. Add to that the fact that you go out on the road for weeks at a time. I mean, say I was married. My wife has a choice between two unattractive options: She could hang onto her life, her career, her friends and stay at home, waiting for me to call before each show. Or she could give up everything and tag along on the tour. Sure, we might be together, but that's not a life.

She ends up being nothing more than a groupie with a ring on her finger. I don't mean any disrespect there, but as I said, this business is…"

"All-consuming," Randy echoed.

"Is that what happened with you and Beth?" Diane asked.

Beth Morgan had actually been a dormmate of mine, one of many I'd introduced to Mitch Black, the man and his music. A physical therapy major, she was a chubby-cheeked blonde who quickly became a fixture at every place he played in town. I'm not sure how long it was after she first saw him play that they'd become an item, but in many ways they complemented each other beautifully. She'd massage his back and shoulders after a set, he'd sing her blues away when college got tough.

"How'd you hear about her?" Mitch queried. "No, wait, let me guess…'Behind the Music,' right?"

"I think it was an E! 'Celebrity Profile.'"

"Fair enough. And yes, that is what happened. I regularly gave away everything I had—all my emotion, all my energy—to my audience, without ever thinking to save some for her. It was a rookie mistake; I was far too committed to my career to be committed to another person. That doesn't mean it didn't hurt when she cheated on me, or when she left, but she did what she felt she had to—and it's hard to fault someone for that."

"And to ease the hurt, you wrote 'Lonely Hours.'"

"Well, yes and no. To ease the hurt, I *started* writing 'Lonely Hours,' but even that became too painful. That's why the song remained unfinished for so long. It took maybe three or four years before I was finally in a place where I could revisit those feelings again without beating myself up."

"You mentioned that the other day," I said, my mouth still full of Pad Thai. I finished chewing, washing it all down with ginger ale. "You said that something happened in Phoenix which helped you put a new perspective on things. What happened?"

Mitch finished his wine and took a breath. "There was a young woman who killed herself."

Diane and Jeannie gasped; the prickly sensation on the back of my neck was an alert that my brain had gone into full cop mode. I was sure Randy was feeling it, too.

"She, er, threw herself off the roof of my hotel. I saw her fall."

The chatter of silverware and side conversation stopped, as if Mitch's revelation were a sponge that soaked up all sound. In fact, the only noise in the room was the gluttonous grunting of J.T. as he attacked his dinner; he'd heard it all before.

CHAPTER 13

▼

Before Mitch continued with his story, we cleared the table, put the fixings away and started the kettle and coffeepot. I'd burned through my caffeine withdrawal period, so I wasn't exactly itching for a cup of joe, but I could taste the French roast from the instant I opened the can. However, there was still a matter of doctor's orders, which had long since become personal annoyances. One more night to get me out of the 72-hour window, and I could start living again.

Diane had offered to wash dishes, but I told her that I'd take care of them. I wrapped up the remaining Pad Thai—just enough for one—and put the wok in the sink. The bottom was scorched, but it wasn't anything a scrunge couldn't handle. While the coffee brewed, we repaired to the living room.

"Jennifer Marx was 22 when she died. She'd come to the hotel to see me, but security turned her away. She didn't try to con anybody, or offer sex for a free pass. She just said, 'I need to see him.'"

"Which I'm sure they'd heard before," I said.

"Precisely. Everybody's got an angle, everybody's got a reason for wanting a piece of the limelight—whatever part might rub off from a chance encounter with someone like me."

"And when she couldn't get in, that sent her over the edge?" Randy asked.

"Literally and figuratively," Mitch replied, and Randy immediately regretted his choice of words. "She took the elevator as high as she could, then the fire stairs up to the roof. From the police reports, she never hesitated. She just marched straight across, climbed up the outer wall and jumped. I happened to be standing out on my terrace and…it was the worst thing I've ever seen."

Randy and I both looked over at Diane, and suddenly her devotion to Mitch's music seemed positively normal. "The press must have had a field day with this one. At least the tabloids," I said, retrieving the coffeepot and pouring out four cups.

"Unfortunately, they did, but not like you'd expect."

"They went on about what a psycho this Marx chick was," J.T. added. "Somehow they found out about all the letters she'd written him. Hundreds of 'em stacked up at the record company. And then they went on about this girl's history. How she got bounced around from foster home to foster home, probable history of sexual abuse. Total whack job."

"What they missed," Mitch said after a hesitation and a sip of coffee, "is that she wasn't quite as crazy as everyone thought."

This took even J.T. by surprise. "Meaning what?"

"After some of the heat had died down and her picture stopped appearing on page three, I stopped in at Vertical and took a look at this mountain of correspondence. Most of it was the usual puppy-love, 'Oh, you're so wonderful' sort of sentiment that girls usually outgrow by the time they're 15. But mixed in with the curlicues and the I's dotted with little hearts was a confident tone, a commitment to the notion that she was a meaningful part of my life, that somehow she and I shared an intense secret."

Jeannie gave her teabag another dunk and pressed it with her spoon, bleeding a little more apple-cinnamon into her cup. "But you'd never met her before, so how could she possibly…?"

"That's what I thought. But then I went back and looked at her picture, wracking my brain for someplace I might have bumped into her, some way we might have come in contact. Finally, I went back through a few of my notebooks, thinking there might be a clue."

"And there was," I said, seeing it in his eyes.

He tapped out a gentle beat on his leg, and began to sing.

> "You brought me in, in from the cold
> Took pity on a wounded soul
> A smile to melt the hardest heart
> Mending what was torn apart.

You brought me in, in from the cold
When I thought I'd lost all control
It took a stranger to make me see
The light beyond reality.

I may be sitting here alone
But I'm no longer on my own
No matter where I go, you'll always be
The one who came and rescued me.

As I picture your face and eyes of blue
With these words and notes I promise you
Someday I'll return to have and hold
The girl who took me in…in from the cold."

It was a song we all knew: "In from the Cold," the lead single from his most recent album. In the friendly confines of my apartment we were all tempted to sing along, but instead greeted the intimate, impromptu serenade with applause, gasps and, in Diane's case, tears. Randy cradled her softly and we all waited with anticipation for Mitch to explain.

"I don't know why I didn't see it sooner. Maybe it was because the picture they ran in the paper looked so sad. It was missing everything that'd made me notice her in the first place."

"Wait a minute," Randy said, leaning in, "are you saying you knew this girl?"

"Knew her? If you allow for a little poetic license, everything I wrote about her is true."

Wouldn't be the first time he hooked up with a space case.

The news was pretty tough to digest, especially on a full stomach. If nothing else, it explained why "In from the Cold" had disappeared from the set list of his recent shows. Just watching Mitch tell the tale there in my living room, it was plain how horrible he felt about the whole situation—even to Jeannie, Randy and Diane, the ones who hadn't known him for years. It may be hard to drum up sympathy for someone who makes more dough in a single night than you're liable to see in a year, but from where we sat, the monkey on his back was looking a lot like King Kong.

"It was during a stayover in Philadelphia—we were doing a back-to-back at the Spectrum. The reviews for *Sticks and Stones* were on the tepid side, and the tour wasn't going all that well. Gil was talking about leaving."

"Our bass player," J.T. offered, though as members of the fan club, we didn't need to be told.

"And I was getting bogged down in the bullshit of this business. It just didn't seem worth it anymore."

Perish the thought!

Mitch got up and paced, some of the agitation in his manner fading as he reflected upon the memory. "And I quit. I stormed out of the hotel, saying good riddance to a life that had drifted. I was tired of fighting. Tired of playing toady to everyone except myself. I was so hot and bothered that I got half a mile into a Philadelphia winter before I even felt the cold. I stopped to figure out where I was and a gust of wind sent me shivering into the first open door I could find. It was, I don't know, 1 in the morning and a diner seemed as good a place as any to disappear."

I nudged Jeannie and we both got up to serve dessert. Mitch stopped his narrative while we cut up the apple crumb, and picked up the coffeepot to freshen everyone's cup. We passed the plates around in bucket-brigade fashion until everyone had a slice, then resumed our positions. We were like kindergartners at story time, restlessly waiting for the teacher to show us another picture of Corduroy or Clifford the big red dog.

"I sank into a booth and ordered coffee without even looking at the waitress' face. All she said was 'Coming right up,' but there was something melodic in her voice. Something pure and wholesome. I don't know if she'd just gone on shift, or if she'd just gotten the job, but everything about her said that she was as happy as she could be, just wearing her polyester blue uniform and pouring coffee for the dregs of humanity. Made me think about the last time I'd truly been happy. And in so doing, I was able to grab hold of a dream that had all but floated away, that thing that drove me to write music in the first place. The more I watched her—from her smile to the little sashay she did around the end of the counter— the better I felt. She was my rejuvenating spring—and sometime between the cheese steak and the chocolate cream pie, I heard the notes...the chords...and I had to borrow her pencil just to get everything down—four or five napkins' worth."

"Wow," Diane said. "Did she even know who you were?"

"If she did, she never let on. She just brought me my food, always with a winning, winsome smile. By the time I swallowed the last piece of pie, it was like I was about to head out on my first tour, not in the middle of my sixth one in six years. There was hope…and possibility."

"I hope you left her a big tip," Jeannie remarked.

"A hundred bucks, and even that didn't seem like enough. I couldn't have paid for that kind of therapy. Plus, I countersigned the check."

"You what?" J.T. asked.

"You know how in restaurants, sometimes the server will sign the back of your bill? That's what she did. It said, 'Thank you, J.M.' And so I wrote beneath that, 'No, thank <u>you</u>,' and signed it."

"Talk about being in the right place at the right time," Diane said romantically. "Imagine."

"Hey, for all I know, she stuck it on the spike next to the register and it got filed with the day's receipts. But it was the least I could do. If I'd had any backstage passes or tickets or anything, I'd have left those, too. But I said goodnight and found my way back to the hotel, where I copied all of my napkins into a notebook and had the best night's sleep I'd had in months."

"I don't mean to be rude," Randy said, standing up to meet Mitch face to face—or close, anyway, since Mitch is a good six inches taller—but how does Jennifer Marx go from slinging hash in Philly to pitching herself off your roof in Phoenix? That's kind of an oddball coincidence, don't you think?"

"All I know is that the police reports said she was living in Phoenix at the time of her death. Who knows? If she'd still been a Philly waitress, maybe she'd still be alive."

The doorbell rang at around 10:30, with Sondra arriving to collect her prize stallion. I invited her in for a cup of coffee and the crumbs of the crumb, which she accepted with a stern look at Mitch and four or five at her watch.

"Everyone," I said, "this is Sondra Fisher. She's Mitch's liaison with the record company." Turning back to her, I added, "I hope that's right."

"More or less," she grumbled.

Randy got up and offered her his seat, but she chose to stand in the entryway, just on the lip of the carpet. She took the cup of coffee I handed her and sipped with brittle determination, as if she might spill it all over her pale gray suit. At this point, J.T. crossed and got right in her personal space. "He doesn't need a babysitter, you know. I can make sure he gets home in one piece."

"You?" she chirped, looking for someplace to set down her cup. "He's due on 'The Big Show' at 7, and 'Regis and Kelly' after that. I need him fresh and focused, not hung over and smelling of cigarette smoke and knockoff perfume."

J.T. glanced over at Mitch, trying to find some deviant flaw that only Sondra saw. "In the seven years, the seven loooong years, you've been doing this Mother Superior act, has he ever shown up late, acted unprofessionally in public or done anything else that might embarrass the record label?"

"No," she said, her voice steely and cold, "which is why I still have a job. On the other hand, if it was *your* name on the marquee, we'd probably all be arrested for crimes against morality."

While they continued their lovers' quarrel—personally, I'd have put money on Sondra in a cage match, and definitely would have paid to see her kick J.T.'s ass—I crooked my finger at Randy and gestured for him to join me in the kitchen. He wound his way through the living room—which was pretty crowded with seven occupants—and followed me.

"Jeannie seems great," he said in an exaggerated whisper. "I like the way she plays off you."

"Thanks. Feels like I've known her a lot longer than two days, but there are still a lot of mysteries to be revealed."

"That's a good thing, isn't it?"

"Oh, yes," I said, feeling on top of the fridge for the card Mitch had given me. I felt inside and pulled out two of the tickets, which I presented to my partner. "I realize, after tonight, these may come as anti-climactic, but I'd like the two of you to be there. I'd have given them to you earlier, but I think Diane would appreciate them more if they came from you. Besides, why shouldn't you be on the receiving end of her gratitude?"

Instead of taking the tickets, he cast his eyes downward and kicked at the floor. "You really know how to make a person feel like a shit, don't you?"

"I've had years of practice," I said, jokingly shaking his arm. "But what makes you say so?"

"That," he blurted, pointing toward the living room, "and those. You just gave us a double dose of fantasy, and I couldn't even be bothered to remember your birthday."

Oh. That.

"It wasn't that memorable," I said quickly, before he accumulated any more frequent guilt miles. "If it hadn't been the day I met Jeannie, I'd have written it off entirely." Hearing a shuffling of shoes in the other room, I ventured, "Come on, it sounds like Sondra's about to get out the leash."

"For Mitch or J.T.?"

"Which one do you think needs it more?"

"For J.T., I think a muzzle might be more suitable. That and a rabies shot."

The three of them were indeed getting ready to leave, so we said our goodbyes with hugs and kisses. Mitch started to say that he'd see everyone on Saturday, but I cut him off with a head shake, retaining the element of surprise. Instead, he gave me the universal phone signal and I knew I'd be hearing from him shortly.

"I could kill you," was the two-way barrage I got as soon as the door closed; Diane was still too star-struck to let loose.

"We've been partners for two years, and you don't even think to *mention* that Mitch Black is a personal friend," Randy said with just a sprinkle of wounded pride. "I thought we told each other everything."

"How much meaningless drivel came out of my mouth?" Jeannie countered. "He must think I'm a complete idiot."

She batted my hand away on my first move, then let me wrap my arm around her waist. "Nobody thinks you're an idiot," I said softly. Then to Randy I charged, "If I'd told you the truth, would you have believed me?"

That shut him up, but it happened at the same time Diane found her voice. "Amanda, I don't know how to thank you. I feel like I won a contest, or finally got the bigger end of the wishbone. You have no idea what this meant to me."

Just wait 'til Randy gets you home.

"Not that there's any way we could top that," Randy added, "but we did want to wish you a belated happy birthday." Diane handed him a card she produced from a pocket on her wheelchair, and he passed it along to me. Jeannie looked over my shoulder as I opened the envelope, finding a picture of three babies smiling beneath the word "Friendship." The gushy verse inside wasn't really my style—Diane must have picked out the card—but it found the soft spot it was aimed at.

"Thanks, guys," I said quietly.

They looked at each other quizzically before Randy piped in, "There's something else in the envelope."

That something else was a gift certificate for a rock-climbing lesson. One hour of private instruction at the climbing school at Sports Center at Chelsea Piers, on what was billed as "the world's most challenging climbing wall."

"Hey, wow," Jeannie said, "that looks like fun."

"Goes with all the rocks in my head."

Diane wasn't quite sure what to make of my reaction. "You like it?"

"I'm not going to be able to use it for a while, but absolutely. I've always wanted to try it, but it's not something I'd ever do on my own."

"Good," she said as Randy rubbed her shoulders. "I'm glad."

"You're not all that easy to shop for," Randy offered.

"You done good."

There was another round of goodbyes, with the four of us agreeing to hook up again in the not-too-distant future. Jeannie was already fitting in with my friends, which wasn't necessarily a big hurdle, but an obstacle I was happy she cleared.

We carted the dessert dishes into the kitchen and added them to the pile in the sink. "Wash or dry?"

"Dry," she said, and we both groaned.

We talked as we worked our way through the mound; she was easy to talk to, and a good listener. She also didn't mind a little bit of dirty work—it was no small stack of dishes. By the time we were done and my fingers had turned to prunes, it was after 11:30.

"Thanks," I said as we shared a dishtowel to wipe our hands. "This would have taken me forever."

We stood in the kitchen, doing the post-date dance of indecision and hesitation. "You know, I've been climbing once or twice. It's been a few years and I could certainly use a refresher. Maybe we could do that class together."

Together. I like the sound of that.

"Like I said, that's going to be a while in coming, but there's something else that I was hoping we could do together." I found one of the remaining concert tickets and eased it into her hand.

Her smile was delayed, but no less bright than I remembered. She didn't say anything, but rather sidled shyly in my direction. When her eyes met mine, she sealed the deal with a kiss—softer than we'd shared Monday night, but twice as electric.

"Amanda, my dear, your little soiree this evening earned you entrance to my parlor. This, though, entitles you to one complimentary orgasm."

With the way she said it and the seductive intensity in her gaze, I nearly had one on the spot.

CHAPTER 14

▼

Dr. Calamari would never have approved.

Jeannie delivered on her promise and then some, her hands, fingers and tongue exploring every part of my body, finding nary an out-of-order sign. I'd been charged from that last moment in the kitchen until we collapsed in each other's arms some four hours later, and there wasn't an instant in between that wasn't magical. Involuntary abstinence is like hitting yourself in the head with a sledgehammer; it feels so good when you stop.

Fortunately for Jeannie, out of practice doesn't necessarily mean incapable, and I managed to rock her world on more than one occasion. It wasn't my best effort—but I figured it was enough to bring her back for a second helping.

She was spooning me when I woke, her nipples tickling my back as she breathed, her left arm draped across my chest. I laid there for at least ten minutes, feeling her, trying to get a picture of her dreams. Was I a part of them? Did her black-and-white visions foretell a full-color future for two? Time might tell, but the virtue of patience was wasted on me.

We tumbled out of bed at around 9:15, still caught up in each other's wonder. We were no longer strangers in the night, yet there was none of the been-there-done-that casualness that sometimes follows sexual conquest, and the glances we exchanged were as tender as a loving caress. Even morning breath couldn't dampen the chemistry.

"Good morning," Jeannie said, nuzzling me once again.

"It certainly is." Outside of a funeral I had to attend, it was, in fact, just about perfect. I was a bit disappointed she wouldn't be accompanying me ("You have to wait until at least the sixth date to get me to a funeral," she'd said), but she did promise to model her "little black dress" for me at a later date.

We both had places to go on that rainy Thursday morning, otherwise I might have accepted her invitation to join her in the shower. Instead we took turns, and I was toweling off, she poured cereal and put up water for tea. I offered her a sweatshirt so she wouldn't have to make the post-coital "walk of shame," but she declined with an answer that would have charmed the pants off me, had I been wearing any: "Beauty is nothing to be ashamed of."

We dallied over breakfast, longer than we should have, such that I barely had 15 minutes to pull together an outfit and hoof it to the church. I pulled on stockings, panties and bra, followed by black slacks and a rust blouse. Jeannie pointed out a bleach streak on the side of the blouse, so I adopted the previous day's sweater as a cover. With black flats on my feet, I was just about set. However, while I rummaged for my raincoat, I made sure Jeannie jotted down her phone number.

We left together, with Jeannie saying she'd give me a ring during one of her office hours that afternoon. Our goodbye kiss was just a peck, which startled her.

"Always leave 'em wanting more," I shouted, tripping my way east on 61st Street. "Mitch taught me that."

The church's stained glass windows were covered in condensation from the gloomy November rain. The walk over had been tough enough, with icy gusts trying to defrock me at each corner, but I felt sorry for anyone who was going to stand outside for the burial.

With neither a legion of admirers nor a lengthy list of enemies, Charlotte Kilmer wasn't due an SRO memorial service. Her family and close friends—including Pete, Janice, her husband John and their kids—didn't even fill up the first two pews. There were maybe 40 people in all, including a few faces from the neighborhood and, I assume, contacts from the book world. Toward the back was a smattering of misfits—including a pair of elderly funeral groupies, Jason Perelli and myself. He and I sat side-by-side in the last row, within earshot of the pulpit but far enough away that we could talk shop without disturbing the proceedings.

"How're you feeling?" he asked as the organist began his rendition of Generic Funeral Music, Volume One. Everything about the place, from the flowers to the blow-up photo of Charlotte—displayed on a Sunday school easel—felt cookie-cutter thoughtless. In their hour of grief, John and Janice had likely taken the simplest way out, with the funeral director saying the magic words: "Let us take care of everything."

"All things considered," I said, shrugging my shoulders toward the casket, "pretty good. How about you? Any progress?"

"No hits, no runs, no errors," he replied dejectedly. "Couldn't uncover a thing on the explosion or Vic Renzo. Though not for lack of trying. Until we have some kind of motive, we're just grasping at straws. Christ, you're the closest thing we have to a witness."

"What about the device? Can't you trace its origins?"

"We've got a partial serial number we're trying to pin down. Forensics says it's a piece of the detonator, which should help us narrow down the possibilities. But with all the stuff available online, who's to say where the damn thing came from?"

Just as the priest approached the altar, a pair of stragglers came in—a couple in their early 60s—and slid into the pew opposite us. She had hair the color of used charcoal, fancifully fluffed in front and shorn in the back, baring a leathery neck. She wore dark-rimmed glasses and earrings with flat black dangles. He had a darker coloring, and was dressed in a modest gray suit with a maroon shirt. His hair, still reasonably brown, surrounded a bald spot the size of a small saucer. Only his smoky sideburns, which splashed down around his big-lobed ears, belied his otherwise hearty and youthful appearance."

"I wonder who they are," I whispered. "Couldn't be her parents, could they?"

"What kind of parents would be late to their daughter's funeral?"

"Good point."

"Actually, her parents beat her into the afterlife. The mother died of ovarian cancer in '93 and the father died in a construction-site accident mishap two years later. That's the official version, anyhow. There's a lot of speculation that he died accidentally on purpose, that he never got over losing the missus."

While I ruminated on that family skeleton, the priest began his eulogy. He looked sober and solemn enough, but his black hair was combed in an almost-pompadour and I kept expecting him to break into "Are You Lonesome Tonight?" Instead, he delivered a speech that was full of warm memories of Charlotte, even as his recitation was devoid of warmth. As far as I could tell, he'd never actually met the woman, and all the anecdotes he related were spoon-fed from John and Janice. Chances are, he got some things mixed up, confused a few names, but he gave Charlotte a reasonably reasonable sendoff—one she herself might have appreciated. Perelli and I kept our conversation to a minimum while the priest spoke, though we each peeked over at the mystery couple from time to time. Their attention was at the front of the chancel, but they didn't seem particularly moved by the proceedings.

When John Kilmer got up to speak, he was the very model of devastation. While he had his wife and children for comfort, his sister was the third horrible death he'd contended with in less than a decade. If his spirit wasn't broken, it had at least spiderwebbed, and it showed in his stooped posture and quavering voice. He was a big man, probably 6'3", maybe 230 pounds, with dark hair and a goatee, and it was heartrending to see such a hulk laid low by circumstance.

"For those of you who don't know, Charlotte was my baby sister," he began, reading from a folded sheet of paper. "And as her big brother, I always took it upon myself to protect her—from bullies on the playground to the boys who came calling in high school. She even played on that a few times, deliberately inviting guys she didn't like back to the house so that I might scare them off."

There were subdued titters among the crowd, and John waited for quiet before he continued. "But Charlotte was more to me than a sister. She was my friend. So many nights we stayed up late, talking about all the places we wanted to go, all the things we wanted to do. She told me how she wanted to be a writer, how she wanted to make the world a better place with words. Even as she got older, she never let that dream get away. She'd make up stories as she put Pete to bed—fantasies to fill his slumber—and if she'd had a hard day, she'd send me e-mails about the adventures of Reader Girl, the world's most grammatically correct superhero.

"But this superhero wasn't bulletproof." He was starting to crumble, and I could see Janice shifting uncomfortably in her seat, as if she needed to rescue her big lug. "And her dreams will have to remain just that. But know this, kid, you did make the world a better place—with your self and your son—and it's much colder without you in it. Watch the roads, Charlotte—"

He barely got the last four words out before collapsing into heaving sobs, and Janice rushed up to be by his side. It was odd to see her be the rock, standing nearly a foot shorter than her husband, but she gently led him back to the front row of pews, where their two children and Pete collected for a group hug. The priest returned to his post to thank us all for coming and to give details about the interment. He followed that with a moment of reflection and a couple of obligatory hymns.

After the service, Perelli and I hovered near the back, waiting for family to disperse, seeing if there was any information to be gleaned from the designated mourners. Neither of us really thought so, but we did get to view an additional piece of melodrama: the latecomer couple hesitated in their seats, and from what we could overhear of their dialogue, they were unsure of whether they should make their presence known. In the end, they opted for a quick exit, deciding it was neither the time nor the place to put in a formal appearance.

"Now what?"

I turned to look at Perelli. "You're asking *me*? This is *your* case."

"The question was meant to be rhetorical, but I'd be happy to hear your thoughts on the subject. Like the world without Charlotte Kilmer in it, this case is getting colder by the day."

I shook my head, even though I did have an idea. But it wasn't anything I could discuss with him—not unless I wanted to put *two* badges on the line. We said our goodbyes and I bundled myself up as best I could for another foray into the chill. I was about to exit, stage left, when I felt a tug on my sweater; Pete was on the other end of the tug.

"'Manda," he said.

I squatted down so I could look him in the face. "Hi, Pete." He's a cute kid, though without ever having seen his father, it's hard to tell which features came from which parent. His brown eyes were more inquisitive than sad, as if the whole significance of the funeral had just passed him by. I might have gone on believing that, had he not quickly changed my mind.

"My mom's in heaven now."

"Is that what your uncle John told you?" I wasn't about to mess with family rituals and explanations.

"Uh-huh. My aunt Janice, too."

"Well," I said, groping for something appropriate to say. "Heaven is a good place to be. It means she can always keep an eye on you."

"I wish she was here instead of up there."

"I'm sure she does, too, honey."

He fidgeted in his suit, which looked new enough to have been bought for the occasion. "Does it hurt?"

"Not anymore, sweetie. Nothing hurts in heaven."

"But *you* got hurt."

Think fast, 'Manda.

"It happened so fast. Your mom never felt a thing." I sincerely hoped it wasn't a lie.

"My mom used to call my uncle John her guardian angel. I thought all the angels were up in heaven."

"Some angels are, and they look out for us when we're alone, or when we're traveling. Then there are others…good people who make sure nothing bad happens to the ones they love. We call them angels because they do the same job as the ones in heaven."

"Do we get more than one?"

"Some people only need one, but kids like you get a bunch of 'em, just to make sure you get off to a good start."

"'Manda," he said in a voice that just barely registered a whisper, "are you one of my angels?"

I didn't know how to answer the question, but no sacrifice could be too great for the chance to earn my wings.

CHAPTER 15

▼

Despite my good and angelic intentions, I still had several hours before I could start actively hoofing it on my road to Hell. The frigid gust that ripped through me as I departed the church reminded me that I was still here on Earth—unless, of course, Satan's backyard had just frozen over. Maybe it was just my imagination, but the weather seemed to have gotten a good deal colder over the previous few days. Perhaps John had been right, and we were all feeling the absence of Charlotte's warmth. More likely, it was just, as Gordon Lightfoot put it, "the gales of November come early."

By the time I got back to my apartment, my ears were ready to fall off and my sweater felt, in spots, like a used sponge. I shed my outer layers and quickly nuked a can of split pea soup to heat up my insides in hopes that my outside would soon follow. I scanned the newspaper as I sat and slurped, pausing to read Charlotte's obituary—no other family listed besides Pete, John, Janice and their brood, and no mention at all of Vic Renzo. I wouldn't have expected an ex-husband to be given a "beloved wife of..." citation, but stranger things have been printed—especially in the New York press.

The news section of the paper was still jammed with reportage from Ground Zero, about the combined rescue and cleanup efforts, and profiles of the victims. The stories tried to sound hopeful, as though someone might still be found beneath the rubble, nearly two months after the fact. Meanwhile, virtually everyone knew that no survivors had been found since September 12, but when evil appears to have the upper hand, I suppose false hope is better than none.

After I washed out my soup bowl and shook off the last vestiges of autumn chill, I set myself to a task I'd truly missed: old-fashioned detective work. I started with a theory: Mitch said he was inspired to finish "Lonely Hours" after Jennifer Marx pitched herself off the hotel roof. Gordon, reportedly, claimed that Mitch stole "Lonely Hours" from him, thereby ruining his life and setting him on a path of murderous vengeance. Since these two scandals had a common element, could they possibly be related in some other fashion? This syllogism didn't stand up to logical scrutiny, but it made as much sense as anything else had in the last 72 or so hours.

I picked up the phone and dialed 411, and James Earl Jones thanked me for using the information service. Next an automated voice asked what listing I'd like. "Main branch of the Phoenix Public Library in Phoenix, Arizona," I said, then proceeded to hold while the "operator" looked for my number. I reached for a pen and jotted it down, rather than paying the phone company to dial it for me. The clock on my stove read 12:45, and as my connection went through, I tried to remember whether Phoenix was two or three hours behind New York.

"Library." The voice sounded efficient and polite—female, probably in her late 40s or early 50s. A lifer.

"Yes, I'm trying to get some information from back issues of the paper there…what is it, the *Arizona Republic*?"

"That's the one. We have all the back issues on microfilm if you'd care to come in…"

"Ma'am, I'm calling from New York City."

She laughed. "For some reason, I don't think you'd make it here by closing. Um, why don't you go to the Web site? The paper's bound to have an online archive you could search."

I resisted the temptation to stick my tongue out at the phone. It wasn't her fault I'm a techno-moron. "I'm not sure if the archive goes back far enough. I'm looking for articles from about six years ago."

"Oh, I see."

"And, truth be told, I'm not much of a computer person."

"They don't bite, you know. You ever think about taking a class?"

"What a great idea," I said, as though I'd never thought or done anything of the sort. "I'll definitely look into it. In the meantime, you think you can help me with this?"

"Not from where I'm sitting. I'm up in the children's section. Let me switch you down to reference. I'm sure Gladys can get you what you're looking for. Hang on."

She put me on hold and I was treated to about three measures worth of classical music before another woman came on the line.

"Reference. This is Gladys."

From the name, I'd pictured a grandmotherly sort, around five feet tall with a thatch of gray hair and lookover glasses on a chain. However, the voice on the other end sounded much younger—maybe my age. "Hi, Gladys. I hope you can help me. I'm looking for information from back issues of the *Arizona Republic*."

"I'd be glad to pull it up, but it might be faster if you went to the paper's Web site."

Instead of the same old song and dance I'd gone through with the book lady a few moments before, I tried a different set of steps. "My computer's down and I need the information right away."

"Oh," she said. "Um, sure thing. You working on a story or something?"

This was one of those times when the lie would be easier to finagle than the truth. However, the badge is usually better for getting abject cooperation. "I'm a police detective in New York and I'm looking for information on a woman who committed suicide out there."

"You're going to have to give me a little more than that. I'm sure New York's got its share of suicides and, unfortunately, so do we."

"This was about six years ago. She, er, killed herself by jumping off the roof of a hotel."

There was a long pause before Gladys offered anything more, though I could hear her drumming a pencil on her desk. "This woman you're asking about," she offered slowly, "her name wasn't Jennifer Marx by any chance?"

Jackpot.

"That's her," I said. "Did you know her?"

"More by association than through any personal contact. Friend of a friend, you know. Maybe I ran into her at a party or something. She hadn't been in town all that long when she offed herself, I remember that much."

"How about when it happened? You have any idea?"

"Let's see…that would be September or October of '95, I think. No, wait, definitely September. Yeah, it was right before Faith got married and Hope was walking by the hotel on her way home when it happened and she just *totally* wigged out. They had no idea if she was gonna be okay to stand up at the wedding. But I mean, Faith *is* her sister, and she *was* the maid of honor."

"So she made it?"

"Oh, you bet. I mean, Charity was ready to step in, especially 'cause she wanted that first slow dance with Eddie Kissena, who was best man. And if she wasn't already miffed that Faith skipped her over in the first place, Charity was the one who'd been soft on Eddie since she was in kindergarten. But the folks had already put it in the program that Hope would be maid of honor, and after all they spent on the band and the country club, and all the people they invited, they'd have been too embarrassed to admit why they had to switch daughters."

Faith, Hope and Charity? That's embarrassing enough.

"Thank you, Gladys, but I really need to call up the papers from back then…what'd you say, September '95? Whatever the papers ran on Jennifer Marx's death."

"Oh, right. That's gonna take me a few minutes. Why don't you call me back in about 15? I'd call you, but we can't make long-distance calls anymore. This girl Shelley…"

"That's fine, Gladys," I said before getting any further into the hijinks of Phoenix's citizenry. "I'll call you back." A blabbermouth can often be a cop's best friend, but only when she has something remotely useful to say.

I didn't really have another angle to play, so I flicked on the Game Show Network and watched most of an old episode of "Match Game," just to fill the time. Listening to Brett Somers, Charles Nelson Reilly and company spout double entendres as the contestants tried to match their answers, I realized just how many blanks I needed to fill in myself—and Gene Rayburn couldn't possibly help.

Especially since he's died and gone to blank.

I called the library again and asked for reference, and I was quickly connected with Gladys the gossipmonger.

"Reference. This is Gladys."

"Hi, Gladys, this is Detective Ross, calling from New York."

"Oh, yes, I found those articles you were looking for…now, where did I put them? Oh, here they are. You want me to read them to you?"

"How about a recap? I'm just looking for names. Any friends that were interviewed, any police officers involved in the investigation, that sort of thing."

I could hear mumbling as she read to herself, the tap-tap-tap of her pencil given added thwack by the papers in front of her. "There's a Lieutenant Roberto Dominguez who's mentioned in the first article—that's the day after it happened, September 19th. The next day, there was a little profile piece, talking about her mental problems, how she'd been in and out of foster care and, oh, I don't believe this!"

"What?"

"That freakin' liar! Everybody knows she'll do anything to get her name in the paper, but this is low even for her."

"Who?"

"Donna DeMarco. She is such a publicity slut. She says that she and Jennifer Marx had been 'best buds' since high school, but she never imagined that she'd take her own life."

Even I knew that wasn't true; from Mitch's account of things, Jennifer Marx wasn't from Phoenix originally. "Not what I'd call a reliable source. Anybody else?"

"Huh? Oh, right. Um…toward the end, there's a little something from someone named Ingrid Jakubowski. I don't know her."

"What'd she say?"

"'All Jennifer ever wanted to go was get close to him' and then they put in brackets 'Mitch Black. She felt she was a part of his music, that somehow they were connected. Maybe now she can watch over him. Be the guardian angel she always wanted to be.'"

That sounded like the troubled soul Mitch and J.T. had described. "Thank you, Gladys," I said, just before asking her to spell Ingrid's last name for me. "You've been a big help."

"That's why they pay me the big bucks."

It sounded like sarcasm, but in truth I had no idea how much librarians got paid. I was just about to hang up when I realized that Gladys and I had one unfinished piece of business. "Out of curiosity, how did the wedding turn out?"

"Whose? Faith's? You wouldn't believe this. After all that bickering over Eddie Kissena, Charity goes into the ladies room and finds Denise Slater on her knees, giving him a hummer. Right there in the country club! Of course, Charity starts bawling and blames Faith and Hope for this, how if they'd let *her* be the maid of honor, she'd never have let Eddie stray. And Hope blamed Faith for inviting Denise in the first place, especially since she'd stolen at least one boyfriend from each of them. Before their parents could stop them, they'd started kicking and scratching and throwing cake. Faith spent her wedding night in the hospital, getting stitches and a tetanus shot."

So much for the cardinal virtues.

CHAPTER 16

▼

I wasn't sure how much help Lt. Dominguez would be, but I decided to try him first, hoping professional courtesy might extend some 2,500 miles. It took two calls to information and a pair of relays through his precinct before they were able to patch me through to his cell phone.

"Dominguez."

"Lieutenant, this is Detective Amanda Ross with the 11th Precinct in New York."

"Yeah, and?" There were voices in the background, and what sounded like people moving furniture.

"I'm calling to ask you about an old case of yours, from about six years ago." He didn't respond at first, and I thought I'd lost the connection. "Lieutenant?"

"Go ahead. Ask."

Not exactly blessed with Gladys' gift for gab, is he?

"I'm sorry, is this a bad time?"

He exhaled, perhaps realizing he wasn't going to get me off the phone that easily. "It is for Mr. Dwayne Allstot, whose wife just splattered his brains all over their bedroom wall with a shotgun. Looks like one of those Spin Art things my kids used to make."

Glad to hear somebody was still doing real police work. "I don't mean to bother you at a crime scene, but I'm trying to gather information on a suicide you investigated. Young woman by the name of Jennifer Marx."

"Now *that* was a splatter. Twelve stories of gravity and a spread of asphalt."

I expect that was his idea of poetry. "What can you tell me about her?"

"Not much. There wasn't a lot to investigate. She fall down, go boom. End of story."

"Was there any kind of note, or explanation as to why she jumped?"

"No, so we're pretty sure this was spur of the moment. Our chain of events doesn't have too many links. A hotel desk clerk spots her in the lobby. A few minutes later, she was turned away by that rock singer's security. What's his name again?"

"Mitch Black," I said, wondering if the call was even worth the long distance charges.

"Right. Black's bodyguards give her the brush-off, and less than 10 minutes after that, she's airborne."

He had nothing new to add, but the story sounded a little *too* familiar. "Your memory on the subject's pretty good, Lieutenant. I'm surprised you've got that much detail in mind after six years."

"Detective," he said with more than a touch of condescension, "you've been on the job long enough to know that nothing you or I will ever do can stop human nature. Murder, that's in our biology. Just about every species feeds on the weak and vulnerable. Half the people we tag and bag, we're better off without. But suicide? That's something that defies explanation. A true waste of human life, and we're the only animals who are capable of coming to the conclusion that death has a greater appeal. That's why I remember Jennifer Marx, Detective. When someone snaps, they usually point the gun in some other direction."

I wasn't sure if I bought his psychobabble, but I couldn't fully discount it, either. Seven years of personal experience on the job only lent credence to Dominguez's most trenchant point: Violence toward others is far more common that violence toward oneself. The notion clung to my mind like a barnacle, and I wasn't about to bring Ingrid Jakubowski or anyone else into that dark place—a workout presented itself as the most positive way to clear my head.

It had been too long since I'd picked up my weights and, given the bleeder in my brain, I didn't want to push it too much. Just enough to work up a sweat and send out an invitation to any endorphins that might wish to drop by. I pulled off my stockings and pants, and tucked the blouse aside in hopes a dry cleaner could undo the bleach damage. I dug out a tanktop and shorts, cued up Styx's *Pieces of Eight* on random play and set myself to the task. To the hard-driving guitars of "Renegade" and "Blue Collar Man," I did curls and straight-arm lifts; the buoyant "Sing for the Day" helped me get through the more difficult squats. I had just settled into a rhythm of ab crunches when the song "Queen of Spades" came on,

its somber mood and heavy lyrics reminding me that I was still chasing a ghost—
one that few people seemed to care about. It was only Mitch and myself who
were still hounded by her, but he'd had no choice in the matter. I, on the other
hand, had appointed myself exorcist.

There were two Jakubowskis listed in the Phoenix area, but no Ingrid. Still, I
took down both numbers and tried Charles first, thinking he might be an uncle
or a cousin. A woman answered on the third ring. "Yeah?"

"Yes, hi, I'm looking for Ingrid."

"Well, ma'am, you're looking in the wrong place. She moved to Pennsylvania
about three years ago."

"Really?" I said with just a bit of curiosity. To me, Phoenix has always been
the last stop on a person's lifetime itinerary, rather than a place you moved away
from. Maybe it's all those "most livable city" surveys that give it that reputation.

"Yep. Met a boy on the Internet and took off for the Northeast. You ain't selling somethin', are ya?"

"No, ma'am. I'm a police detective."

"Now, now, now I know there's been some kind of mistake. That girl may not
have an ounce of sense when it comes to findin' herself a husband, but she sure as
shootin' ain't criminal. I can vouch for her that much."

"And you are?"

"The given name's Lucille, but you might as well call me Lou. Everyone else
does."

"And Ingrid is your…"

"She's my niece on my husband's side."

"Lou, before you say anything else, I just want you to know Ingrid isn't in any
trouble. I'm not after her for anything. I just want to talk to her. I'm picking up
on an old case and I came across her name. I just want to see if she knows anything, so I can be sure I've covered everything. If you have a phone number,
that'd be real helpful. If you're not comfortable giving it to me, I understand.
You can have her call me, if you prefer. I'll give you my number."

I could hear her chewing something while she made up her mind; I must have
caught her in the middle of lunch. "Give me the number and I'll pass it along.
Mind you, she's not too good at returning phone messages. Says she prefers
e-mail."

Not surprising for an Internet bride. "She'll want to return this one," I said,
rattling off my name, rank and home phone. "Tell her it's regarding Jennifer
Marx."

If the name meant anything to Aunt Lou, it didn't register. "I'll give a call over there now, before I forget. She probably won't get it until later."

"Not a problem," I said, and clicked off. It was nearly 3:30 at that point, so I took a quick shower, just to rinse away the fine oily layer that had settled on my post-workout skin. I dressed in a plain white T-shirt, jeans and sneakers, and teased my hair as best I could. The result was trashy but not overly so—the perfect camouflage for an uptown hunting trip. Before I left, I grabbed my leather jacket, my badge and gun. I probably didn't need the firepower—I didn't feel like a cop, and Lord knows I didn't look like one—but sometimes when you're out on safari, the game shoots back.

I locked up and took the elevator down, leaving home behind for the subway—the underground dwelling I found myself inhabiting more and more frequently. It took three trains to get from Columbus Circle to the Upper East Side: the 2 down to Times Square, the 7 across to Grand Central and the 6 up into East 80s, so it was nearly 5:00 by the time I strolled into Bad Habits.

The bar had, at one point, been home to a topless revue, but the former mayor had sent the strippers packing, thus taking a huge bite out of cash flow. The owners had tried to hang onto clientele by adding satellite TVs and a Sunday buffet. This strategy worked okay on weekends, but left other nights wanting. Most of the weeknight patronage came from folks trying to drown their sorrows from all the death and dying at nearby Lenox Hill Hospital.

The person—if you can call him that—I was looking for was Phil Lentini, a low-level lowlife who held a majority stake in Bad Habits. He was sitting at the bar, dealing out a game of solitaire when I walked in. I'd hoped to be a little less conspicuous, but I arrived at a time when the joint was about a quart low on estrogen; I could immediately feel half a dozen sets of eyeballs checking out my merchandise.

So glad I dressed for the occasion.

Phil Lentini looked pretty much as I remembered him from his mug shot: scrawny and short, with dirty blond hair feathering back across his narrow scalp. He had beady eyes, a pointed nose, small ears that hugged the sides of his face and stubby yellow teeth. As a complete package, he was the very embodiment of the nickname that had stuck in his fur for all the years he'd scurried around the bottom rungs of the criminal ladder: the Ferret.

I approached the bar slowly but confidently, all the while trying not to gag on the heavy cigarette smoke in the air. The bartender, a ridiculously tall man with shaggy red hair and an unkempt goatee, was waiting for me. "What can I get you?"

I flicked my eyes in the Ferret's direction, just making sure he was paying attention. "Seven of hearts."

"Come again?"

"Seven of hearts," I purred.

He reached up a lanky arm and scratched his head. "I'm afraid I don't know that one."

Neither did I. It was something I'd seen in a liquor ad on one of the trains.

"Remy Red and 7-Up," the Ferret growled at his employee, saving for me his sweetest smile, which had all the charisma of a rotten apple core.

I took out a ten and wove it through my fingers as the bartender mixed my drink. He served it in an old-fashioned glass with ice; it was pink and fizzy and tasted mildly of cherry cough syrup. I lifted the bill, yet before Stretch could take it, the Ferret hissed, "On the house." To me he added, "You stumped the chump."

"Thanks," I said with as much grace as I could muster. The only reason I could play so well with others was that I'd just gotten laid; two days earlier, I'd have been far too frustrated to flirt with the savage beasts. "I could still use a couple of bucks worth of quarters."

The bartender glanced over at his boss, who gave an approving twitch, and returned with eight singles and eight quarters. I pocketed the bills, leaving one for a tip, and sashayed over to the pool table. After finding a cue stick that wasn't too warped, I rammed home a dollar in change, sending the billiard balls tumbling down into the well. I racked up all 15, and proceeded to make an almost total ass of myself—if they gave out an annual bimbo award, I'd have been a shoo-in—deliberately missing easy shots, leaning much further over the table than I had to, giggling to myself when I "accidentally" sank a ball.

My God, I'm a beer commercial!

The act worked, sort of. Before I'd cleared half the balls, two guys had already "punted," stacking quarters on the edge of the table for a shot at dethroning—or, looking ahead a few hours, deflowering—the queen. I took my time in playing off the rest, hoping for a bite from Phil Lentini; I'd gone hunting for a ferret, but succeeded in snaring a chimp and, based on the amount of cologne he'd marinated in, a musk ox.

There was a method to my madness. In addition to his pursuits as a bar owner and wannabe ladies man, Phil Lentini was also an underling of Sam Pelillo, a mob captain whose influence could be felt from West Side Highway to FDR Drive, for everything above the southern border of Central Park. It was Pelillo I really wanted to get close to, for if anybody knew anything about the bomb in

Charlotte's apartment, he'd be the man. He was sure to have the lowdown on such an event—either by association, in which case I was probably screwed, or by omniscience, because he liked to have his finger in every piece of criminal pie in northern Manhattan. Out of respect, he usually got a taste. That's why I thought he might be willing to hear me out about Charlotte's murder. Nobody seemed to have profited from it and that might, at the very least, pique his interest.

The problem with my plan was that I couldn't approach the Ferret directly. The department's profile labeled him as skittish, and quick to bolt when things went awry. He was hardly a criminal mastermind, and did very little of his own volition, but served his capo loyally—usually as a driver or a gofer. If I let him come onto me, I might be able to wangle a sitdown without the critter getting wise.

The brown 7 ball was still on the table when a pissing contest broke out between Hairy and Stinky.

"These are my quarters," clucked the simian in training, "and they were there first."

Stinky was bigger than his rival, and sweat was beading down from his forehead as he popped the little man in the shoulder. "You ain't seein' things straight, pal. Those are your quarters over *there*," he said, pointing to the opposite side of the table, "and *here* is where the next shooter stands."

Bonzo threw all his weight behind a shove to the other man's chest, and met an immovable object. "Says *you*. I've got her next."

"Keep dreaming."

"Boys, boys," I said with no lack of irony.

"What do you say, doll?" asked the ox.

"Oh," I said, leaning on my cue stick, "I wasn't really watching. I was keeping my eye on the balls."

I half expected the two of them to come to blows, as they stared each other down, nostrils flaring, facial muscles tight, teeth bared. The only sound I heard was the scrape of a bar stool.

"What'd I tell you about hassling the broads?" asked the Ferret as he ambled over to join our little billiard klatch. "And you wonder why there's never any pussy in this place."

It's unusual to find someone capable of being so perceptive and so offensive at the same time. Under normal circumstances, he'd have ended up wearing my little pink drink, but my Wile E. Coyote plan was starting to work and it was no time to let indignation get in the way of progress.

"Hey, Phil, I didn't mean nothin'," said Hairy, and I took it as his version of an apology.

"Yeah, we just wanted to show her a good time," Stinky agreed, taking a step back.

"That's *my* job," the Ferret corrected, puffing himself up. "As owner of this little establishment, I personally see to it that all of our female patrons are well taken care of."

Geez, how many times did you practice that speech before you actually got a chance to use it?

"Now, if you'll pardon me," he continued, snatching up one of the stacks of quarters, "this game's on me. You wanna break, or should I?"

"You go ahead," I effused. "I like the way you handle yourself."

His second smile was far more sincere than the first, and I detected a store of true warmth beneath the bravado. "You're not so bad yourself."

I called the shot: Ferret in my hip pocket.

CHAPTER 17

▼

Now I'm no Loree Jon Jones or Karen Corr, but after years of late-night practice with my fellow officers at Pete's Ale House, I can handle a cue stick pretty well. I was working an old-fashioned hustle, but since I wasn't looking for a financial windfall, I hoped my deceptive tactics might go undetected.

"What do you wanna play for?" the Ferret asked as he chalked up his cue.

"Oh," I said with a startle, "I thought this was just going to be for fun."

"It will be fun. Tacking on stakes just makes it interesting."

Before going for broke, I figured I should probably size up the competition. I hemmed and hawed and chewed on my nails a bit before responding to the competition. "Is $20 enough to make it interesting?"

"Sure thing."

The key to a good hustle is not to embarrass the mark. Do that, especially when you've been sandbagging, and you might as well kiss your take goodbye. That's why I wanted Phil Lentini to break, so I could get some idea of his ability and go skill to skill with him without making him feel like a sucker.

It was obvious from the start that I could outplay him. He bridged under his fingers, resting the shaft up against the nock between his index and middle fingers. Novices tend to find that position more comfortable, but it creates a lot of friction and is far less accurate than an over-the-knuckle style. In addition, he put no English on the cue ball as he broke, so the rack didn't scatter. There were clusters of stripes and solids just waiting to be sunk. I looked for the easiest setup— the yellow 1 ball was pretty much hanging over a corner pocket, so I plunked it in, giving the cue ball extra side spin, so that when it came it rest, it nested amid several others, leaving me no shot.

So it went for the rest of the game—setting myself up with crappy leaves and impossible shots, making the Ferret look good by comparison. I still had two balls on the table when he knocked in the 8 on a called shot. I took out a Jackson and laid it on the table, smoothing it with my hand while donning my best pout. "Good game," I said softly.

He put one hand over mine on the bill, then reached out a hooked finger and lifted my chin so he could look me in the eye. "Hey, I'll give you a chance to win your money back. Don't worry."

"Double or nothing?" I mewed.

"You bet."

Once again, I let him break, and even though he actually sank a ball on that first shot for an immediate advantage, I was able to finesse a victory without too much trouble. I'd wanted him to have one ball on the table when I pocketed the 8, but it was risky. If he made a couple of shots in a row, I'd have to make an emergency run to the ATM, and that definitely constitutes bad form. Fortunately, his bank shot on the 13 caromed a little too wide, missing the side pocket and coming to rest just off the rail. I dropped the 2 and 8 in succession, both with angles a child could have managed.

"Even Steven," the Ferret remarked as he slipped me back my original $20, "only I don't like things even. Too neat."

"So we'll make it two out of three."

"Only how 'bout we raise the stakes this time?"

I closed my eyes, then opened one, looking at him sidelong. "What did you want to play for?"

He eyed me up and down, then ran a finger along my bare arm. My skin was crawling and whatever warmth I'd tapped into earlier had gone missing; he was cold-blooded through and through. "You."

Somehow I'd known it would come to that, but was I really ready to play with fire? I stalled. "What do you mean?"

"You give me your marker, your IOU. Call it a favor."

Even if I was into guys, I wouldn't want this creature touching me. The whole notion made me want to retch. Saying yes would amount to prostituting myself for a case, and that was one of those black holes I'd never escape from—if I lost. Words I'd often seen in front of a church on East 34th Street flashed in my mind. "Stand up for what is right, even if you are standing alone." Finding out who killed Charlotte was the right thing to do. It *had* to be. "And if I win?"

"Name it."

"A meeting with Sam," I said coolly.

He forced a snicker. "Sam who?"

"Don't be like that," I said, stroking his cheek. "Nicky told me you were a standup guy." I hoped the bluff would work. Nicky Avian was one of Sam's runners who owned a magic shop in my neighborhood. From what I could recall, the various task forces had determined that Nicky and the Ferret had recently crossed paths on a job. Neither one had had any direct contact with Sam Pelillo, which is why these particular pawns were still out on the chessboard.

"How do you know Nicky?"

"Let's just say that I fell for one of his magic tricks and leave it at that." Nicky Avian regularly held court at a bar called The Raven's Nest, and used his skills at sleight-of-hand to lure women into his bed. He was legend on the Upper West Side, though few people knew about his sideline gig. I didn't know him, certainly not in the sense I suggested, but it was the most plausible thing I could come up with—one the Ferret wasn't likely to double-check.

He lifted his cue stick over his head and draped his arms around it, resembling nothing so much as a poor man's Christ figure. "Why do you need to meet with Sam?"

"I don't think that's any of your concern."

"Hey," he said, swinging the butt of the stick in my direction, "don't tell me what is or isn't my concern. I ain't about to okay somethin' like that until I know what the game is."

"The game is 8-ball," I retorted, brushing him off. "You win, you get your way with me for one night. I win, I get the meeting with Sam, no questions asked…and $500."

"Nuh-uh, no cash. We're just exchanging favors."

"I've got more to lose."

It took him so long to respond, I thought I'd pushed too hard, and made him realize that this particular piece of tail was too much trouble and not worth the price. I was almost offended. Only when Phil Lentini realized that Hairy, Stinky and the rest of the bar was watching—and listening—did he find his voice again. "Deal."

Everything I stood for and believed in hung in the balance of the one game. I was on auto-pilot when I racked the balls, desperately rummaging through my mental excuse pile for an out, just in case I lost. There wasn't much need; if the Ferret downed the 8 ball before I did, the hematoma, coupled with severe shock, would (hopefully) kill me instantly. I slid the triangle back under the table and turned away, closing my eyes and clenching my teeth. I heard Phil Lentini put more chalk on his stick and place the cue ball. I heard him smack the cue ball into the others. I heard the clack-a-clack of multiple ricochets. And, after a brief silence, I heard the plunk of a ball as it rolled into a pocket. I spun around to assess the damage, quickly scanning the table for the missing ball. What I saw, or rather didn't see, nearly made me cry.

The cue ball was gone. He'd scratched on the break.

The Ferret stood agape, his tiny eyes as wide as they could be. Behind him, some of the patrons started coughing and making other noises, stopping just short of calling him a choke artist. I graciously stepped away, returned my stick to the wall rack and waited for him at the bar. He might have welched on the bet, claiming the game didn't count, or asking for a mulligan—but he didn't, realizing that in front of his customers, he could afford to lose half a grand. What he couldn't afford to lose was face.

The bartender didn't talk to me, and there were no congratulatory backslaps or high fives from the barflies. I was relieved if not thrilled by the results. It's one thing to beat a man at his own game, in his own bar; it's quite another for him to lose. After a minute, the Ferret came over and sat next to me. "So how do we do this?" I asked. "You call him? He calls you?"

"I call," he growled. "Gimme a number and somebody'll be in touch."

"Fair enough," I said, jotting down my name and number on a bar napkin. "And the other?"

"Ike, we got five-C in the till?"

The bartender punched open the register and took a glance. "Uh-uh, boss. Two-fifty tops."

"Let me have two," he said, reaching into his pocket for his personal money roll. He peeled off three hundred-dollar bills and added them to the stack of 20s that Ike handed him. I folded them together and stuck the wad in my jeans pocket, then recovered my jacket from the bar stool where I'd left it. I thanked him and the bartender for their hospitality and got up to go.

"You know somethin', honey?" Phil Lentini said to me before I was out of earshot. "I've been working that hustle for years and you're the first gal who's ever taken the bet. I don't know whether to respect your *cojones* or call you a whore."

Me neither.

The triple-subway ride home was even lonelier since I'd left my self-respect at Bad Habits. The only person who could possibly empathize with my actions had been put in the ground earlier that day. When I got home just after 7, I was hungry, but didn't feel like eating. I could've nuked either the pasta or the Pad Thai, but there was no reheating my pride.

The light on my answering machine was blinking repeatedly. As much as I wanted the world to just disappear, I couldn't ignore the possibilities of who might be looking for me. The first message was from Jeannie, who was sitting in her cluttered office, once again waiting for students to show up, students who never would. Now that students had e-mail, they sent in their questions, rather than stopping by. This was especially the case for her as part of the computer department. Yet protocol dictated that she maintain weekly office hours, even if it was just an excuse to get some work done, undisturbed. She added that she missed me, and that she looked forward to seeing me again. The feeling was more than mutual, and I saved the message, preserving her voice for the pick-me-up I knew I'd need.

The second message was from Ingrid Jakubowski, returning my call. She wasn't sure how much help she could be with Jennifer Marx, especially since they only knew each other a few months before Jennifer died. But she left home and work numbers, and said I could get back to her whenever it was convenient.

"Amanda, it's me," the third message began, and I immediately recognized Mitch's voice. He sounded weak and hoarse, almost as if he'd been crying. "You'd better get over to my hotel right away. Sondra's dead."

There were no additional details on the tape, but according to the machine's voice imprint, the message had been left just 15 minutes earlier. I was out the door in a flash, barely taking the time to stick the $500 in a drawer. I was already armed, and as prepared as I could possibly be. I jogged east to Broadway and turned south, toward midtown, hoping to snare a cab without too much difficulty. I finally caught one around West 55th, and barked out the name of the Grand Hyatt. With the theater-district traffic, plus the usual snarls around Grand Central Station and the Chrysler Building, I might have done better on foot.

When we finally got close, the night was flooded with flashing red, blue and yellow emergency lights, 42nd Street piled with police and EMTs. In that moment, my hope of continuing a quiet, below-the-radar investigation was dashed. The can was open, and there were worms all over the place.

CHAPTER 18

▼

The Grand Hyatt lives up to its name in opulence and convenience, but one is left to wonder about the location. It's nestled atop a major subway stop—the 4, 5, 6 and 7 trains all run beneath it—and it's situated right next to Grand Central Station, which has dozens of Metro North and other tracks, carrying people to Westchester, Connecticut and other nearby locales around the clock. It's not surprising, then, that the hotel is known by the formal name of the Grand Hyatt at Grand Central. By dropping the "Station," the marketing people must have hoped to conjure up a hub of importance, a place where people with gobs of money could spend it without having to go too far, rather than a common railway terminal bringing riffraff in at all hours. Somehow, this had even carried over to the building's address—Park Avenue certainly sounded regal and hoity-toity, but the hotel wasn't actually on that well-to-do boulevard. Then again, it's doubtful anyone would pay upwards of $325 a night for someplace with a 42nd Street address. Even in post-Giuliani New York, the famed thoroughfare retained its tawdry and tacky reputation.

The badge gained me access but not information. I had no idea where the crime had taken place or where I might find Mitch. The more blue-shirts I asked, the more attention I'd have coming my way—and that was the one thing I didn't need. Not only was I out of my jurisdiction, but invisibility was supposed to be my secret weapon.

I weaved my way through the cops, valets and bystanders, going up a short flight of stairs to the lobby. This was mainly a huge seating area, with comfy couches and chairs tastefully arranged around chrome-and-glass tables. Enormous vases, filled with white and green flora, stood on seven-foot pedestals. To my immediate left was a coffee bar; in front was the concierge's kiosk, with the registration and video checkout desks recessed in the smooth, wood-paneled walls. Opposite me, I could see the brighter lights of a gift shop, and a counter where guests could pick up theater tickets. A uniformed officer and his plain-clothes superior crossed by me toward an extensive bank of elevators and I followed, pausing with them near the right-most doors; a video monitor indicated that these elevators went to the upper floors. A door slid open and we boarded. I immediately pushed the button for 36 while the uniformed cop pressed 33.

I rode up to my chosen floor, pretending to pay attention to the mute broadcast of CNBC showing on another monitor inside the car. The two officers disembarked three stories below, but I let them go, only to double back and get off at 33. There was a lot of hubbub around the corner and I followed the voices, keeping my badge in hand only to fend off any inquiries. Most of the young-uns were quick to let my gold detective shield lead the way.

Just past the ice and vending machines—two dollars for a Pepsi?!—a narrow corridor broke off from the main hallway, and I could see the center of action. Another dozen officers clogged up the passage in front of Room 3330. It struck me that there were an awful lot of cops on the scene, but when a celebrity is involved, I guess no one's above the lure of a little privacy. Some of them might even have been autograph hounds, dreaming of an encounter with the music man himself.

I squirmed through the crowd to get a glimpse of the crime scene. One of the suite's double doors was open, but it had a gaping hole through it. I couldn't be sure of what had happened afterward, but someone had definitely blasted away with a heavy-gauge shotgun. Sondra Fisher had had the misfortune of coming to the door just before it was used for target practice. Her body lay several feet into the room, blown back by the force of the shot, covered in wood fragments and blood. From what I could see of the suite, Vertical Records had spared little expense in making Mitch feel comfortable. The place was probably two-thirds the size of my aparment, with a big potted plant on the fringe of the "living room." The only visible evidence of Mitch's having been there was a guitar case resting on the couch.

The scene was an almost perfect setup. The suite was right across from the fire stairs. Gordon, if this was indeed his handiwork, could have been gone in a split second, with no labyrinth of green carpeted hallways to navigate for an escape route. In addition, because of those stairs, there were fewer rooms in the vicinity, making it less likely that anyone would be around to hear and/or report a very loud noise. What bothered me was the timing. What was Sondra doing in

Mitch's room? Weren't they out on an all-day promotional tour? And shouldn't the killer be able to recognize a woman's voice before taking aim at the front door?

It was only a matter of time before somebody realized there were too many detectives in the neighborhood, so I framed my mental picture and slithered out of the way. The coroner's office would take care of the body, but I doubted Mitch would be sleeping there. Before I could figure out what to do next, however, and what he should do to keep himself safe, I needed to find him. Fortunately, his story about that night in Philadelphia gave me the clue.

It was well into the dinner hour at the Commodore Grill & Lounge, the hotel's main restaurant. Guests certainly had their choice of alternative (and less expensive) fare—Houlihan's and McDonald's were among the options across the street, and there were a number of eateries in the Grand Central terminal—but if you could afford the rooms at the Grand Hyatt, you could sure as hell afford to pony up for a pricey meal ticket. Even with the mood lighting, it wasn't hard to pick out Mitch among the patrons. He was sitting off in a corner, with a female cop, in uniform, at his table. They didn't appear to be having any kind of idol-fan conversation, so I presumed that she'd been assigned to babysit him. Until the lead investigator had something more to go on, Mitch would be on the short list of suspects. He might tell them about Gordon, but until some kind of hard evidence turned up—proving Gordon's existence, if nothing else—Mitch would be kept under close watch. He was drinking beer from a glass, and if my timing was right, it wasn't his first.

"Can I help you?" the cop asked, bolting up at my approach. She withered back into her seat at the sight of my badge, and I went over to be with my friend.

"You okay?" I asked, taking the chair next to his, across from the overeager girl in blue.

"No," he said softly. Then, after a beat, he pounded the table with his fist. "Fucking Gordon."

If he was right, then his five-year disappearing act had only delayed what Gordon had vowed to finish. "It's not your fault."

"It *is* my fault," he said, a touch too loud for comfort. "That bullet had my name on it, not Sondra's."

"You don't know that," I replied, doing my best to keep any notes of falsehood out of my voice. It didn't work; Mitch fixed me with a sarcastic stare, and I knew I wouldn't be winning any sort of consolation prize. "Okay, okay, I suck at sympathy."

That got him to smile a little bit, and our dinner companion looked at us with utter confusion. "Amanda," Mitch said, "this is Officer Yellin. Officer Yellin, Detective Amanda Ross."

She was about my height and build, with flat brown hair drooping down from the sides and back of her topper like cooked spaghetti. "You two know each other?" she asked.

"Since sometime around the last ice age," I remarked in an attempt to keep Mitch's spirits up, and prevent him from drowning himself in drafts. I don't think the information fully processed in her head, but she settled down and let us continue our conversation.

"You want anything?" Mitch asked me, pointing toward his glass.

"No, I've already liquored up for the evening, but if you're ordering food..."

"Mine's on its way, but by all means, join me. I'm having the sea bass."

That didn't surprise me. He usually went for seafood when he was feeling down. "Um, sure."

"Officer Yellin," he said, "would you mind getting Detective Ross here a menu?"

"You don't have to do that," I said.

"He's kinda my responsibility," she replied. "They told me upstairs to keep an eye on him. Make sure he doesn't leave the hotel. If he goes missing, my C.O.'s gonna put my butt in a sling."

"Don't worry, he won't go anywhere. Even if I have to handcuff him to a pepper mill."

She took assurance in that and left her post in search of a menu. I hated treating junior officers that way, but there was no other way Mitch and I could really talk without everything we said flipping back to the contingent on the 33rd floor.

"So, what happened?" I said, pulling my chair closer.

"And start at the beginning. My readers will want to know." We turned to find Andy Devane at our table, hands in his pockets. He had on the same black windbreaker he'd been wearing three days earlier, over a striped shirt and charcoal pants. "Hello, Mitch."

I blinked, my brain quickly trying to make the connection. When the memory fell into place, I almost laughed. "I'd forgotten you two know each other."

"That was one of our first dates, Amanda," Andy recalled, taking the fourth seat at the round table, on my left. "You took me to hear this guy sing. You said then that he was going to be something...and you were right. Andy Devane."

"I remember," Mitch said, offering his hand. "Betsy here didn't bring by too many men."

Andy didn't seem to pick up on the hated nickname, so I was more than happy to let it go. "That was a long time ago. Andy's been doing the crime beat here in New York for what, six years now?"

"About that," he said, keeping his attention focused on Mitch. "You have anything to say about what happened here tonight?"

"Nothing on the record," Mitch said, and we were both glad to see Officer Yellin return. Andy looked disappointed, but Mitch cheered him up. "I'm not talking to anybody about this right now, but when I do have something to say, it'll have your byline on top of it."

"In the meantime," I added, "the story's up on 33, not down here."

"I'm sure," Andy said, "but I just figured I'd check on the living first. Besides, I knew I'd find you here. Same old Amanda. When things get messy, just follow the gravy."

He left us, but Mitch and I both knew there'd be other reporters on their way soon. If we wanted to accomplish anything, we'd have to ditch Mary Poppins. "Let me ask you something, Officer, do they do this to you a lot?"

"Do what?"

"Stick you on the sidelines somewhere, away from the action?"

I could see she felt uneasy about ratting out her chauvinistic superiors, but she wasn't completely above being petty. "Yeah, sometimes."

"And that really burns you, doesn't it? I mean, that's not why you joined the force, is it? To be treated like a glorified secretary?"

"Of course not."

"Then do something about it, Yellin. Make a scene, make a name for yourself. When you're somebody, you're a lot harder to shove off."

"But how do I do that?" she asked, before remembering a trace of decorum. "Detective."

"You know that guy who was here when you got back?"

"Yeah."

"Talk to him. He's a reporter and he's a friend of mine. He'll take care of you."

She shifted uncomfortably. "I'm not supposed to talk to reporters."

"You're not *supposed* to be a flunky, either, Yellin. You want to be fetching coffee and fingerprinting perps the rest of your career?"

"No, Detective."

"Then be somebody. Get into the game. Now."

"Yes, Detective," she said, getting up and marching away. She got about three steps before retreating. "What about…?"

"He won't leave the hotel. He promises."

Mitch didn't say anything at first, so I stuck him in the ribs with a fork. "I promise."

"I'll look after him. Now go, Yellin, and make a splash."

And just like that, she dove in, and was out of our way. Mitch looked down to make sure I hadn't punched holes in his shirt, then peered up at me. "Now what?"

"There any place we can talk?"

"Without leaving the hotel? Only place I can think of would be Sondra's room."

"Perfect." Before we left the restaurant, we made arrangements to have Mitch's sea bass and a New York Sirloin for me, plus an appetizer of Crispy Calamari Asia, sent up to room 2903. We made a quick stop at the front desk, where Mitch finagled a copy of the card key for the late Ms. Fisher's room, and then proceeded up to 29 ourselves.

The room was right off the elevators, and the hallway was empty, save for a sitting chair and glass table, so we were able to sneak in without being seen. The room was appointed in a similar manner to Mitch's suite, but with less furniture. Just a bed, dresser, nightstand, desk and dinette table with chairs, plus a TV and some lamps. Sondra had unpacked completely, rather than live out of her suitcase, so her personal effects were everywhere to be seen.

"This feels very wrong," Mitch said, sinking onto a corner of the bed.

"It *is* very wrong, but until we have some concept of what's going on, we have to blur that line. So tell me what happened."

"Well, after we left last night, we came right back here and then to sleep. J.T. was out late, as usual. He found a bar nearby called—guess what—J.T.'s, so he was carousing 'til I don't know when. That's why I never room with him on the road. So, we're up early and to the radio station by, I don't know, 6:45. I did the interview with Scott and Todd, talked about the upcoming shows, how I might be working on a new album, the usual chatfest. Then we took it over to NBC and it started over again. It was like that all day, one station right after another."

I was trying to check out the room without being too disrespectful. "You didn't perform?"

"Nope. That was part of the deal. Besides, Gil and Tommy and Kelly aren't even coming into town until later on tonight. Around the same time as our gear, hopefully. J.T.'s only here because he chose to be."

"So when did you and Sondra part company?"

"Our last stop was Q-104, and I was supposed to do the drive-time show with the Dasher. But the one thing I'd forgotten was the stack of bumper stickers I'd signed for a giveaway. I'd left 'em in my room. So Sondra tells me to go do the show, and she'll get the bumper stickers. I give her my card key and she left me there in the studio. That was the last time I saw her alive."

At that point, room service brought up our food and we ate, though not with much gusto. Mitch's fish came with a lobster risotto in a red coconut cream sauce, while my steak was accompanied by stir-fried vegetables. As we dug into the Calamari Asia, I was reminded of my ER doctor. "I've already broken at least one of his directives, and though he didn't rule out sex, he probably wouldn't have recommended the blood rush."

He crunched one last piece of squid. "Sounds like you're falling pretty hard for this girl."

"Feels that way, too. Weirdest part is, I think she feels the same."

"It's about time you had a little happiness in your life."

"I could say the same about you."

He let that one pass, and I retreated to the bathroom to pee and wash my hands. He was stacking up the dishes when I returned, and pointed out Sondra's laptop.

"She keep a lot of business stuff on there?" I asked.

"Oh, yeah. Itineraries, correspondence, you name it. I'd always see her with it."

I gathered the power adapter and other peripherals and stacked them together with the machine. "Then we'd better take it with us."

"Why?"

"First off, we don't want anyone else to have access to your schedule."

"Okay," he said, but not with any confidence in my reasoning.

"And second, it may give us some insight into why Sondra was killed."

He stepped in front of me with a defiant glare. "What do you mean? Sondra was killed because she came to the door when Gordon knocked and not me."

"I don't think so," I said, gesturing for him to sit. "Now maybe you were the intended target, but if that's the case, I don't think Gordon was the shooter."

Mitch hard a hard time swallowing after I delivered that opinion. "Why not?"

I put my hand on his arm. "I'm no profiler, but here's my take on Gordon: He's been after you for five years, and in all that time, his hate has been growing. Festering. I don't know any better way to say this, but a seemingly blind shot like today just tells me that he's gotten even more fearless and more reckless. But also more determined to see this through."

I could feel Mitch shake, and for a moment I thought he might pass out, or at the very least, throw up the dinner we'd just shared. I wouldn't have blamed him.

"The thing is," I concluded, "for someone like him, there's only one way to satisfy the blood lust. He actually needs to see you die."

CHAPTER 19

▼

Removing evidence from a crime scene? Guilty. Obstruction of justice? Probably. Violating police procedure? You betcha. Given my actions, I probably should have gotten a note from Wacky Jacky stating that I was patently insane and not responsible for anything I said or did. It'd be my only defense in front of a review board.

I took the laptop and proceeded with Mitch down to the lobby, where we sat and waited until the locals came to get him for a formal line of questioning. There was nothing incriminating in his story, and various TV and radio stations could certainly verify his whereabouts for most of the day. Once the coroner established a time of death, Mitch would be cleared of suspicion, if he was even a suspect to begin with.

I left him with Detective Jerry Winston, a genial and competent-looking fellow who'd had the misfortune of catching this case. He'd found us there in the lobby after leaving his partner upstairs to secure the crime scene and to handle one Officer Denise Yellin, who was ranting about being marginalized. Winston was tall and paunchy, with a full head of dark gray hair, glasses and a soft baritone of a voice. I explained that I was a friend and on medical leave from the job, and that he could call me if there were any concerns.

Was I any closer to knowing anything? It was hard to tell, even if my hunch about Sondra's death was spot-on. The possibility existed that someone besides Gordon had done the murder, but the chance of Mitch crossing paths with a second psycho was too James Patterson in its coincidence, too much for me to contemplate. That meant that Gordon had killed Sondra and, more to the point, wanted her dead. But why? It was as if my jigsaw puzzle was just starting to look like the picture on the box, only I'd just found a stray piece under the carpet that didn't seem to fit anywhere.

Before going to the subway for the trip home, I called Jeannie from a payphone.

"Hello?" The female voice on the other end didn't sound familiar. Probably one of her roommates.

"Can I talk to Jeannie, please?"

"Um, yeah, hang on a sec…who's calling?"

"Amanda."

Through the receiver, I heard muffled thuds and thunks, along with snatches of conversation, as the phone was passed around to Jeannie. "Hi there," she said.

"Hey there. Sorry I missed your call. It's been a long and wearying day."

"No problem."

I held up a finger to the well-dressed man who was anxiously pacing behind me. "I'm on a payphone, so I really can't talk, but can you come over? I need you to do a little hacking."

"Is that what you kids are calling it these days?" she asked bemusedly.

I took her intimation—that thought wasn't far from my mind. "We'll talk about *that* later, but I do need your computer skills."

"Sure thing. 'Bout a half-hour?"

"Great. I'll see you then. Looking forward to it."

"Me too."

As much as I loved the sound of her voice, something in it didn't register quite right. Maybe she was distracted. Maybe she'd been getting ready for bed. Whatever tricks my head was playing, they weren't worth dwelling on. Yet as I waited on the platform for a 7 train, a singer with an electric piano—the New York equivalent of a busker—drove home doubt with his mangled renditions of Billy Joel and Beatles tunes. He wore a sweat-soaked lavender T-shirt, baggy blue shorts, gray socks and black Puma sneakers, an ensemble almost as odd as his performance. He had neither the range of Paul McCartney nor the abandon of John Lennon, and his "Let It Be" was as lifeless as Denise Yellin's hair. It was his "She's Always A Woman" that got to me, though, with its pointed lyrics and muted melody. "She can ruin your faith with her casual lies," he sang, and every niggling doubt came to the fore. Granted, we'd only known each other for three days, but some chemical reactions are, unfortunately, short-lived.

The 7 and 1 trains got me home at around 10:30, and Jeannie arrived shortly thereafter. She looked every bit the college student in jeans, a black top and pink sweatshirt. We kissed and held each other, and in that embrace, everything felt right, as if the previous night's ecstasy had yet to end. And just like that, my doubts retreated to the shadows.

"What is it?" she asked. "Why are you shaking?"

"I did a terrible, horrible thing," I moaned, my words carrying the salty sting of tears.

She wiped my cheek with her hand. "I'm sure it's not that bad...and whatever it is, I forgive you. Now come on, sit down and tell Dr. Jeannie all about it."

"Doctor," I said, attempting a laugh, "you don't even have your master's."

She shook her head with a groan and led me to the couch, where she sat and I rested my head in her lap. The rest of my body instinctively curled into the fetal position. I told her about my trip to Bad Habits, about The Ferret and his repugnant bet, and how it was killing me that I'd said yes.

"Let me ask you this," she said, gently stroking my hair, "do you still want me?"

"More than anyone I've ever known."

"And would you ever in your life willingly sleep with that piece of shit? Even if Regis were to hand you the million-dollar check as soon as the deed was done?"

"No."

"Then welcome back to the pink triangle. It's a bad, bad world out there, hon. You're safer here at home with me."

"I know."

Doctor, can I get a lifetime prescription of whatever it is you're dispensing?

I sat up and humped over next to her, and when I got there, she deposited her head onto my shoulder. It was a long time before she spoke. "I've got a confession to make, and I'm not sure what you'll think of me after I tell you."

I lifted her head up so I could see her face. "Are you sure you want to tell me?"

"I have to. I've been lying for too long."

She only reveals what she wants you to see.

I don't think either of us expected the night to become a communal bath, but she had begun adding tears to the pool. "Jeannie, what is it?"

She didn't answer at first, and I gave her time to cry it out. In the aftershock of my bombshell, she was hurting pretty bad and there was little I could do but hold on—hold on to her for dear life. Finally, just when I thought the sound of silence would drown us out forever, she whispered something.

I'd been on the verge of drifting off when she said it, so I didn't hear. "What?"

"Nobody knows I'm here."

"Oh, sweetie," I said, taking her face in my hands, "is that all? Did you need to let your roommates know where you are? You can call them if you like." Gauging by her reaction, I probably should have glanced over to see if I'd sprouted a second head.

"I mean nobody knows I'm *here*," she said, waggling her finger back and forth between us. "In the pink triangle."

Some detective you are.

"You mean you're still…in the closet?"

"Hanging right next to the little black dress."

She probably expected me to feel hurt, betrayed. Maybe a little confused. And in truth, I likely did have some of those responses—but they were snuffed out by a big old blanket of relief. It explained everything that had been worrying me: Why she hadn't given me her number right away. Why her roommate hadn't known who I was when I called. Why there'd been no sweet nothings spoken over the phone. It may have also explained why she'd had such a sympathetic ear for the audio version of my journey into self-loathing. "If that's the way you want it to be…"

"Of course it's not. I wish I had your candor. Your courage. The only reason I was capable of coming on to you that night at Houlihan's was that there was no one around to rat me out."

I got up and went into the kitchen, putting on a kettle of water for tea. While I was in there, I also raided my cookie jar—a hideous porcelain thing depicting two cows drinking coffee—and put together a plate of Oreos and Chips Ahoy. "I can see why you might not tell your folks, or friends in your hometown, but why not your roommates? Not that it's any of their business, but aren't they, you know, safe?"

"When Caitlin and Michelle and I first decided to get a place together, I figured I'd tell them. My roommate up in Plattsburgh freshman year didn't know and besides, up there in the boonies, you're not going to find too many gay bars where you can pick up a partner for some mattress dancing. After that, I moved off campus, so it was no longer an issue. But here, the three of us found a great place with three bedrooms, but the rent was too steep. That's when Michelle told us about this girl Carol she knew, who was looking to get in on some kind of share. It was supposed to be a great arrangement—Michelle and Carol would take the master bedroom and Caitlin and I would each take one of the smaller ones."

I delivered the cookies and sat down, waiting for the water to boil. "What happened?"

"Two nights before classes started, and we'd just spent all day getting the apartment all spruced up, unpacking boxes and sorting through dishes and stuff, when we order a pizza for dinner. The delivery girl comes, and she's got her T-shirt sleeves rolled up, and her hair's cut really short, and after Michelle paid for the pie, Carol says to her, "You give Butch a big tip?"

"You're kidding."

She split apart an Oreo and took a lick of creme filling. "I wish. The next day, I have a meeting with my thesis advisor, and Carol's got something to do at school, too, so we walk down together. I'm still pretty miffed about the night before, but I'm not about to make a stink. Not when I have to share a roof with this bitch. But there we were, walking down Broadway, and she makes a crack about how this woman in front of us has got on these 'dyke-y shoes.'"

The water was boiling, and so was my blood. "She's the ignorant cow, and you're the one who has to cover your tracks." I'd almost chosen another noun to describe this woman I hadn't met, a noun I'm loath to use because of just how demeaning it's become. Still, it almost escaped my lips, before the "cow" jumped over my tongue.

Maybe Eve Ensler's right. Maybe it's time we reclaimed "cunt."

"It's my own damn fault," she said, following me into the kitchen, where she pulled out two mugs. "If I hadn't been so afraid to tell anyone, I'd have been able to avoid this kind of thing. Or at the very least, she'd have avoided me."

As I poured, I considered how her secret might affect us. "Look, if you want to keep me to yourself, it's not my place to say. But yes, I would be uncomfortable if you started introducing me to people as your 'friend.' I've been down that road before, and the scenery is pretty ugly."

A casual psychologist could see how she was beating herself up, the way she dunked her teabag so violently, the hot water nearly slopped up over the rim. "So tell me," she said, letting go of the string and apparently dropping the subject, "what's this hacking you need me to do?"

I indicated the laptop sitting on the living room table, and explained that it had belonged to the now-deceased Sondra Fisher.

"You mean that uptight woman who roped Mitch out of here last night?"

"Yeah," I said, not really wanting to go into the details, "she was shot and killed this afternoon. And I'm looking for something that might be on her hard drive, in her e-mails, somewhere. Something that got her dead."

As I watched her hook up the computer and cables, and power the machine up with its familiar clicks and whirs, the conflicted, scared woman who'd cried on my shoulder melted away, leaving a strong, confident and competent hacker, diving headlong into a challenge.

She hides like a child, but she's always a woman to me.

CHAPTER 20

▼

We didn't make love that night, but in some way what we shared was far more intimate. After the tea and cookies came truth, though I did a lot of the talking. I told her what it had been like coming out, first to Andy Devane, then to my parents. When I was assigned to the 11th Precinct, I explained, there'd been the expected knucklehead bullshit, a classic case of ignorance beating common sense to the punch. Over the years, the homophobia had faded for the most part, except for one event—where Janet Seeber, a rookie at the time, now a friend on the force, thought I had sexually harassed her—and so, my orientation became a non-issue among my fellow officers. After that, the rest of New York had been a snap.

Just after midnight, long after I'd given up on trying to decipher everything Jeannie was doing, brushed my teeth and gotten ready for bed, I was hit by a sudden silence. The rapid-fire typing and techno-babbling stopped and Jeannie sat motionless, her fingers poised above the keys, her panic-stricken face taut, as if she'd been cast in porcelain. Then, just as suddenly, her features softened and she even smiled. "Fuck it," she said.

She wasn't giving up on Sondra's laptop, but on the lie. Her parents would still love her. Carol wasn't worth hiding from. And everyone else, well, they'd learn to deal with it. With her bloodshot eyes and wrinkled brow, she was hardly the cocksure dynamo I'd encountered that first night. And she'd recovered enough of herself to leave behind the weepy and lost little girl who'd spilled all her secrets. I was staring at someone in between, someone I could give my heart to without regret.

She declined my invitation to share a blanket, instead working late into the night at cracking through Sondra's passwords and security measures. When I crawled into bed at around 1 a.m., she was charged to the challenge, enthusiastically dunking a Chips Ahoy in her tea with the gusto of positive energy.

Still, even wired programmers have to crash sometime, and when the Sandman decided to kick me back into the waking world, shortly before 10, Jeannie was still within his clutches—dead asleep on the couch. I fetched a blanket from the bedroom and tucked her in—only a few hours too late. In doing so, I noticed a pad on which Jeannie had scribbled a number of incoherent notes, strings of numbers and letters that read more like a bowl of alphabet soup than any kind of language. On the bottom of the page, she'd jotted down an e-mail address: angermgmt@redrum.net. While it seemed important—she'd drawn boxes around it and arrows pointing to it—she hadn't conveyed its significance. Did it belong to Sondra? Gordon? Mitch?

Rather than giving Jeannie the third degree, I repaid the favor of her late-night detective work and let her sleep. I wanted to try Ingrid Jakubowski, anyhow. On my way to the kitchen, I noticed a rust-colored piece of paper that had been slid under my door. Plenty of takeout menus arrive that way, and I nearly tossed this one out before even looking at it. Fortunately, a few things caught my eye. First, my name was inked across the top. And second, where the restaurant's hours were listed, the abbreviation Fri. was circled, as was the time of opening—11:30. Based on my scant knowledge of Sam Pelillo's habits and taste for local cuisine, I suspected that this was, as the Ferret had put it, someone "getting in touch." Which meant that I had my sitdown—at Ollie's Noodle Shop, about six blocks away, in less than 90 minutes.

I picked up the phone to call Ingrid, only to find that I had no dial tone. I hit the flashhook a few times before I noticed that the phone wasn't plugged into the wall. Instead, a flat gray cable snaked its way out to the living room, dead-ending at the back of Sondra's laptop. Whatever it was that Jeannie had done during the night, it was more than just keystrokes and mouse clicks.

I unplugged the cable and re-attached the phone, quickly dialing Ingrid's number. A woman answered on the third ring. "Hello?" The voice sounded congested and hoarse.

"Ingrid?"

"Yes?"

"This is Detective Ross in New York. Your Aunt Lou gave you my number."

She didn't answer right away, but after a few seconds, I heard the distinct honking and sniffling of someone whose nose desperately needed blowing.

"Sorry," she said, "I didn't go to work today because I'm sick, and the stuff I took last night made me kind of foggy-headed on top of it. I'm a mess."

"I've been there," I replied, trying to come up with a way of being both thorough and expedient. "You said in your phone message that you didn't know Jennifer Marx all that well. But could you fill me in on what you do know? What do you remember about her?"

She coughed, and on reflex I moved the receiver away from my head. Obviously, I know that her germs weren't going to book a one-way passage through my phone line, only to vacation in my respiratory tract. But my instinctive aversion to doctors, hospitals and all things illness-related wasn't taking any chances. Even a "widdle cold" could dull my senses enough to make me less than effective in sniffing out Gordon before he snuffed out Mitch. "She and I worked at the same restaurant in Phoenix, that's how we met. She didn't know anyone in town when she got there, so I'd show her around when we got off shift. Took her to some of the hot spots, couple of parties, introduced her to a few people. You know, made sure she didn't feel like such a stranger."

"Was she a happy person?"

"That sounds like what the reporters were asking way back when."

"I guess what I'm asking is, were you surprised when you heard about her death?"

A sneeze, followed by more coughing. "I was at first, but then when it came out that Mitch Black had been staying at that hotel, it all made sense in a weird sort of way."

"How so?"

"Oh, Jen was, like, *totally* obsessed with him," she said. "Talked about him all the time. She even claimed that he wrote one of his songs for her. Every time she'd meet someone new, she'd tell this story of how he came into the diner where she was working and how even though she never said a word to him, she knew that she'd made an impression on him. I must've heard that story six or seven times. We all thought it was just a bunch of B.S."

A true story that no one ever believed.

"But if Mitch, er, Mr. Black was in town, why wouldn't she just go to the concert and sneak backstage or try to bluff her way into the hotel?"

She blew her nose again. "She thought all that groupie-chick stuff was beneath her, and that it didn't dignify the artist. Still, she did say she was going to see him that night. Said that her sister was in town, and she was going to introduce the two of them."

"Wait a minute. Jennifer Marx had a sister? I know she bounced around the system, but I never heard about any blood relatives."

"Foster sister, I guess. She didn't have any real family...That's right, she said she'd been with these people in Florida for a couple of years, and there was a girl there, a few years older. The two of them were pretty close, to hear Jen tell it, and they kept in touch."

"But how's the sister going to introduce her to Mr. Black? What'd, she work at the hotel or something?"

"No, no...Jen said that her sister worked at his record label, and she was coming into Phoenix on his tour bus."

Suddenly, the dots were starting to resemble something. "She must have been a big deal to be riding with the band."

"Oh, she was. She was his, um...what's the word? Not his assistant. She was the one who handled all the back-and-forth stuff between him and the record company. The, uh, it's on the tip of my tongue..."

"Liaison?"

"That's it. Liaison. Jen said that Sondra always followed Mitch around on tour, at appearances, kind of looking out for him and reporting back if there were any problems."

Sondra.

"You happen to recall Sondra's last name?"

"No. I don't know if Jen ever mentioned it." She sneezed.

"Gesundheit. It's okay, Ingrid. Not important. You've been very helpful. Take care and feel better."

I was about to hang up when I heard Ingrid on the other end. "Detective?"

"Yes?"

"If you don't mind my asking, why the interest in Jennifer now? The police couldn't have cared less six years ago."

I could hear Jeannie stirring in the other room, so I had to get off quickly. "I can't really talk about a case, Ingrid, but since Jennifer was your friend, I'll tell you this: That story she used to tell, about Mitch Black and the diner in Philly? She wasn't making it up."

The shock on Ingrid's end registered as more of a wheeze than a gasp, but I knew the point had been taken—and that she'd never hear "In from the Cold" again without thinking of Jennifer. In Mitch's lyrics, she'd become immortal.

I hung up and scampered into the living room, catching Jeannie in mid-stretch. "Morning, you."

She gazed up at me, then down at the blanket which had magically appeared. "What time is it?"

"About 10:30."

"Shit!" she said, throwing off the blanket and darting into the bathroom. "I've got a class to teach!"

I followed her, offering a spare toothbrush and hairbrush. "Any luck last night?"

"That depends," she said, double-timing all the morning ablutions she could manage. "There's an e-mail address I jotted down, over on the pad. See if it means anything to you."

"Jeannie, just because you gave me an e-mail address on Monday night, that doesn't mean I have any use for it—or others of its kind."

"Well, Sondra'd been exchanging correspondence with that user for a while. Most of it venomous."

"How'd you find that out?"

She took a washcloth and dabbed at her face and neck. "Once I got her password, I was able to sift through all of her e-mail stuff. Now either she was careless or lazy because she left a virtual paper trail. There was nothing in her inbox, and her Deleted Items folder was empty. From her system settings, I was able to determine that the folder cleaned itself out every time she shut down."

I joined her at the mirror, assessing the night's damage to my hair. It was a disaster. "So where was this paper trail?"

"In her Sent Items folder. Every e-mail she'd sent over I don't know how many months was in there. And I'll say this: From what she wrote, she placed Mitch right up there with Osama bin Laden in the evil department."

"Because of her foster sister," I said, mostly to myself. "Which means that she's the insider who was feeding Gordon information. Who got him a job on the road crew that last date. Who let him know what hospital Mitch was recuperating in. And that means the e-mail address you found is probably him."

"I tried tracing it back to the source, but with some of these fly-by-night ISPs, there's no information tied to it. It's quite possibly a vanity production."

I turned on the shower and let the water run while we finished up. "Meaning he's the only user, right?"

"Right. Just about anyone can get themselves a domain, at which point all bets are off. As is any kind of regulation of content, violence, profanity or anything else."

"Was there anything about Gordon's plans? Is he coming to New York? Is he planning to pull anything at the concert tonight?"

"No, nothing like that. I think he's a little too smart for that. Too crafty to leave so much information out there."

"Unlike Sondra," I said, swiping my hand under the spray and making it a little hotter. "Okay, thanks."

"Any time, darling." She turned my face to hers and kissed me.

"I've got to call Mitch as soon as I'm out of the shower."

"Don't forget to hook up your phone again. I used the jack to log on last night. And let me tell you this: 56K dial-up sucks!"

"Whatever that means. And I already undid your handiwork. Now go. Get to class."

She departed, and I pulled off the T-shirt and panties I was wearing, getting ready to step in the tub. Just then, out of the corner of my eye, I saw Jeannie lurking around the doorframe, taking in my strip show. I whirled on her, catching the Peeping Tonya in the act. "Gotcha."

She smiled. "No, I've got you. And this little snapshot will carry me through my day."

And that little ego stroke will do the same for me.

CHAPTER 21

▼

Despite all the new information I'd recently gleaned, there were still a lot of questions. How could Sondra have continued to work with Mitch for so long, believing him to be responsible for Jennifer's death? Was Gordon the one who'd blasted through Mitch's hotel room door? Sticking with my theory about Mitch *not* being the target, had Sondra been killed on purpose, or was she just in the path of the projectiles? If the former, why would Gordon want her dead? She'd been his in, his access to Mitch for years. Had he gotten so confident that the deed would be done that he no longer required a Gal Friday? After all, she had more incriminating stuff on him than anyone else, including the police. Maybe he was afraid she'd turn on him, pick him out of the crowd and use the e-mails as evidence. Or perhaps she had chickened out, and told Gordon they couldn't go through with it. No, with six years of hatred behind her—she was the charter member of the Mitch Must Die fan club, not Gordon—I couldn't see Sondra suddenly letting it drop. And if she *had* planned on switching sides, Gordon's messages would be stored somewhere on her laptop, to be used against him later, rather than zapped from the hard drive at every opportunity.

Then there was the most pressing question of all: What does one wear to have lunch with a Mafioso?

After I showered and brushed my hair, I retreated to the bedroom and dug out my other gray blouse, and conservative gray slacks. Then, for a splash of color—so somebody might notice and remember me dining with Sam Pelillo, just in case I got gunned down on my way home—a cable-knit peach cardigan. It was out of season and looked ridiculous, but I had to admit, it was hard to miss.

Once I was dressed, I put a call in to Mitch or, more accurately, I called the Grand Hyatt and asked to be connected with a Mr. James Mitchell. Granted, this alias was juvenile in its construction—James is Mitch's middle name—but it usually served its purpose in keeping inexperienced hotel clerks from inadvertently pointing groupies in his direction.

"Hello?"

"Mitch, it's Amanda. I don't have a lot of time, but I wanted to fill you in on everything that's happened. But before I forget, what time is your sound check?"

"2:30, at The Bottom Line."

"Okay, I'll be there, but be sure to have your crew go over every piece of equipment. If there's anything, and I mean *anything* that strikes you as out of the ordinary, get the hell out of there. If you see any roadies or tech guys you don't recognize, find out who they are and fast. If no one else can vouch for them, call the cops."

"Yeah, sure, will do."

His response struck me as surprisingly subdued. With good reason, he'd been something of a Nervous Norman every time I'd had him one on one. "Everything all right there?"

"Sure. I'm just relaxing is all."

"Well, that's good to hear. After last night, I thought you'd be, well…"

"A basket case?"

"Yeah, something like that."

"Ten, eleven hours ago, you'd have been right," he said. "After I got done with Detective Winston, I was wound so tight I thought I'd bust a spring. So I knew I had to loosen up. And who better to help me in that regard than the loosest person we both know?"

Why not? J.T. can always be found on the path of least resistance.

"So you went out with the little drummer boy, and…?"

"Say what you will about him, the man knows how to have a good time."

"Well, good, I'm glad to know he can do more than lay down a rhythm track."

"It'd been so long since I'd done the night owl thing," Mitch mused, "that I'd forgotten how much fun it could be…when you're in the right company."

Ah. "Eight million people in this city, someone's bound to get lucky once in a while. What was her name?"

"Ariel. But you might remember her better if I called her Inky Boo."

I swear there are mice gnawing at my Swiss-cheese memory, because I had no idea what he was talking about. Inky Boo? After scrunching up my brow and staring at the phone for more than a minute, I nearly gagged in distaste. "You mean that"—I chose the next word very carefully—"dish from Tower Records? The one with the marker fetish?"

"Mmhmm."

"I thought you didn't do that sort of thing," I said, shaking my head.

"I don't, but a little female companionship seemed like just the thing to get my mind off the whole Gordon thing."

"And from the sound of it, she succeeded."

"Oh, trust me. She's a *very* healthy distraction. Some of the things she does, you'd have to be dead not to sit up and take notice."

Which I'm sure is exactly what Little Mitch did.

Before I could tell him about Sondra, Mitch regaled me with how he'd run into Ariel and her friend DeLynn at J.T.'s. How they'd talked, how they'd danced, how her boyfriend had broken up with her over a certain signature. And how J.T. himself had had no problem whatsoever with crowning DeLynn Miss Congeniality.

It was just after 11 when I finally got him to shut up and listen. I told him about Sondra's e-mails, and how she was almost definitely the one who'd been spoon-feeding Gordon whatever inside information he'd needed. I reiterated my earlier warning about his equipment and his crew, and wrapped it up with the juiciest tidbit of all.

I waited while Mitch picked up the phone after he'd dropped it. "Sondra and Jennifer Marx? Sisters?"

"Foster sisters, but close enough for her to hate you."

"But...how? How did Sondra hook up with Gordon?"

"Probably from that radio call-in show. After Jennifer tried to fly, Sondra might have killed you herself. My guess is, she didn't have it in her. But you pick up a caller on line three, and suddenly she's got a willing accomplice. She might have gone through the station's logs, or found some other way to track Gordon down, but all she had to do was put two and two together. She enlisted herself a hunter and made you the prey."

I had succeeded in extinguishing whatever afterglow had still been burning in Mitch's hotel room. That hadn't been my intent, but I needed him on his toes, alert and focused. He needed me to be the same, otherwise these might be Mitch's last hours on Earth. I told him I'd see him at 2:30, then hung up and got my ass out the door.

Outside, it was cold and damp, a funereal air left over from the day before. Still, foot traffic on Broadway was heavy and I had to bob and weave and zig and zag to move any faster than an urban crawl. In doing so, I blew by a newsstand, only to be drawn back by the morning's headlines and cover shots.

"Deadly Hours" proclaimed the *Daily News*, with a big photo of the door to suite 3330 and thumbnails of Mitch and Sondra. "Number One With A Bullet" read the *Post*, which somehow had gotten hold of a crime scene photo of Sondra's bleeding corpse, and offset it with a snap of Mitch and Jerry Winston talking in the hotel lobby. *Newsday* took a slightly more tasteful approach, shrinking the splintered door shot down to an inset, with an outdoor pic of the cops and porters at the Grand Hyatt taking up most of the page under the banner "Blown Away," not coincidentally, the title of a song on Mitch's first album. Since I didn't care to show up to lunch looking like a vendor, I didn't buy any papers; I'd get them on my way home.

Ollie's Noodle Shop & Grille is a chain, with several locations around Manhattan. Primarily serving Chinese food, there's at least one that has a much more extensive menu, complete with Italian and American entrees. The one near me, however, between 67th and 68th, has more traditional Far East fare.

The front of the restaurant offers casual dining, with a large pickup window looking in on woks, deep fryers and other tools of the trade. The two dozen plastic tables and chairs were unoccupied, it being right after opening, so rather than wait, I proceeded to the back. Sam Pelillo was seated toward the rear of the dark dining room, accompanied by a younger man with pale blond hair. I hesitated for just a second before walking over.

"Over here," said Sam, gesturing to the chair opposite him while remaining in his place. The other man stood, but not out of chivalry. Before he let me take a seat, he patted me down for wires, weapons and, more than likely, just to cop a feel. Given what I'd been willing to say and do just to get this meeting, I could live with the grope. Had his Roman hands gone anywhere near my crotch, though, I was ready to retaliate. Fortunately, he turned out to be a gentlemanly perv; only my boobs got the once over.

"Thank you for seeing me, Mr. Pelillo," I said as I sat, keeping my eyes on Mr. Frisky, who kept his gaze on me until I'd settled in.

"Frankie," he said with a quick head tilt toward his blond lieutenant. "It's Amanda, right?"

"Right." I was surprised he needed the prompt; there couldn't be that many other strangers ballsy enough to ask for a moment of his time.

"From what Phil told me, you had an important matter to discuss." His appearance was jovial, but his tone was clipped. He was nattily dressed in a dark blue suit, and he carried his weight well. A shade under six feet tall, he probably tipped the scales at around 270. In looks and demeanor, he was the mirror image of his companion—a sinewy sort with a stern face and rough hands. The man looked uncomfortable in a shirt and tie, and I could see a tattoo peeking out from his French cuffs.

A waiter came by and poured tea for the two men. I kept my cup inverted and asked for a Coke. I was in for a long day and wanted all the pep I could get. He brought my soda and menus, then departed to let us continue our conversation.

"Here's the thing," I said, feeling like I belonged in a David Mamet play. "A woman in my building was killed on Monday morning. A bomb in her apartment. She had a 7-year-old boy, and his father is nowhere to be found. At this point, the police have no idea who did it, or even why. I was hoping you might know something about it, or be willing to ask around. You're always on top of everything in this part of this city, so if anyone's going to be able to find out who's behind this, it'd be you...sir."

"Nice whitewash," said Frankie, whom I took to be Frankie Dean, Sam's chief enforcer and button man. "Of course, all the snow just makes the bullshit stand out."

Sam contemplated, and I wasn't sure whether he was mulling my request or absorbing his cohort's colloquy. Finally, he spoke. "Ordinarily, I couldn't care less about Phil Lentini and his bar bets. The guy's mouth is twice as big as his brain and he's liable to fuck up a job as often as not. He's kind of like the mangy mutt you've had around for 10 years but you can't bring yourself to dial up the vet and have him put down. Still, he's loyal, doesn't bark in the wrong neighborhoods and doesn't shit on my lawn."

"I see," I said, starting to feel that my plan was as shaky as the San Andreas.

"No, I don't think you do," he said, his voice taking on a Rottweiler snarl. "Even if I had tits and a box, I wouldn't fuck the Ferret for a million bucks, much less five hundred and a game of pool. Not only that, but from what I hear, you're more likely to cooze over that 'Friends' chick than her pretty-boy husband."

What the...?

"Hey, if pussy is your thing, knock yourself out. But I gotta wonder how fucked in the head you gotta be to put that kinda thing into play."

"I...I don't know what I was thinking. I'm sorry," I said, and I buried my face in my hands like I'd just sprouted a zit the size of Macy's. I took a breath and stood on weakened knees, hoping I might make it to the street before I threw up.

"Sit down, Detective," I heard Frankie say. It wasn't a request.

"What?" I glanced back, startled by what he'd called me.

"Detective Amanda Ross, 11th Precinct. How stupid did you think we were?" My tongue had turned to stone, and it was like pulling my feet from half-dried cement to move my body back toward the table.

"You have got to be the dumbest cop I've ever seen," Sam said as he cracked each knuckle on his right hand. "Either that or the craziest. Given that you took a psycho leave shortly after 9/11, I'll give you the benefit of the doubt."

I'd completely lost control of the situation, something I'd been totally afraid of as I walked over. Yet somehow, in the wry smile that had crept across the face of Sam Pelillo, I could sense that my lapse in judgment may well have saved my life.

"Stones are stones, Detective, and you've got 'em," Sam said as he picked up his menu, "no matter what's wrong with your wiring. Now let's order so I can hear your story out while I'm still feeling charitable."

CHAPTER 22

▼

I'd been made. I was a pathetic excuse for a cop. I wanted to bury my head in the fried noodles.

Make like an ostrich all you want, the world still won't go away.

Sam signaled for the waiter, who came over, pad in hand. Rather than doing the chivalric thing, he went right ahead and ordered, starting with Pickled Cabbage and Shredded Pork with Noodle Soup, followed by Diced Chicken in Hot Pepper Sauce with Peanuts. True to his reputation, the boss liked things hot. Frankie Dean chose the Crispy Chicken & Wonton Soup and Beef with Scallops in Brown Sauce. I'm not sure what I'd expected a cold-blooded killer to have for lunch. Somewhere I'd read that a large percentage of convicted murderers order peach cobbler as part of their last meal.

Still, in listening to the two men make their menu choices, I saw through the smokescreen. Sure, they were likely both armed (Frankie was for sure) and they could probably make me disappear in a New York minute, but they were, after all, just men. Filled with all the insecurities, vanity and pride that comes with a Y chromosome. They were just like the Ferret, only with more firepower. However, since they'd also unearthed my other dirty little secret, I had no way of using sex as a weapon.

"And for you, miss?" the waiter asked.

"I don't think she's got much of an appetite," chortled Frankie.

At that point, I reached into my bag of tricks to find the Mafioso's method of choice: bluster.

"Hey, Frankie," I said, "when I need a dietitian to remind me of what I ate and to measure my last bowel movement, I'll schedule you for an interview.

Right now, we're all on the clock, so let's skip the unpleasantries, hm? Sliced Lamb with Sha Cha Sauce."

I glanced over at the waiter to make sure he took it down. "Something to start?" he asked with just a hint of smile, his thin lips parting ever so slightly, set low beneath a slender nose in a round, ageless face. He'd seen these characters before.

"Little Bit of Everything Soup."

"Very good," he said, flipping his pad closed and moseying toward the kitchen.

"Look," I said once my co-conspirator was out of earshot, "I didn't bring the badge to the table because I'm not coming to you as a cop. My interest in finding out who bombed my neighbor's apartment has nothing to do with my being on the force. Finding the fucker responsible is the only way I can be sure the kid'll live to see his next birthday. And, if you manage to flush out his MIA father in the process, he might just have something worth coming home to."

"Hold on there, honey," Sam said with a snort, "why the personal interest? Can't be just because she lived next door. What, you show her how the other half lives? Teach an old dog some new tricks?"

For these two Neanderthals, it would be the simplest thing, letting them think Charlotte and I had grappled between the sheets, and that I was due a lover's vengeance. But I wasn't about to give them any Spice Channel fantasies. "When the bomb went off, I was standing in her doorway. A few feet closer, and I'd have been collateral damage. As it is, the blast knocked me into next week and left me a bleeder on the brain as a souvenir. So you're damn right it's personal. I don't take near-death experiences lightly."

The waiter brought our soups in steaming bowls, served with squarish porcelain spoons. As its name indicated, mine had something for everyone: beef, chicken, seafood, vegetables, noodles. It was flavorful and filling, and just the thing to keep the fire burning in my belly.

As Sam slurped up the last of his soup, he glanced over at Frankie Dean, not looking for approval or reassurance, more to let his man know a decision had been made.

"You give us the information on when and where this happened, and I'll have some guys ask around. But in the meantime, I'd like to know exactly how you plan to repay my generosity."

I didn't expect to get away from the lunch without feeling the pinch, but neither had I bothered to come up with a suitable peace offering. "A favor's what I ask, and a favor's what you get. In whatever way I can be of service."

"Detective Ross," he said, "and I don't call you that out of respect, but to remind you of your intrinsic value. When I come to collect, your badge better be on the table."

"I don't follow," is what I said, even though I followed him perfectly.

"What he means is," said Frankie, eager to cobble his way back into the conversation, "that a cop favor is a helluva lot more valuable than a crackpot dyke favor. You're of a lot more use on the job than off."

It should have been an easy call, what with all the rules I'd bent and broken over the years. My sexual wager with The Ferret should have been the last possible line I could cross. The fact that I was even associating with Sam Pelillo and Frankie Dean without first clearing it with my lieutenant as well as IAB would mean that I'd be in for a rectal probe from my favorite cheese-eater, Lt. Donald Dingman, once I reported back for active duty. Yet some part of me, some long-forgotten innocence I'd stowed away beneath the basement steps, was still clinging to the notion that my professional integrity was intact. That my oath to uphold and defend was still sacrosanct, and that my badge, though dented and dinged, still shone pristine. Could I live with myself if I jumped off that bridge and into mob-infested waters? Maybe, but would I want to? Is there such a price that's simply too high to pay?

If you report back for active duty.

"What you see is what you get, gentlemen. You know who I am, so you know my limitations."

I was accorded a few more minutes of virtue, as the waiter arrived with our entrees; I could savor my lamb while Sam took his time in turning the screws.

"Whoo!" I said after the first bite, after the spicy barbecue sauce they called Sha Cha had scorched my taste buds. I gulped down some water and chomped on a handful of fried noodles to put out the blaze.

"If you can't stand the heat..." Frankie snickered.

"Not what you were expecting?" Sam queried.

"Exactly what I was expecting," I panted, "only more so."

Sam smiled, knowing that he had bested me in terms of tolerance for spice. After that, the three of us ate quickly and quietly, save for my numerous requests of a water refill. It was a good thing I hadn't made any plans with Jeannie for that night; my tongue was bound to be out of commission.

"Detective Ross," Sam said as he reached into his pocket and produced a silver cigar tube, "I didn't come here to be insulted, and dumb-broad bullshit aside, you're smart enough not to insult me. You screw with me in any way, or try to go back on this little deal of yours, you'll be wishin' to God that the Ferret had won your bet, 'cause that'd be the only way you'd be fucked."

The boss took the cigar from its holder and placed it between his lips, Frankie taking that as his signal that they were leaving. "As for me collectin' on this favor of yours, you will do what I say, when I say it. I don't care whether you're still on the force, working overnight security or living in a rubber room at Bellevue. I own your ass until I say otherwise. So you can take your limitations and stick 'em up your girlfriend's twat."

The two men left without so much as a parting glance, and the waitstaff immediately came over to start clearing the table. At the moment, I wasn't sure which horrified me more: What Sam Pelillo had just said, or that he'd stuck me with the bill. I was reaching into my jacket for my wallet when my friendly neighborhood waiter returned.

"Is taken care of," he said, touching me lightly on the shoulder. "Mr. Sam not usually have guests for lunch, but for Mr. Frankie."

"Oh," I said, nearly letting the wallet slide back into my pocket before I realized what an ally I had. I pulled out $20 and a business card, and slipped the man both. "The service was excellent."

He noticed the bill and quickly stashed it in the pocket of his uniform. "Thank you, miss."

I didn't really expect the $20 to buy me anything, but maybe he'd remember me if my mug ever appeared on TV or in the newspapers after I'd been whacked, and he'd recall whom I'd had lunch with. Not bloody likely, but he could perhaps be called upon to forget he ever saw me—especially if the shit started raining down from above because of my alleged mob connections.

As I stepped out onto Broadway, I was nearly waylaid by my own foolishness. Always the drama queen, I'd systematically gone about making these wildly absurd gestures—potentially forfeiting my life, my job and my virtue in the process—while at the same time letting Police Work 101 slip from my mind. I hurried off in the direction of the church, praying—if you can call it that—that God was in good humor.

Had I been the detective investigating Charlotte's death, I'd have attended the funeral as part of the procedure I'd set down for myself. After all, when else are you going to have all the deceased's nearest and dearest assembled in one room? Sitting at the back, you can usually observe half a dozen mini-soap operas as people's heightened emotions often lead them to divulge just how they feel about each other—and the person in the box. Ostensibly, I'd been there as a mourner, and even though I'd sat through the service with Jason Perelli, my powers of observation were muted by the occasion.

It was nearly 1:30 by the time I made my winded way up the steps of Our Lady of Lourdes. There was no service in progress, the only people I could see were a few random fixtures—elderly women who virtually lived there, trying to fill the holes in their lives with a spiritual gusto. I could admire their dedication to the faith, but I could also see them empty at the end of the day, no more fulfilled than when they'd entered, however many hours before.

"Can I help you?"

The question came from a young man with prematurely thinning brown hair, a high forehead and wire-rimmed glasses that sat in front of benign eyes. His face was thin and pale, almost angelic, save for a Diablo goatee that he kept closely trimmed. He was dressed entirely in black, and I'd have pegged him as clergy even if the book he was holding was a Danielle Steel novel instead of a bible.

"Yes," I said, producing my wallet and badge. "My name is Amanda Ross and I'm a detective with the 11th Precinct. I was here yesterday for a funeral, and I wanted to know if it's possible to look at the sign-in book—the, um, registry, that was out front here."

"Father Samuel," he said, barely glancing at my ID. "Father Donald usually handles funeral services, so I'm not exactly sure how everything is arranged. But I would imagine that the registry would go home with the family, so they could send out cards to the people who attended the service."

"That's what I was afraid of," I said, hoping to avoid a schlep out to Janice's place in Queens. "You don't think there's any chance they forgot it or anything, do you?"

Father Samuel smiled softly. "We all react differently in our time of grief. One certainly couldn't be blamed for having other things on his or her mind. You might want to check with Mrs. Baxter, downstairs in the church office. She takes care of all the clerical duties here."

"Thank you," I said, craning my neck to see a staircase going down beneath the congregation. "You've been a big help."

This time, his smile carried just a hint of impishness. I could almost see him contemplating a witty retort, something along the lines of Gladys' "big bucks" line. Instead, he just bowed slightly and said, "We should all do what we can for each other."

I turned to go, but Father Samuel called me back with a whispered, "Detective Ross."

"Yes?"

"You said you were here yesterday for the funeral. Tell me, what was your relation to Ms. Kilmer?"

The question, though valid, was unexpected. "She was my next door neighbor," I said.

"Were you close?"

Any closer and you'd have had a double feature, padre.

"Getting there. We were about to spend the day together when the…" He didn't need to hear about an exploding microwave. "When she died."

He took my hand and patted it gently. "I'm sorry for your loss."

My loss?

I'd been so wrapped up in caring about Pete that I hadn't noticed the elephant in the room, the one with the black armband around its front leg. I practically had to steady myself as I descended the wooden stairs, reeling from the obviousness of my antics. Why should I cry when I can distract myself with lunatic behavior and obsessive worry?

I tried to suck it up, and regretted it almost immediately; the church office reeked of cigarette smoke, reminiscent of all the bingo parlors my grandmother took me to throughout my childhood. Mrs. Baxter might have only been in her mid-40s, but the damage done by half a century or more of Kools had creased her leathery skin. Like the teeth she hid behind pale lips, the tobacco had stained everything about her yellow. The open pack of smokes on her desk led me to believe that if I waited a few minutes, she'd be scurrying out to the church steps for a drag. Even as a churchgoing woman, she'd probably never forgiven the Surgeon General, the Mayor's office and whomever else was responsible for taking away her right to light up in a public place.

"Mrs. Baxter," I said, gently tapping on the door. I secretly wondered if all those years of sucking down nicotine gave her the ability to breathe fire.

"Yes?" she said, turning and seeing me. Her voice was low and raspy, almost like the early rumble of an earthquake.

"I'm Detective Amanda Ross with the 11th Precinct. Father Samuel sent me down here to see you."

She stacked up a pile of papers and tottered over to a filing cabinet, keeping an eye on me so that I wouldn't disturb her system. "He's new," she said with a lung-taxing exhale, followed by a string of coughs. "I still have to remind him where we keep the incense and wafers."

How many priests had she outlasted? "He said you could tell me if, by chance, the registry from yesterday's funeral got left behind."

She stared at me through thick lenses, cataracts clearly visible across what once were beautiful blue eyes. Was she sizing me up? Trying to determine if I was a good Christian woman? "You're in luck, detective," she said finally. "The registry usually goes home with the family, but from what Father Donald tells me, there was a mix-up over who was going to drive to the cemetery and who was going to ride in the limo. There was an aunt or a cousin who wanted to ride, but with the sister and her husband, plus the kids, there just wasn't enough room. But they stood there on the steps arguing about it, by which point everyone else was already on their way. So they had to make tracks to get in front of the procession. And in the rush, they forgot the registry." She produced the book from on top of the file cabinet. "I was about to give the sister a call and see if she wanted me to send it, or if she was going to come pick it up."

"I know she lives out in Queens, so I suspect she'd want you to send it."

"They *always* want me to send it," she groused. "This is a church, not a post office." Perhaps the gold Zippo did more than light her cigs; there was still some spark and spunk to this crotchety old broad.

"Do you mind if I take a look? The investigation surrounding Ms. Kilmer's death is still open, so I need to check every possible lead."

"Yeah, sure, help yourself," she said, dropping the registry on a rickety wooden chair. "I've read enough Joseph Wambaugh and Ed McBain to know when to get out of the cops' way."

I picked up the vinyl-bound book, the words "In Memoriam" inscribed in some kind of gold leaf. I stood, rather than risking my weight on the chair, which looked like it had survived the Great Chicago Fire. I knew it was pushing my luck to hope for something helpful, but I couldn't leave this stone unturned. In fact, I wasn't really sure what I was looking for; most of the names connected with Charlotte's past would be as foreign to me as if I'd just skimmed through the phone book.

Still, there was one name I definitely *wasn't* expecting to find: Renzo. Mr. and Mrs. V. Renzo.

CHAPTER 23

▼

"Can I borrow your phone?" I asked Mrs. Baxter, making another mental note about finally listening to Randy and James and getting myself a cell phone.

Mrs. Baxter gestured toward an old brown rotary job with light-up buttons along the bottom and handwritten numbers for each of the church's three lines. As I picked up the phone and dialed, I noticed a clay jar with coins in it. Etched on the front were the words "Hell to Pay." While my call was ringing through, I fished a quarter out of my pocket and plunked it in.

"20th Precinct, this is Mimsy."

I wasn't expecting to get her, and the mere mention of her name started my brain rolling through what I remembered of "Jabberwocky." Somewhere between the slithy toves and the jubjub bird, I remembered why I'd called. "Detective Perelli, please."

"I'm sorry, Detective Perelli is not in at the moment. May I take a message?"

"Mimsy, it's Detective Ross from the one-one. Can you patch me through to his cell phone?"

"Oh, Detective Ross, how are you? How's your head?"

I could have done without the doting, and the saccharine sympathy in her voice, but there was no point in being rude. "Everything's just peachy."

"You been getting enough rest?"

"My bed and I are very well acquainted, thank you. Now if you could just put me through…"

"'Cause I was talking to my Uncle Wally down in Florida. Well, he's not really my uncle. More of a close family friend, and he's a doctor, and he was telling me you can't be too careful with a hematoma, you know. Too much strain on the brain and you could really be in a pickle."

That's me, one big gherkin.

"Mimsy, I'm kind of in a hurry, so if you could please get Detective Perelli…"

"I'm already dialing, Detective."

How a woman like her ended up working for the New York Police Department instead of teaching kindergarten somewhere, I'll never know.

"Perelli."

"Jason, it's Amanda Ross."

"Hey, Amanda, how are ya?" From the noise behind him, I surmised that he was in an office somewhere; I could hear the electronic whine of a fax machine as it picked up, and the rapid clack-clack-clack of people typing on computer keyboards. A crime scene? "Didn't get enough of me at the funeral, huh?"

There was an awkward pause on my part. I hadn't told him I was gay, and that put me at a loss for a suitable response to his playful machismo. I knew it didn't mean anything, but I didn't want to say anything that might rub him the wrong way—especially since I was about to butt into his investigation. "Certain things you can't ever get enough of."

"Like black-and-whites," he said. "I'd have one with every meal…if I wanted to weigh 400 pounds." The two-toned treats he referred to are a New York staple; you can find them in any bakery worth its salt and sugar. Around various holidays, the white icing is dyed for the occasion, so you end up with black-and-pinks for Valentine's Day, black-and-greens for St. Patrick's Day and, most fittingly, black-and-oranges for Halloween. I'd seen my last of those only a week or so before.

"I know what you mean," I said, wondering how much Mrs. Baxter was listening to the conversation. Her puttering around the office had a deliberate quality to it, as if she were trying to justify her continued spot on the church's payroll. "I'm the same way with cheese."

"Mmm-mmm. Give me fat and cholesterol over fiber any day," he said, smacking his lips. "But I'm sure that's not why you called, to talk about food." A phone rang in the background.

"Where are you? Sounds like you're in the middle of a steno pool."

"Close. We finally got an address for Vic Renzo. He's still nowhere to be found, but when we searched his apartment, we came up with an old pay stub, so we're looking to talk to the guy who hired him. See if he can point us in the direction of the Invisible Man."

"What about Renzo's parents?"

"What about 'em?"

"You talk to them?"

"Sure. I reached them on, I guess, Tuesday afternoon. They don't have any idea where he is, either."

"You have any idea where *they* are at the moment?"

"I'd imagine at home or at work—which is somewhere in the hill towns outside Albany, if I recall. Why?"

I took a breath. "Yesterday, they were here in New York. They were *at the funeral.* They even signed the guestbook."

"Huh," he said, and I could just picture him making a face, maybe sliding his lower jaw to one side. "Doesn't make much sense that they'd come all this way if they weren't going to see their son."

"Unless they had another reason. Which is why I want to get in touch with them. Find out what brought them to town. You mind?"

"Knock yourself out. As far as I'm concerned, they're just fringe."

"Fringe?"

"Not part of the fabric of the case, but something decorative on the outside. Fringe is a waste of time. You ever try to vacuum a rug that's got fringe?"

I pulled the phone away from my ear and stared at it, unable to even hazard a guess as to why the conversation had taken this particular left turn. "Um, no, Jason, I can't say that I have."

"My in-laws went to Pakistan some years back and brought home these great-looking area rugs—except they've got fringe on two ends. Whenever you try to vacuum the fringe, the strands either get snarled in the mechanism, or they get knotted up on their own. Either way, you're down on your hands and knees combing the stuff to make it look nice."

"As you said, a waste of time. You got a number of the Renzos?"

Perelli riffled through the pages of his notebook and gave me a home number and a cell number, both with 518 area codes. As much as I wanted to get the matter squared away ASAP, I was already running late for Mitch's sound check. Plus, I didn't want Mrs. Baxter to get in trouble for making long-distance calls. Maybe my years on the force had made me cynical—or else my experience on the streets had clued me in to a reality best learned early: Until they prove otherwise, people are scum. Mrs. Baxter was probably calling distant lands whenever it suited her, and closing up shop each night with paper clips, Post-Its and Wite-Out tucked in her control-top hose.

Fortunately, I hadn't strayed too far from my usual subway line, so I skedaddled to the nearest station and hooked a C train heading downtown. I nearly missed it, since my first two Metrocard swipes were too fast for the reader. My third swipe was down to speed and the turnstile let me through so I could slide onto the train just ahead of the doors closing. I found a seat next to a dozing, middle-aged man. He had on a black leather jacket and a brown cap, which showed just a whisper of gray sideburns. His glasses slipped down his nose as his head pitched forward with the motion of the car, but somehow the man's bushy mustache kept them from clattering to the floor.

West 4th Street is a pretty big station, what with six trains coming in and out, including a crosstown S. When I surfaced, I was actually on 6th Avenue, and it took me a moment to orient myself. Few of the area businesses had changed since my younger days; there were still plenty of pizza shops and tattoo parlors. The two most prominent features of the local landscape are Washington Square Park—not huge, but it covers three short blocks and contains the Arc de Triomphe replica where Meg Ryan dropped off Billy Crystal in the first part of *When Harry Met Sally…*—and the main campus of New York University. It may lack the ivy-covered walls and green-copper roofs of more prestigious academic institutions, but NYU is a downtown fixture, with many turn-of-the-century buildings that are used for everything from administration to student housing to performance space. The Film School is considered one of the best in the country, and the arts curriculum gets high marks across the board.

The Bottom Line was a few blocks from the subway stop, and as much as I like to lollygag along those streets, sometimes stopping to watch the chess hustlers in the park, my pace was more of a brisk stroll—and I frequently found myself two-stepping along 4th Street to make up for lost time. The venue is on the corner of 4th and Mercer, and except for an old-fashioned signboard announcing upcoming events—white plastic letters stuck into a black felt background—it tends to blend in with its surroundings. Some of the NYU spaces have marquees of their own, as do a couple of the nearby cabaret spots, so The Bottom Line hardly seems out of place. I walked in and tapped my badge against the box-office glass; the scraggly redhead inside barely looked up from his textbook before waving me through.

I'm not quite sure what I expected to hear upon my arrival at 2:45, presumably a quick run-through of the set list for that night's concert. That presumption was incorrect, as the first notes to hit my ears were the opening piano riff from Al Stewart's "Year of the Cat." I didn't recognize the young man at the keyboard—he wasn't one of the original band members, but from what Mitch had told me, he'd been with them for the past several tours. Kelly was his name, if memory served, and he wore a shallow black cowboy hat atop long curls of black-and-blonde hair. His chin bore stubble that aspired to be some sort of facial hair, and his thin frame bobbed and weaved with each bouncy chord.

One by one, the rest of the band joined him—Gil laying over a jazzy bass line, Tommy's electric picking on his six-string and J.T. with brushy cymbal and snare. The casual feel of the bare stage and empty seating area, combined with the memory of A.M. radio days, left me awash in '70s nostalgia. It was only when Mitch's familiar tenor tackled Stewart's film-noir lyrics that I was whisked back to the present. I stood and swayed to each precious note, wrapped in a solitude of sound, pretending the boys were playing just for me—rather than the guys at the sound board.

When the song ended, I clapped, the sound ringing out into the silence before I embarrassedly realized I was applauding alone. This pre-show ritual was nothing new to the band or crew, but to the longtime fan and closet groupie, I'd been given keys to the kingdom, and I was going to take the grand tour. Mitch acknowledged me with a wink before J.T. counted down the beat for the sonic assault that served as the intro to "Anywhere But Here." The rip-snorting Mitch Black original, always a crowd pleaser, brought two more people onto the stage: a pair of female backup singers. One was dressed like a '60s holdover, with long, straight blonde hair, no makeup and a green-and-black pullover whose design resembled a burbling lava lamp. All I could say about the other was that if her voice was nearly as stand-up-and-take-notice as her body, skin-tight pink T-shirt and jeans, she'd have her own record deal and be in heavy rotation on MTV within a year. And if she wasn't already a notch on J.T.'s bedpost, he'd likely been angling toward it since she joined the group.

I don't have the best musical ear, but it was obvious that Plain Jane was the better of the two singers, swaying and grooving to the rhythm track while Miss Hot Pants did little more than practice her runway pout. Still, they provided fine backup for Mitch and company as they plowed through the early number and proved that, even after a five-year hiatus, they didn't have much rust to shake off.

Tommy took the final guitar riff, and played it right into the dirty distortion of an '80s chestnut I'd almost forgotten: John Parr's "Naughty, Naughty." While the song allowed Tommy to show of his flashy fretwork, it also provided an opportunity to showcase the singers through the raucous, catcall chorus. As they played, I roamed the space—seemingly cavernous when empty, definitely intimate when filled with 400 or so people sitting, singing, standing and making their way back to their tables with drinks from the bar that ran along the side wall. I took the time to introduce myself to each of the roadies, all of whom had nicknames—Toad, Hangdog, Slappy, Tiny—that they seemed to prefer to whatever their real monikers might be. Most of them were wearing T-shirts from various concerts they'd worked, the others kept to a basic black. The crew was stripped down from Mitch's arena setup, maybe a third as many people, but every one of them seemed to be a veteran hand. When I asked who was in charge, they all pointed me in the direction of an older guy who looked to be involved in every aspect of the show. Everyone called him Merlin.

He was a short, paunchy man, with sparse gray hair scratching its way around the outer rim of his scalp, then framing his face and mouth in a beard. He had rough, powerful hands that had scars from the battles he'd won with electrical and scaffolding equipment. In directing traffic backstage and through the technical paces, to tackling key jobs himself, he carried a quiet authority that no one seemed to question.

"Merlin?" I said to him as he approached the sound board from the back of the house.

"Yeah?" His response wasn't unfriendly, just a little gruff and full of preoccupation.

"Amanda Ross. I'm a friend of Mitch's, and he asked me to be another pair of eyes for this whole thing."

"Yeah, he told me. As senior member of the road crew, I feel responsible for what happens to the performer. And after what happened with that flashpot, I've made it my business to see that it doesn't happen again."

"You sound pretty dedicated," I said as I watched him confab with another sound tech, twiddling dials and sliding levers on the board.

I could see him hesitate before going into any details, scrunching up and blinking his seen-it-all eyes, but he resigned himself with a sigh—either because Mitch had told everyone to come clean with me, or perhaps there was another reason. "Yeah, well, that's because Mitch took a chance on me when no one else would. I've been in this business for a long time, and with some of the things I've done..."

"Such as?"

"Look, not everybody in this business is as clean and sober as your boy there," he said, gesturing toward Mitch on the stage. "Early on, I was hitting it pretty hard, and being on the road, there are so many temptations to help you pass the time. I could party as hard as anyone, and I did. Thinking back on it now, the amount of poison I sniffed and shot into my system, I should have been dead a dozen times over."

Isn't once enough?

"Plus, I'd been a total shit to everyone who ever got close to me. Had a kid with a woman I barely knew, and didn't even think about decent things like supporting the two of them. It was all about the open road, moving on from town to town, never throwing out an anchor."

"So what changed?"

"I hit the anchor, so to speak. Actually plowed into it at about 65, when I lost control of my rig on I-70."

"Were you stoned?"

"I didn't think so. More like I was coming down from a high, so that my senses were pretty dull. I blew off the highway and into a ditch, and never even realized that my tires had left the pavement."

"What were you hauling?"

"What else? Band equipment. Got my ass fired for my troubles, but it may have been the best thing, since it got me seriously looking into getting clean."

I admired his candor. "Rehab?"

"I take it every one of those 12 steps at a time."

"So where does Mitch fit in?"

"After I dried out, nobody wanted to hire me on. I was an insurance risk, despite the fact that I came out my haze a little older and a lot wiser. Mitch was just starting to hit the big time, then, and his people were looking for someone who'd been up to bat. So here I am."

"That why they call you Merlin?" I asked, hearing the song come to a close with yet another guitar solo. "Because of how you managed to transform yourself?"

"No," he said with a laugh, "though you're not the first person to think so. The name really is Merlin. Merlin Skye."

"Silly me. With all the nicknames…"

"Like I said, you're not the first."

I followed as he made his way to the stage, getting up and checking the transmitter on Gil's belt-clip amplifier. "You mind if I ask you one more thing?"

"Long as I can keep working," he said, clambering back down to the sound board.

"You manage to make peace with your past? Make all the apologies and everything?"

For the first time, his mind let go of all the cables and switches and he kicked out another sigh. "Some things you spend the rest of your life apologizing for. And some mistakes you made, well, there may come a time when you're glad you made them. Like now. Now that I've got my head screwed on straight, and it's been that way for a while, I managed to make a connection with the daughter I left behind. Her mother was a decent enough sport to let me back into their lives, and I'm not letting a second chance go to waste."

"So you get to see her?"

"Maybe more than her mother might have wanted. You see, she wants to be a singer…"

"I see. So you're going to talk to Mitch about…?"

"Been there, done that. My little girl's not so little anymore, but she can take care of herself. Especially on stage, don't you think?"

I nearly got whiplash from swooping my neck up toward the band, which closed the number with a final downbeat. "You mean…?"

"In the green and black," said Merlin, smiling as only a proud papa can. "And I'm going to see to it that she doesn't make the same mistakes I did."

CHAPTER 24

▼

So Merlin had another reason to keep Mitch safe on stage. And that reason was enough for me to take him at his word when he said that he'd checked over all the equipment to make sure that nothing was rigged, and that any pyrotechnics on stage—though not called for in such a small venue—would be deliberate and easily controlled.

The rest of the songs the band played were a mixed medley, with a few of Mitch's songs tossed in with a variety of tunes from decades past, apparently catering to the whims of the group members. They harkened back to the '60s' with "California Dreaming," as Tommy and Gil traded Mamas-and-Papas vocals with the two backup singers; took a sidestep toward proto-punk with Joe Jackson's "Got the Time"; and let Mitch cut loose with a raw, raunchy take on Billy Idol's "Rebel Yell." By the time they were done, all the levels were set, the adrenaline was flowing and I was in a musical rapture.

Mitch grabbed a bottle of water and hopped down off the stage, coming directly toward me. "So, how'd we sound?"

The circumstances were unique, and Mitch and I are old friends, but the question still struck me as outrageous, as if I'd just taken in a Picasso, only to have the artist sidle up beside me and ask, "What do you think, more blue?"

There had been a joy in his playing and performing, a free-flowing exuberance that comes from doing what you love and being exceptionally good at it. Sure, the critics hadn't always been kind to Mitch—despite hitting #1 on the pop charts, "Lonely Hours" was generally dismissed as "treacle"—but I'd always found his gift pretty darn amazing. He had enough innate musical ability for the both of us, which was a good thing, since I had none. After elementary school, where music classes had been mandatory, I gave up on a singing career, and Mr. Perkins was only too happy to have me cease my assaults on my school-issued viola. "Sounded great."

"Felt good," he said, bouncing in place to keep himself pumped.

"So what happens now?"

"If anybody has anything they want to work on, now's the time. Once we're all satisfied that we're not going to suck, we head back to the hotel for a little rest before the big show. J.T. usually likes to have something to eat...you know, carbo-loading before his workout. Gil and Kelly usually join him, while Tommy calls his wife and has a snooze."

"I know you don't like to eat before a show."

"Yeah, that hasn't changed," he said. Fortunately, he also stopped his Tigger imitation, which had been making me nauseous to watch. "Although sometimes I'm starving by the time we hit the finale, it's just that if I have anything before I go out on stage, it feels like I've got a brick sitting in my stomach."

"Got anything on the agenda?"

"You know me, I'll probably chill out at one of the museums. I want to check in with the concierge at the hotel and see if there's anything worth catching while I'm in town."

"What about this place? Is all your gear safe?"

"Don't worry, Merlin will keep an eye on everything while we're gone, and if he has to step out, he'll make sure someone's on watch. Even without thinking about Gordon and a possible booby trap, we've still got in the neighborhood of 75 grand worth of equipment between the instruments, the amps and everything. Pretty appealing for a thief, someone who wants to make a quick buck selling the stuff on eBay."

I was still listening, but I'd drifed toward the stage to look at the array of guitars, keyboards and drums that were piled there. "I don't think they traffic in stolen merchandise. Unless, of course, you wanted to set up a sting to catch the guy."

Mitch gave half a laugh. "I think I've already had enough questionable press. Not everyone yearns to be front-page news."

That reminded me of the grisly crime-scene photos I'd seen—which only augmented my memory of the previous night's events—and suddenly I was jolted back to the present, and something else I had to do. "Can I use your cell phone?"

"Huh?"

"I have to make a long-distance call, and I imagine the management here frowns on that sort of thing." Mitch still had a slightly puzzled look on his face, so I added, "It's for that other matter I'm looking into."

"Oh, sure, come on, it's, er, back in the dressing room."

We got up on the stage, where Tommy was still making a few adjustments to his guitar straps. He was the quiet member of the group, a short, chunky guy with a country-bumpkin face and a thatch of reddish-brown hair, and though I'd known him peripherally since he first joined Mitch's ensemble, we'd barely exchanged more than ten words. He offered a fey smile of recognition, but kept his attention focused on the Stratocaster he had slung down around his waist.

We ducked back behind the scrim and teasers, and down a hallway to the small rooms that served as prep areas for The Bottom Line's main attractions. In general, the acts that play there are blues and jazz musicians, including some pretty big names, but Mitch was someone who could easily fill 100 times as many seats. But he felt that his "return" should be something more intimate, especially when it was for such an important cause. There were already huge benefit concerts in the works with performers ranging across the rock and pop spectra, and from what I gathered, Mitch might join one of those all-star lineups, but he didn't want his own safety concerns to override what it was really all about: helping those whose lives collapsed when the towers fell down.

Mitch pulled his cell phone from his jacket pocket, while I retrieved the numbers that Jason Perelli had given me for Mr. and Mrs. Renzo. I stared at the keypad which, even though it was laid out like every telephone I'd ever used, still looked as foreign as the bridge computer on the starship *Enterprise*.

"Just dial the number, and then hit Send," Mitch said, picking up on my confusion.

"I knew that," I said. "I was just admiring the design. Thinking I might get one and I wanted to see what sort of features there are."

"I've been in the music business for 15 years, Amanda. I know bullshit when I hear it."

"All right, fine." I turned my back to him in mock peevishness and dialed the Renzos' home number. There was no answer, and I half considered talking to their oh-too-cheery answering machine, but I figured I'd check their cell before deigning to leave a message at the beep. It took another staring contest with the phone before I realized that the End button was probably the way to terminate the connection. I punched in the second number, pushed Send and hoped that the Renzos were still in range.

"Hello?" The voice was older, male.

"Mr. Renzo?"

"May I ask who's calling, please?"

"My name is Amanda Ross, and I'm a detective with the 11th Precinct."

There was a brief pause, and I could picture him covering the mouthpiece to repeat my information to the missus. "We've already spoken with a Detective Perelli, and told him everything we know."

"That may be the case, but I'm looking at things from a different perspective, if you will. I live next door to Charlotte, and I was in her apartment the morning she was killed, so I have something of a personal stake in seeing this matter through. From what I understand, Charlotte and your son were divorced and hadn't seen each other in years."

Another pause. "That's correct."

"Which would lead me to believe that you didn't have much of a relationship with Charlotte, at least not after the split." Mitch gathered up his things, gulped down the rest of his water and swished the bottle into the wastebasket. It was the happiest I'd seen him in a long, long time.

Getting laid does wonders for the soul.

"Is that so unusual, Detective Ross? For parents to cease contact with their child's ex?"

"Not in my experience, no," I said, "but it does leave a powder keg in the 'Questions To Be Asked' column. Namely, what were you doing at Charlotte's funeral?"

I could hear the two of them trying to regroup, so I decided to save them the trouble. "Mr. Renzo, you still there?"

"Yes." His voice was softer, more hesitant.

"If you really didn't want to be noticed, you wouldn't have signed the register at the church. Which leads me to believe that you had some ulterior motive in making the drive down. I think I know what that is, and if you're still in town, I'd like to talk to you, face to face."

"My wife and I picked up some half-priced theater tickets for this evening, so we were getting dressed for an early dinner before the show. Maybe get in a little celebrity gawking along Broadway. A friend of mine tells me he saw Barbara Walters and Elliot Gould last time he was in New York."

Would I even recognize a celebrity if we brushed elbows on the street? Heck, I didn't even know Baba Wawa lived here. "What about tomorrow?"

"We're going back first thing in the morning."

Ugh. "I don't need a lot of time. Is there any way you can squeeze me in? I've really got Pete's interest at heart here."

Say the magic word and win $100.

There was a lengthy tennis match between the Renzos before he—the more affable of the two, from what I could tell—got back on the horn. "We're having dinner in the Greek restaurant downstairs. We'll be there in about 10 minutes, if you'd like to catch us there."

"Um, downstairs where? What hotel are you at?"

"Oh, sorry, it's called the Wellington. It's on Seventh Avenue and…Wendy, could you look at and see if you can read the street sign? I know we're on a diagonal from the Carnegie Deli."

"I know the neighborhood," I said, giving Mitch an indication that I was nearly done running up his bill. "I'll find you."

"How will we know it's you?"

"Don't worry. I know who I'm looking for."

It was on the far side of 4:30 by the time Mitch scooted me out the door and out onto West 4th. Neither one of us had a lot of time to take care of business before the show."

"Which way you headed?" he asked.

"Uptown."

"Me, too. Wanna share a cab?"

"Wrong side of the park, darling. My museum pieces are on the West Side."

"Careful, Betsy, you're going to be old with grandkids someday, too."

"Keep calling me that," I said through clenched teeth, shaking a fist at him, "and you won't live to reproduce."

I headed back to the subway terminal before he could shoot down my theatrics. Truth is, I'd been making such veiled and not-so-veiled threats ever since he came up with the nickname a decade earlier. It was my own fault, too, setting myself up for the obvious. At one of Mitch's early gigs, I'd done a bit of emergency stitching on his shirt, which he'd snagged on the back door of the club. "You're a regular Betsy Ross," he'd said and, despite my protestations, the moniker stuck. It didn't help my case that the last name was already in place.

Two trains and some 25 minutes later, I was climbing up the stairs from a subway platform just outside the Wellington, on 55th. I peered in and spotted Mrs. Renzo—one-half of the elderly couple Perelli and I had noticed at the funeral—sitting in a booth. I assumed her husband was opposite her, doing the gentlemanly thing. Somewhere in a Miss Manners-type column, I'd read that the woman should always face out so she can see and be seen.

Perhaps chivalry isn't dead in the Capital District.

The 55th Street entrance was closed, so I entered the restaurant on Seventh Avenue and wound my way toward their table. They still had menus, so they probably hadn't even ordered.

"Mr. and Mrs. Renzo? I'm Amanda Ross."

The two looked just as formal as they had the day before, if not quite so somber. I imagined that for them, a Broadway show was a pretty special occasion, one that called for their best duds. From what I'd seen at some of the theater district restaurants of late, the Renzos were indeed a dying breed. As the Great White Way tried desperately to appeal to a younger clientele, the infusion of new blood had brought with it a relief from the stodginess previously been associated with "the theater crowd." Thus, audience members with jeans and sneakers were becoming a more common sight, with just people like Wendy and Vincent to make them feel self-conscious. "Detective," he said politely. "My wife, Wendy."

"Hello," she said, her manner brusque but somehow open; I was a necessary evil. I'd gotten similar reactions in the past when telling people my profession—the acclaim in Monday's computer class notwithstanding.

I stood there awkwardly, waiting for one of them to slide over and make room for me, while at the same time not wanting to interrupt their meal. "You said something about Pete's best interest," Mr. Renzo lobbed.

"Have you ever met him?"

"Only once," he replied, "but not because of any doings on our part. We came down shortly after he was born, and stayed for a few days. That's how we knew about this hotel. When they were married, Vincent and Charlotte lived not too far from here."

"Wait a minute. Vincent? His name is Vincent?"

"Yes. Vincent Edward Renzo. Junior, in fact."

"I'm sorry, I'd always heard him referred to as Vic, so I assumed his name was Victor."

"He and my husband had an argument, sometime when Vincent was in the seventh grade," the mother piped in. "He was starting to rebel, trying to get out of his father's shadow, and so he got all of his friends and teachers to call him 'Vic,' instead of Vinny or Vincent. And God forbid you should call him 'Junior.' In the eyes of a 12-year-old, that made him his own man."

At that point, I was tempted to just sit on their tabletop, but Mr. Renzo made a subtle shift to his left, making room for me on his bench. It didn't go unnoticed, as Wendy gave him a disgusted look when I sat down. "That probably explains why everyone's been having such a hard time finding him, but if we could get back to the original question…"

Mr. Renzo returned a defensive stare before explaining. "By the time Pete was born, the marriage was already falling apart. When they divorced, it wasn't so much a matter of 'why?' but 'what took them so long?' My son, you see, is a bit eccentric in how he deals with people."

At that point, a Latino waiter came over, inquiring if we were ready to order. Mr. Renzo glanced over at his wife, with a slight head jerk in my direction. I hadn't asked to join them for dinner, and despite their familiarity with the world of Emily Post, they weren't quite sure how to handle a table crasher.

"You two go ahead," I said. "Really, don't let me interfere with your schedule."

Vincent deferred to Wendy, who asked for moussaka and a Greek salad. He then ordered spanakopita with an appetizer of hommus to start. Lunch with Sam Pelillo and Frankie Dean was but a gastronomic memory, especially since I didn't recall eating all that much.

"He doesn't deal with people," Mrs. Renzo said once the waiter had left, thinking she could rid of me faster if she didn't bother to wait for my questions. "He's all about ideas. You remember what he was like in high school. First he was into skateboarding. Got all the equipment, subscribed to three different magazines. He wanted to build ramps in our backyard. It was his obsession...for about six months. Then he got the photography bug, and he set up a darkroom in the basement. It consumed his every waking hour. That lasted, I don't know, nine months. He was into weight lifting, baseball cards, bowling, filmmaking. Each time, he'd eat, sleep, breathe his passion. And eventually he'd burn through his interest. But computers, that was something else. That he stuck with. Just as obsessively as the other things, but at least it gave him direction...and a career.

"In a sense, I think that's how he approached marriage and even fatherhood, as something new to try. So no, it didn't surprise me when he tired of it all. Even less that he signed away all custodial rights to our grandson without so much as a court date. To him, Pete was just ballast, weighing him down in one world when there were still others to explore."

I suppose we all have fantasies of being able to drift from one experience to the next without having to look back or ask permission, but in the case of Vic Renzo, it struck me as more sad than adventurous.

If I'm never tied to anything, I can never be free.

"That's what brought you here, isn't it? You wanted to give Pete the family your son never could." They were both silent, and Wendy's frosty façade was beginning to fade. "Besides his uncle John, you're the closest family the kid's got...and if you can give him a good home, a good life, then by all means do it.

Give the Kilmers a call. They're good people, and they want what's best for Pete, too."

They grasped hands, and Wendy began to tear. "You think they'd be home now?" Vincent asked. I nodded, and I could see his hand shake as he pulled out his cell phone. "Will you watch the table?"

I smiled as the two walked lovingly outside to make their call, past a man in a brown corduroy suit who was just paying his check. As the hostess rang up his order, the old-fashioned cash register dinged.

A bell, for this angel who'd just earned her wings.

CHAPTER 25

▼

The phone call was shorter than I expected, but at least as productive, with the Renzos re-entering the restaurant wearing smiles that lit up Seventh Avenue. They explained that they'd be traveling out to Queens the next day to have a sit-down with John and Janice, and that they'd spoken to Pete for the first time. It was a flawed family portrait, what with the boy's father still lurking about somewhere, but to a child who'd lost just about everything, an instant pair of loving grandparents was the closest thing to a miracle.

Since I'd already donned the social worker's mantle, it came as little surprise when the happy couple started filling me in on their background, as if this were some impromptu homestudy. Vincent had worked for the State of New York for nearly 35 years, and Wendy was a teacher just a year away from retirement. They had a house in Slingerlands, "just off Route 85, a couple ticks outside the city," with plenty of land for Pete to play on and, benefiting from rural zoning regulations, a horse.

The picture they painted was almost too idyllic, leaving me to wonder how such an elysian environment could produce a societal misfit like Vic Renzo. Then again, I'm as citified as they come; if I'd had to live out in the boonies, miles from decent Italian food or a gourmet grocery store, I might have become an *uber*-weirdo myself.

"How did you happen to hear about Charlotte's death?" I asked, conversation being the only thing keeping me from diving headlong into Vincent's hommus.

"I have a friend, Evelyn, who retired from the Albany school district a few years ago," Wendy replied. "Back in the '80s real estate boom, she and her son went in on a fixer-upper in Park Slope. Three family house. He did the maintenance and rented out the two apartments to cover the mortgage. After her husband died and she said goodbye to the classroom, Evelyn moved down there to Brooklyn to be near Jeff and his family. Anyhow, she was flipping through the paper on Wednesday morning and noticed Charlotte's obituary. She called me straight away—it was 9:30 in the morning and I was in the teacher's lounge, grading papers. 'Charlotte Kilmer,' she said. 'Didn't she used to be your daughter-in-law?'"

"We couldn't believe she was dead," Mr. Renzo piped in. "We never bore her any ill will; she did all she could to make the marriage work. But as we've said, Vincent wasn't an easy person to be married to."

"So I looked up the obit online, and it said that Charlotte was survived by her son and brother. Trouble was, we didn't know how to get a hold of John, or how to find out if anyone had taken custody of Pete. I called Vincent at work and told him we had to get down to New York right away. If we were ever going to have a relationship with our grandson, we had to do it then. The subject of adoption came up sometime around Kingston."

Although both of my parents were alive and well, I felt as if I were being adopted into this new family, too. "So why didn't you say anything at the church?"

"A little bit of cold feet," she said.

"And we didn't want to look like vultures, swooping down out of nowhere just because the boy's mother died. We were looking for a suitable opening, but there just wasn't time."

"And we might not have followed up on it if it weren't for you, Amanda," Wendy added, taking my hand. "Thank you."

There wasn't anything more to say, and we all had places to be, so I wished them well and was on my way. If things worked out between the Renzos and the Kilmers, I was pretty sure I'd be kept in the loop.

If the match made in midtown wasn't enough, I was also fortunate in that the Renzos had chosen a hotel that was within walking distance of my apartment. Not that getting on the subway is such a big deal, but I'd been underground so much in the past few days, the rats were starting to look familiar. I cut over to Broadway and double-timed it up to 61st Street, giving myself as much time as possible before my return trip to The Bottom Line. I made a quick detour to James' apartment before heading home, just to see if he'd gotten back from his trip.

"Welcome home," I said as he opened the door. "How was Boston?"

Instead of a reply, he threw his arms around me and clenched. After a few seconds of my gasping for air, he said, "It's so good to be back amongst sane people."

I let him squeeze the stuffing out of me for a little while longer, before suggesting that he follow me downstairs so I could change and get myself ready for the evening's insanity.

"I swear, the cadavers at Harvard Medical Center are more computer savvy than the idiots I've been dealing with for the past three days."

Good grief. Where do I fit on that evolutionary scale?

"Makes you sorry you skipped on my dinner party, doesn't it?"

"Fittingly, the word of the day is 'duh.'"

Thus far in our friendship, I haven't felt the jab of any serious skewers from James, and for that I counted my blessings. He could dish like nobody's business. "So, how was your little soiree? Is Mitch Black as God-forsaken nice as he comes across in interviews?"

"Sure," I said without hesitation, only to realize from the look in James' eyes that such an abundance of niceness wasn't necessarily a good thing.

"I remember when rock stars had an edge. From what you've told me about him, the guy's a butter knife."

I didn't exactly agree with James' assessment, but he did give me a riposte for the next time Mitch called me "Betsy." Or I could just call him B.K. for short.

While James loitered in my living room, I ducked into the bedroom for a quick change into jeans, T-shirt and my leather jacket. That morning at Ollie's, I'd wanted to be conspicuous, but in order to flush out Gordon, I'd have to blend in with all the other paying customers at The Bottom Line. As I pulled myself together, I gave James the Johnny Moschitta version of the past three days, and all my interactions with Mitch, Pete, J.T., Sondra, Sam Pelillo, the Renzos, The Ferret, Randy, Diane and most of all, Jeannie. It had only been about eight hours since I'd last seen her, and I was already missing her terribly. I was in the midst of falling hard for her, and with all the lunacy in my life, it struck me as the sanest thing I'd ever done.

"Unfortunately," James said, putting my discourse into something resembling perspective, "all the sound and fury still doesn't signify a damn thing. You're no closer to nailing Gordon, or finding Vic Renzo, than you were when I left."

"You sound disappointed," I said, mustering a little bit of humor despite the fact that James was absolutely right—all things considered, my *Sturm und Drang* had netted me precious little except a marker to the mob. I couldn't claim responsibility for Pete and the Renzos; if the old folks truly had the kid's best interest at heart, they'd have reached out to him sooner or later. As for Jeannie, well, the past few days had taught me that she was a gal who generally went for the things she wanted; she'd probably have gotten me into her bed even if the carnal consumption hadn't been mutual.

"If common sense came in a pill, Amanda, I'd write you a prescription. I know you like to think of yourself as a cop crusader, never letting the downtrodden stay that way, but come on, really. Your butting your head into the whole Vic Renzo/ Charlotte thing, that was just going too far. Sure, she was your friend, and I know that you care about her little boy, but there's a reason you don't live in your own precinct."

In my best imitation of a snit, I stomped out of the bedroom and confronted my antagonist face to...lower chest; James is a good nine inches taller than me. "You saying I'm out of my league?"

"I'm saying you're out of your mind. You didn't even give Perelli and company a chance to find the man, and here you are making deals with the devil. You've never been one to grandstand, and I'd say your fur is a little too gray for you to be learning new tricks. What gives?"

Woof.

I didn't have an answer, and though I could debate him on my tendency to showboat, this time I had crossed more than my share of lines. It was as if the explosion in Charlotte's apartment had blown away a piece of me, and that my endeavors were a clumsy attempt to make myself feel whole. Not only had I lost yet another person in my life, but as I'd lost consciousness, I'd seen a flicker of the emptiness, the never that rested six feet under. And it terrified me—more than the panic attacks, more than being shot at, more than spending my life alone. I was running scared, and the only way I could go on without being sucked into the vortex was to scribble an "S" on my chest and pretend I could fly. "It's complicated, James. But believe me, when this is over, Wacky Jacky and I are going to have a long talk."

He put his lanky arms around me and pulled me close. For the overly placid James, this was as close to affection as he got. "I need a few more years to work on your eulogy, kid. So try not to rush things, okay?"

It wasn't what I wanted to hear, given the mortal thoughts that had stormed my brain, but it would have to do. "Okay."

It's easy to feel invulnerable when you're packing, so after James had gone back home, I pulled out my Glock, checked the sights and stowed it in its holster. Eternity had come and gone since the last time I fired it—I hadn't even had much desire to go to the shooting range, my home away from home, down below the 11th Precinct. Emptying a magazine or two was a terrific way to blow off steam, but since 9/11 I'd needed whatever energy I could muster—steam, wind, solar—just to keep myself in the day-to-day.

It was approaching 6 p.m., and I had to get downtown. I didn't expect Gordon, if he were going to make a play, to show up until the house lights went down, but psychosis doesn't necessarily equal punctuality or predictability. Yet another subway ride—if the MTA offered "frequent rider" miles, I'd be halfway to Australia by now—and yet another opportunity to mull things over. One way or another, I'd spent most of the past six weeks alone, and had more than ample opportunity to get sick of my own voice as I talked to myself. This time, instead, I listened to the voice of the train that rattled and rumbled with me in its belly. The screech of the wheels along the track, the electronic bells to signal the closing of the doors, the whoosh as the lead car found the oomph to drag the rest of its body along the crisscross of tracks, the hollow thuck-thuck-thuck as we plowed past a station on the express line. It was a mechanical symphony that played at so many points beneath the city, 24 hours a day, regardless if anyone wanted to hear. In most cases, it was far more talented than the so-called performers who peopled the platforms.

The area around Washington Square Park was lively, with a casual mix of Village denizens, NYU students and the hustle-bustle New Yorkers who are always in a hurry to somewhere else, even at 6:30 or so on a Friday night. The businesses' signs and the streetlights effectively erased the darkness, making the scene a virtual playground for party people or, in my case, a local just looking for a slice of 'za. I picked up a pepperoni wedge and a Coke, plus a wad of napkins, and had my feast as I walked along West 4th, doing a little dance to avoid the driblets of grease as they trickled off my paper plate and out of my mouth.

Even though the doors wouldn't open for another half-hour or so, there were people lining the sidewalk outside The Bottom Line. More teens than I expected, but more soon-to-be-seniors, too. It was a jeans-and-T-shirt crowd, with the tops a random sampling of athletic logos, Mitch Black tour souvenirs and silkscreen tributes to fallen heroes. The images of the World Trade Center were haunting, as were the words "We shall never forget." It was still too soon to even try.

I patrolled the line, looking for anyone who, on the surface, could be considered Gordon-esque. His actions and persistence put him on the older side, probably in his early 40s. He fancied himself a songwriter, so he'd likely have an artistic air about him. And given his deep-seated hatred for Mitch and an overwhelming desire to do the deed, I should be able to pick up on an edginess, an impatience with having to wait even a second longer. No one fit the bill, so I breezed my way past, flashed my ID at the door and went straight through, strolling past Merlin and his cronies as they got the gear together, across the stage and back to the dressing area where I'd left Mitch a few hours earlier. The boys of the band were there, along with the backup singers, and they were each going through their pre-show rituals. Tommy joined the two women for vocal warm-ups, the keyboard player worked to keep his fingers limber and J.T. dozed in an armchair. Rather than his usual bass, Gil noodled on an acoustic guitar.

Those who knew me greeted me, and the noise was enough to rouse J.T. from his slumber. "Damn," he said, shaking his head. Upon seeing me, he remarked, "Amanda, honey. I was just thinking about you."

"Likewise, sweetie," I replied, not even looking at him. "Those nature specials on Channel 13 always bring you to mind."

"Animal instincts," he said, sitting up. "What was it? Lions? Tigers? Cheetahs?"

"Octopus."

Mitch came in just then, and his command of the room put J.T.'s and my ongoing lovers' quarrel to rest. "How's everybody feeling tonight?" he asked, receiving generally positive responses from his entire team. "Kelly, how's the throat?"

"Pretty good, Mitch. Kept clammed up all afternoon, and drank plenty. Speaking of which…" He dashed off to the bathroom.

"I want everyone to keep on their toes tonight, because I don't know what kind of crowd we're going to have. Could be pretty sedate, in which case we might shuffle the set list a bit. But if we kick ass from the word go, then rock-and-roll is here to stay."

Watching him, it was almost impossible to believe that Mitch was about to give his first concert in more than five years. Gordon seemed to be the furthest thing from his mind, which was a good thing as far as I was concerned. The Bottom Line had subtly stepped up security, so they would be checking bags and frisking patrons. And there would be enough of a police presence to hopefully keep the madman in check. There were enough of them on the news each night.

After a few minutes, someone from the road crew came back to let us know that the house was open.

"For what these people shelled out," said Gil, "we better put on a good show."

"Raising as much as we can for the widders and orphans," Mitch joked in a mock geezer accent. It was the first time any of them had referenced the tragedy of the Twin Towers, the very reason they were in New York, and everyone grew silent. The magnitude of their cause was suddenly upon them, the responsibility to soldier on and prove that nothing—not airplanes, not bombs, not videotapes of fundamentalist crowds cheering the destruction of what America held dear—could shatter the spirit that held a country together. We were in the center of the universe, and the Mitch Black band was about to pump its collective fist in defiance of the hatred, and spit in the face of those who would oppress us. It was the healing power of music and all that was great about rock-and-roll.

That's when the vibe started, the thrum of excitement and power, starting with J.T. anxiously tapping his leg, Miss Perfect Bod bouncing her locks in time with the rhythm. They were jamming to a riff only they could hear, and only those who lived and breathed the song could ever hope to understand. They let out a cheer and threw themselves at each other in a group hug, with sentiments like "Good show" and "Break a leg" abounding.

That's when the roadie came back and gave a five-minute call. I quickly gave Mitch a buss on the cheek and told him I'd see him later. As I wound my way out of the dressing room and through the curtains to find some standing room by the bar, I realized that I wouldn't have missed this moment for anything.

Neither would Gordon.

CHAPTER 26

▼

Unlike so many other concerts I've seen, where people trickle in through the opening act and the first couple of songs, The Bottom Line was almost full by the time I got out into the audience. As I wormed my way over to the bar, I could hear people talking about the man I'd just left. "Betcha he's lost it," said one. "I hope he does 'Lonely Hours,'" remarked another. All through, there was a genuine air of excitement, as if New York was tired of being a victim, and with a few power chords it might regain its place as the greatest city in the world.

While I continued to scan the throng for possible threats, I realized that James' height would have been an asset. I found myself staring at too many denim-jacketed shoulders to have any sort of vantage. If the muscle at the door was doing its job, I shouldn't have to worry about anybody taking a shot, but there were too many places on the body to conceal a weapon, especially from a by-the-numbers frisk.

I did a quick circuit of the tables, trying to make sure that Gordon hadn't decided to position himself closer to the stage. It didn't seem likely; if this were indeed the night for all his plans to come into action, he'd need to make a fast exit.

What if he doesn't care how many people he takes out?

As the anticipation in the audience built, so did its number, as the club packed itself to capacity. There wasn't an empty chair to be had, and over by the bar it was like a crowded subway at rush hour, everybody rubbing elbows and other body parts as they tried to preserve what little personal space the situation allowed. Somehow, waitresses managed to squeeze their way between the bodies, delivering food and drink orders to both sitting and standing patrons. That's when the house lights dimmed and the applause started.

It wasn't Mitch who came out but a local DJ I didn't recognize. He was pudgy and bald, with an unruly black goatee. He was dressed in black jeans, with a T-shirt bearing his employer's logo. He stood silently for a few moments, waiting for the crowd to collect itself, before speaking into a wireless mike. "Good evening, everyone. On behalf of Mitch Black and the management of The Bottom Line, I'd like to thank you all for coming out for a great night of rock-and-roll, and to benefit a most worthy cause. All of the profits from these two shows will go to benefit the police and fire departments who worked so long and so hard, many of them giving their lives in the line of duty, as they fought to save our fellow New Yorkers."

The audience response was subdued and polite, with soft clapping and murmured support. "Now I'd like to introduce an old friend," the DJ continued. "We had him in the booth shortly after his second album came out, and he's one of the nicest guys I've ever met in the business. I know you've missed him, and so have we, but he's here tonight and hopefully he's back to stay. Ladies and gentleman, Mitch Black!"

The house went black for a few seconds and I could make out silhouettes as the DJ made his way off the stage and the performers got to their instruments. Mitch counted off a "1-2-3-4" and the lights went up just as Tommy hit the opening lick of "Sometime, Anywhere," a popular number off Mitch's *Sticks and Stones* album. The crowd was instantly in the groove, swaying with Gil's throbbing bass and J.T.'s thumping beat. The mid-tempo rocker kicked things off well, and Mitch sounded terrific as he played rhythm guitar and sang of two people whose lives kept intersecting, without the chance to get together. The chorus brought many of the audience members to their feet, and they chanted the lyrics: "I'll meet you sometime, anywhere. I'll look around and hope to find you there."

It was several minutes of pure euphoria, and it wasn't hard to see it in people's faces, why they'd become fans in the first place. Their CDs and cassettes may have a little dust on them, but the music never grew old. Teenagers and graybeards exchanged looks and smiles, singing along together, uniting in enjoyment. When the song ended, the sonic boom of applause was more than even Mitch expected.

"Thank you," he said, with hand gestures toward his compatriots, and everyone took mini-bows to acknowledge a reception that had been five years in coming. "I know we haven't been here in New York for a while. We haven't, uh, really been anywhere for a while. But some things are more important, some things you've just gotta clear your schedule and find the time to do your part. And, uh, I'd like to think that's what we're doing here tonight."

As he spoke, if you looked up the word "lovefest," there'd be a picture of the concert. He was their treasure, and they were what had driven him for his entire adult life.

"We're going to do something a little different now. When we were putting together the set list for this show, I wanted to include something about New York. As most of you know, I'm not from this area, but I'm always happy to pay a visit. And there are so many songs that pay tribute to this place, but as we ticked them off, we realized that so many people had already done them, and done them better than we could. Then J.T. threw out a suggestion, and I swear, you could have heard the laughter all the way from Colorado. But the more I thought about it, the more I liked it. It talks of a city that once was, and a city that will be again. You just watch…and listen."

J.T. clicked his sticks for a countdown and hit a quick roll before Kelly chimed in with strings-laced synths. The two backup singers joined in soul-sister unison for a call of "city rhythm…ooh," and the band began to swing with a '70s sound. It wasn't until Mitch started singing, however, before I recognized the tune: Barry Manilow's "New York City Rhythm." Once the crowd picked up on it, they were all too happy to bounce along with the jump-and-sway melody. Hundreds of heads bobbed when Kelly switched programming for a heavy piano, and Tommy let loose with a guitar solo. With his facility for sound, it was no wonder Mitch picked Kelly to fill out his crew; after Tommy's solo, he pumped up the jam with organ flavor. It was wild and wonderful, and the audience went nuts.

After the last notes faded, Mitch once again took to the microphone. "Over the last five years, there have been two questions that people keep asking me. First, are you still writing songs? And second, do you have a new album coming out? Well, the second one depends a lot on these folks on stage with me, and whether they're willing to spend six weeks cramped in a recording studio with me and my ego." The joke elicited a slight chuckle from the crowd. "The answer to the first question is yes. This next song is brand new, and it's kind of a gut reaction to everything that's been going on around here the last six weeks. I don't even have a title for it just yet, so…well, here goes."

Tommy began with a soft, driving series of chords, and the other players joined in one by one, giving the melody a military cadence. Kelly's keyboards, especially, with funeral organ tones, added sadness and heft, with the proceedings slowly building in passion and aggression before cutting off completely, leaving Mitch to begin a cappella:

"In a moment, everything changed.
It was no longer you and me.
We were united in a common front
Against a grim reality.

Insanity had seized the day
But could not hold it true.
For when the world fell down,
We were more than just me and you.

We felt the thunder in our hearts,
We saw the smoke upon the sky
We watched the news and saw them fall
And stood there asking 'Why?'

How could you steal so many lives?
Or did you even care?
Said we had it coming
And hid behind your prayers

America will rise again
From the ashes and broken dreams.
And justice will be swift
For the man with all the schemes.

You cannot keep us down
For we'll rebuild and we'll repay.
Flush you from your cave, you're nothing to be saved,
In time you'll rue the day.

We felt the thunder in our hearts,
We saw the smoke upon the sky.
A bright day in September
When an entire nation cried.

You saw it as the end,
But now we shall begin
To honor those you took away
And those who tried to save the day.
For America is here to stay
And we will have the final say.

We felt the thunder in our hearts,
We saw the smoke upon the sky.
Tragedy shall turn to vengeance
And maybe then,
And only then,
Can we truly say goodbye."

The lyrics trailed off into a mournful guitar solo, as both Mitch and Tommy wailed in minor chords, with Gil and J.T. keeping a triumphant, we-shall-over-come beat. The intensity and volume climbed and climbed, and then suddenly, unexpectedly, everything went quiet. It was a good 10 seconds before the audience realized that the song was over, or was the moment of silence intentional?

Whatever Mitch had in mind, the experiment worked, and the response was rapturous. Lyrically, he captured the frustration so many of us felt, and musically, he was both soulful and standing proud. He had created an anthem for the time, and I could almost sense the audience wanting to hear it again so they could join in the rebellion.

Rather than discuss the song, Mitch and company launched into a string of rockers that everyone could sing along with: "Sidewinder," "Blown Away," "In From the Cold" and "Sticks and Stones." The crowd devoured every sonic morsel the band dished out, but the sheer perfection of the evening began to worry me. Seven songs into the set list and Gordon had not done a thing to make his presence known. I'd been so sure he'd take the opportunity to strike, yet there was nary a disgruntled murmur to be heard, much less an anti-Mitch screed. If Gordon was there, lost among the throng, he was staying below my radar—cool as the other side of the pillow.

After the last note of "Sticks and Stones" had faded and the band bowed to yet another ovation, Mitch, J.T., Kelly and the two singers left the stage and Tommy and Gil dove into a two-man jam. With fancy fretwork and fast fingers, they complemented each other; Gil's twiddling provided the harmony behind Tommy's full-bodied chords. They were two old pros, two old friends, having fun doing what they'd been doing all their adult lives, and the exuberance was more eloquent than the craftiest of Mitch's lyrics.

While Tommy and Gil zigged and zagged across the musical spectrum, I tried to put myself in Gordon's shoes. If I was about to pull the trigger on someone, even someone I hated through and through, would I feel something? Some sort of reflex to the anticipation, to the completion of a five-year quest? Wouldn't I be pacing the floor, looking for an opening, the perfect chance to pull the string? Even if he'd found some sort of crow's nest with an unobstructed view of the stage—an impossibility within the confines of The Bottom Line—there's no guarantee he'd have the uninterrupted access he needed to get the job done and get away with it. Motive may have been the man's calling card, but without means and opportunity, there'd be no crime.

The man on the marquee returned to the stage just in time to catch the tail end of his compatriots' extended riff. Rather than bowing to the audience, they each hugged Mitch while the crowd cheered. Struggling through the male bonding to reach a mike, Mitch introduced them and egged everybody on to give the twosome its due. After 15 years together, give or take, these partners still had a genuine affinity for one another.

Ultimately, Tommy and Gil ceded the spotlight to Mitch, who turned and watched them go. "Amazing what you can find on eBay," he said. "Although I had to outbid a fan in Ohio, and pay for shipping to get them here." This joke got more sincere laughs than the first, even if he was trying a bit too hard.

What really got the place going was Mitch pulling out a guitar case, for anyone who'd ever seen him live knew what song was coming. "Lonely Hours" was the only thing he played on acoustic guitar, and he saved it special for that occasion. He pulled out the six-string, which he'd named Amy ("Because Lucille was taken," he'd said in more than one interview) and sat down on a stool, strumming and doing a little fine-tuning on the pegs.

"Since September 11th, we've all had a few lonely hours," he said. "Missing friends, family members, people taken away from us, either by the attack itself or during the rescue attempts. And although this song was written about a different kind of loss, some emotions are indeed universal. This one is for all the survivors."

As he reached down for the cable that snaked its way across the stage, I realized that I'd seen the guitar recently. Or, more specifically, the case. It had been in Mitch's hotel room when Gordon shot through the door, killing Sondra. And I hadn't seen the guitar at all during the sound check. I could feel myself go flush with adrenaline as I came to realize why Gordon could afford to relax, why the madman's restlessness hadn't given him away. His work was done; as far as he was concerned, Mitchell James Black was already dead. All the musician had to do was play his part, literally. I was sweating and shivery, unsure of how he'd done it, or if he'd done anything. But that no longer mattered, nor did the 400-plus bodies surrounding me. I had to get to Mitch, for if I was right, the next note he played would be his last.

Just as Gordon promised.

CHAPTER 27

▼

"Mitch!" I screamed. "Don't plug in!"

Although he wasn't able to hear me clearly above the din, the sudden lunatic shouting was enough to make him pause in what he was doing. He looked out at the audience, trying to ascertain the source of the disturbance.

He didn't have to look far. "Drop the guitar!" I called, squeezing my way past dumbstruck drinkers along the bar. There were more than 800 eyes on me, mostly filled with confusion and bewilderment, but somewhere among them was a pair filled with seething rage, an abject hatred that had suddenly multiplied by two.

As Mitch dumbfoundedly put the guitar down, those fury-filled eyes found me, as did more than 200 pounds of body weight, launched in my direction with full force. "You fucking bitch!" Gordon screamed as he knocked me against the bar, and I felt the crunch of bone against bone against wood. As the adrenaline surged through me, short-circuiting whatever pain the impact may have caused, I briefly imagined some kind of pay-per-view death match, a no-holds-barred affair with Mitch's life as the prize.

Lesbo Cop vs. Psycho Killer. Fox'd probably offer millions.

But the contest never occurred, for Gordon took advantage of the one thing still in his favor: As long as he remained berserk and unpredictable, no one was likely to get in his way. To the standing-room concertgoers in his path, he was just a nutjob in the middle of a bad night, rather than someone wanted for murder, both attempted and the done deal. While I reeled from the body check, he pushed aside any arms, legs, heads and bodies that occupied the shortest route to the door. I struggled to my feet—with no help from the people around me, thank you very much—and took off after Gordon at a dead run. I knew I was in no shape for a chase, but sometimes duty and reflex leave logic in the dust.

I could only hope that Mitch wouldn't do something stupid, like plugging in his guitar after I'd already risked life and several limbs to scare him out of doing just that. Gordon had a several-second headstart on me, and with all the criss-crossing streets going this way and that through lower Manhattan, that was all he needed to disappear. But in this game we'd been playing over the last week, I held the master trump. I knew the city, with all its nooks and crannies, and Gordon was just a loon on the loose, far from his home base.

A fast loon, though. He was already half a block up West 4th by the time I made it to the door, so I had to put the pedal to the metal in order to keep him in sight. There were streetlights, and I caught flickering glimpses of him as he passed under each dusky sphere, but with NYU on one side of the street and Washington Square Park on the other, not enough ambient light to keep him out of the shadows.

It was hard to tell with him running away from me, but Gordon was probably about 5'10" and solidly built, with jet-black hair. He had on a windbreaker, jeans and sneakers, and might have otherwise blended into any nighttime street scene, had he not had me chasing after him. My motor was churning at full throttle, my veins burning gasoline as I pounded the pavement. Any sudden change of direction and I might have given myself whiplash, but this guy knew where he was going, following the shortest distance between two points.

The buildings and the park flew by, my eyes barely able to register faces on the bystanders who did their damnedest to clear the sidewalk, lest they be mowed down like skittish squirrels on the Autobahn. I didn't know how long I could keep up my breakneck speed, or if Gordon had enough juice left in his tank to achieve escape velocity. As he zipped through another beam, I noticed something metallic in his hand, and his body go all herky-jerky as he reached back, throwing off his balance.

Somewhere I'd read that the top speed a human being can achieve on foot is something like 22 miles an hour. Not that we were closing in on any land-speed records, but we were streaming down West 4th at a considerable clip, so the kick-back from a gunshot—even a round from the piddly .22 Gordon had produced—can do quite a number on your racing mechanics. I saw the flash and ducked, but it was unnecessary. Hitting a moving target is near impossible for anyone but a trained marksman. Doing so while running at full tilt, you've got a better chance of hitting the lottery. As far as I could tell, Gordon's shot might as well have been aimed at the Chrysler Building.

But his temporary slowdown and recovery gave me the opening to slow my own footwork enough that I could draw my own weapon and keep Gordon in my sights. Our free-for-all sprint made us menacing enough to society without bringing wild gunplay into the picture.

But when in Rome…

As I tried to aim, I realized that all the thump-thumping I heard wasn't coming from two sets of feet. There was a loud pulse beating a bass line in my brain, and the more I tried to concentrate on my quarry, the harder it became to focus.

The street was getting brighter, and I started to recognize the signage of the tattoo parlors and pizza places in the distance. The chess-playing old-timers may have left Washington Square Park for the night (not that I had the inclination to look), but this was one situation where a stalemate or draw simply wouldn't do. If he made it to the subway station, he was gone. I had to win, but I was running out of street.

Even as I tore up the sidewalk, it felt as if my body were melting down. My left hand started to twitch uncontrollably, making it even harder to keep my Glock under control. Gordon may have reeled, but he wouldn't be off his track for much longer. I just had to hold it together.

As we approached Sixth Avenue, the sound of traffic temporarily overpowered the cacophony in my head. Eventually, Gordon would have to slow down, or take the chance of becoming a hood ornament. A U-Haul was moving slowly through the intersection, cutting off our trajectory and forcing us to veer left. I had hoped to catch the sonuvabitch before we got this far, before the number of spectators and obstacles quadrupled. Who knew if anyone from The Bottom Line was even behind us, adding to the scene? Or had Mitch resumed his playing, with a different guitar?

As he bobbed and weaved his way across Sixth, Gordon took a quick look back and for the first time, I had a face to go with the phantasm. Instead of evil, it was rather ordinary. Big ears, dark, scruffy features, widely set eyes. He might have even blended in as an everyday New Yorker had he not been overcome by his misjudgments.

He fired off another round that was again off its mark, but closer to home. A car tire popped and hissed as the air came rushing out.

Gordon was nearing the entrance to the subway platform. At least, one of him was. I was starting to see double, and the blur of magazines from the next-door newsstand left me desperate for my bearings. My heart was doing triple-time, but the blood didn't seem to be getting where it needed to. My legs felt heavy and my gun had gained 50 pounds. My engine seizing, my body in total breakdown, I did the stupidest thing imaginable.

I fired.

Somewhere amidst the sidewalk chatter, the screeching brakes and car horns, I heard a groan. It was a man's voice, but was it Gordon I hit?

I stopped, hands on knees, trying to catch each painful breath. A knife was in my lungs, a bullet in my brain, the system shutting down, overwhelmed by pain and noise.

Paging Dr. Calamari.

Was I still on the sidewalk, or had I ventured out into the street? Gordon was no longer in sight, even as I squinted through the growing group of gawkers and pointers. I had lost Gordon, and I had lost sensation.

Consciousness soon followed.

CHAPTER 28

▼

"Amanda?"

The voice, though quiet and womanly, jarred my senses like a five-alarm fire. It hurt to be awake, to be aware, for every muscle in my body seemed to be playing tag with an electric eel.

"Amanda?"

I forced my eyes open and took in a landscape of fuzzy white and pink. Wherever I was, I wasn't lying in a heap on Sixth Avenue.

"Amanda, can you hear me?"

Yes, I can hear you, but who the hell are you?

My lips were crusty and stuck together, my skin oily, my T-shirt…I wasn't wearing a T-shirt, or a bra, or jeans from what I could tell. The loose-fitting frock I had on was blue and white in some sort of pattern, and it itched. My scalp itched, too, but trying to scratch anywhere would have taken far too much effort.

"Amanda?"

"What?!" The word was creaky and croaky, containing none of the peevishness I'd intended.

"How are we feeling?"

Oh. Hospital talk. I'm in a hospital.

Truth be told, I didn't have an answer to the soft-spoken question. The individual parts may as well have been run through a trash compactor, but the fact that I could even respond, and that all the pieces were present and accounted for, put a big whopping infinity in the "Could Be A Whole Lot Worse" column.

"Where am I?"

"St. Vincent's," said the voice. "We were closest."

I tried to piece together what had happened after I'd squeezed off my single shot, but there were no pieces.

Must have been one heck of a swoon.

Slowly, my eyes focused and I was able to see the woman responsible for disturbing my coma. She was young, younger than me, with long, dark hair held loosely behind with a barrette. Though the white doctor's coat covered a lot, there was a frumpy figure beneath the cheery face, with an extra helping of hips and butt. Beneath the coat peeked a loose-fitting black top and beige slacks.

She must have noticed my change in alertness and lucidity, for she pried her attention away from my chart long enough to practice Bedside Manner 101.

"Amanda, I'm Dr. Brenner. Do you know why you're here?"

"Umm…not exactly."

"We did an MRI and a few other tests when you were brought in last night, unconscious. You have a subdural hematoma. Do you know what that is?"

I was tempted to mock her kindergarten demeanor, but what's the point of sassing the person who dishes out the pain pills? "Bleeding on the brain," I muttered, "or something like that."

"Very good," she said. "Now, when you saw Dr. Calamari on Monday, did he tell you about your condition?"

"Yes."

"And did he tell you to take it easy for a while?"

"Yes."

"And did you?"

"For the most part."

"I see." She scribbled something in my chart, but I couldn't make it out. "Amanda, when you were brought in, your clothes were drenched in sweat, and your pulse and blood pressure were through the roof. Care to tell me why?"

Did she know already, or was she still gathering information? I hated being in the dark. "I'm a cop. I was chasing someone."

"I don't care if you're Marion Jones. You shouldn't be running your mouth, much less your feet. You could have died last night."

Been there, done that, bought the soundtrack.

"Something you need to remember, Amanda. A brain injury isn't like anything else. Brain cells don't regenerate. Ever. So when you hurt your head, there's no such thing as being too careful. When you collapsed last night, it was your body protecting itself from a biological catastrophe. With a condition as delicate as yours, with possible blood vessel damage, you could have had a stroke, or an aneurysm, and you'd have been dead before you hit the pavement."

"I'm already on medical leave," I said, though I didn't think it would carry much weight.

"Then start acting like it, or you'll be going to another police funeral, and it'll be your parents holding the burial flag."

Dr. Brenner had gone from warm fuzzy to cold customer in a matter of minutes; I sometimes had that effect on people. But her words were even more chilling than Dr. Calamari's frostbitten advice, and if I'd been able to feel my spine at that moment, it would have tingled. Still, she was Pippi Longstocking compared to the piranha outside the door.

"Is she awake yet?" I heard someone bark out in the hallway, before barging in without waiting for a verbal reply. His shoes thwop-thwopped on the smooth floor, and even in my sorry state, I could tell that rank was about to be pulled. "What the fuck do you think you're doing?"

He was a stocky man in his 40s, with a big nose and thinning brown hair above a highly wrinkled brow. His long arms probably would have hung to his ankles had he not held them so sternly crossed in front of him. I didn't know who he was, but I was ready for a browbeating.

"Convalescing, sir," I said with as much authority as I could muster. The four-syllable word seemed to throw him, so he glared at Dr. Brenner, probably expecting her to turn on her heel so the chew-out could begin. Lucky for me, if not for her, she stood her ground.

"I don't know who you think you are," she said, "but I will not have you come charging in here and upsetting my patient. Now I will ask you to leave before I call security."

"Lady," he replied, as if that were the only form of address he had for a person with tits, "I *am* security. Lieutenant Raymond Durst."

"You've obviously mistaken me for someone who gives a shit," Dr. Brenner said coolly before replacing the chart at the foot of my bed. "I can see you've got business with Detective Ross, so I'll leave you to it. But don't you dare come in here and think you're in charge. Johns Hopkins Medical trumps whatever charm school you graduated from."

He was flabbergasted, unused to having his authority questioned, especially by a member of Generation XX. It didn't take him long to rebuild his steam, however, and I was the one in for a scalding. "What precinct are you with, Lieutenant?"

"You're laying in it right now, Detective," he said in a tone that was almost civil, but not quite. "And last night you spilled someone's blood in it. So I want answers. Now."

"What was the question?" I tried very hard to make sure that didn't come out like a joke. The shinier the brass, the less humor to be found.

In heeding Dr. Brenner's warning, Lt. Durst looked like he was about to blow a blood vessel of his own. "Explain your actions," he said through tight lips and even tighter teeth.

I felt sorry for the next person who encountered him after the cork was pulled. "I was pursuing a suspect."

The near-smile that crossed his face was scarier than anything Stephen King could have dreamed. "As far as your Lt. Montague is concerned, Detective, you don't have any active cases. In fact, he says you've been on disability for weeks."

Busted.

"I don't like people shooting up my streets. And I don't like cops who think they're above and beyond the chain of command. And I sure as shit don't like smart-mouths who don't know a damn thing about police procedure."

If, among the many push-button controls on my hospital bed, there had been one for disappearing into the mattress, I would have used it. None of the other tongue lashings I'd gotten over the previous several days had left me with scars; this one would. Durst was a superior officer. Not my boss, technically, but someone with the clout to tell me what for, but to dish it out in spades. He'd already spoken with my C.O., so even if I survived my extended vacation, my job was probably dead on arrival.

"If it means anything, sir, I was helping out a friend. Someone who'd come to me and asked for help. I only said yes because I wasn't punching the clock."

"We all have friends, Detective," he said, turning away. "Some of us less than we used to."

I wasn't sure where he was going, but I followed. "Yes, sir."

"And Mitch Black is lucky to have a friend like you."

"Lieutenant?" I coughed, propping myself up on my elbows.

"After the concert, my officers interviewed Mr. Black and his band, along with some of the members of his road crew. None of them had thought anything about that guitar of his."

"Why? What was it?"

"It was electrified. Seems someone had slipped in some kind of transformer, would have zapped him the instant he plugged in. No one saw it coming. Except you."

I wanted to speak, but my mind was a tangle of elation, relief, confusion and terror, and the knot got in the way of any words that might have come out.

"Don't get me wrong, Ross, if you were under my command, I'd bust you down to uniform and worse. But as it is, the Mayor'd never let me break a hero. Montague can deal with your brand of bullshit."

The man was no longer a grizzly, but not quite a Teddy bear, either, so I wasn't about to ask for a congratulatory hug. It felt good to be appreciated, and as I looked around the room, I noticed for the first time that my fan club had more than one member; I counted at least six flower arrangements. "What about…?" I asked hesitantly, not wanting Durst to show his claws again, "What about Gordon? I'm pretty sure he's the one responsible for the murder at the Grand Hyatt on Thursday."

"My detectives are working on that with the folks in midtown," he growled. "Now leave the policing to those of us who are still working for a living." He left as he came in, gruff as a billy goat.

I wanted to listen to Durst's advice. I really did, but I didn't know whether Gordon was the one I'd shot, or whether I'd done any real damage. If Gordon was still alive and well, then Mitch remained in danger. There was a phone on the table next to me, but from what I could tell, it hadn't been hooked up yet. And from what Durst had told me, that was probably a good thing. If the media had picked up on what had happened, and made a connection to Mitch and the Grand Hyatt, and figured out a way to reach me, well, sometimes there *is* such a thing as bad publicity.

The back-to-back confrontations with Dr. Brenner and Lt. Durst must have tuckered me out more than I realized, because the next thing I knew, an orderly was wheeling the lunch cart into my room. The muscular Hispanic man pulled a tray off the cart and, without a word, left it for me on the table.

"Hanging out in hospitals is bad for your health," I heard Andy Devane say, and I swung my head around to see him sitting in one of the orange vinyl-covered chairs. I don't know how long he'd been there, or whether he'd been watching me sleep. The thought of a man doing so usually left me feeling a little violated, but despite his profession, Andy was one of the good guys.

"Tell me about it," I sighed, reaching to pull myself up so I could eat. I couldn't remember having filled out a menu, so I was in for a potluck.

"Actually," Andy said, pulling a folded-up newspaper from his jacket, "you can read about it."

The front page was a two-shot of Mitch and his guitar. Headline: "Unplugged." Subhead: "Assassination Plot Foiled At 9/11 Benefit." I didn't go through the entire article, but the lead said it all: "While performing at a benefit concert for families of victims of the World Trade Center attacks, singer Mitch

Black nearly became the victim of another fiendish plot. The weapon of choice wasn't a jetliner, but rather his custom guitar 'Amy,' which had been rigged to electrocute the player when plugged in. Only the presence and acute instincts of an off-duty police detective kept hundreds of New Yorkers from bearing witness to another tragedy."

Andy's purple prose made me uncomfortable, turning my actions into something more than they were. I'd been doing a favor for a friend, and I didn't feel right with being labeled a hero. Especially put in the context of 9/11, there was nothing extraordinary about my deeds, and nothing remarkable about being in the right place at the right time. As for picking up on the possible danger in Mitch's guitar, it had been a lucky guess. "I don't deserve this."

"Tell that to Mitch's fans," Andy replied casually. "Tell that to the people who'll benefit from the money he raises. Tell that to the millions who just can't stand to hear another piece of bad news. Most of the heroes we've been honoring for the past six weeks are either dead and buried or missing in the rubble, so it's nice to have a warm body to put up on that pedestal."

I slumped back against my bed. "It's too much, especially since the guy is still on the loose."

"From what I was able to gather, the crime lab is analyzing the blood they found at the scene. They'll find him."

"If the blood is even his. I could have shot a street mime for all I know."

"Either way, the world's a better place."

I was glad to be talking with Andy, spending some time with him. He was looking better than he had on Monday, and in my heart of hearts I wanted to believe that his uplifting article had done a positive number on his spirits. "I guess if you need anything for a follow-up, you know where I'll be."

"Yeah, I spoke to your doctor on my way in. Looks like she's going to keep you here, at least overnight, for observation, maybe run a few more tests."

"What'd you think of Dr. Brenner?" I asked, trying to stifle an impish smile.

"She seemed nice."

"Nice is good," I said, then, after a moment. "Nudge nudge."

He did a slow burn in response to my not-so-subtle hint. "Since when did you become a yenta?"

"Since it occurred to me that maybe the reason you always look like you've been run over by a truck is that you need someone in your life."

"Unlike you, who looks that way because you've *been* run over by a truck."

"Seriously, Devane. How come there's no one special?"

"Amanda, on my beat, most of the women I meet are either dead, widowed or about to be convicted of something. Either that, or they're reporters like me, which means they're lacking in the very same social skills. Hook up with one of them and I double the misanthropy in my life."

I sat up as best I could, and tried to shrug away the stiffness in my shoulders. "Which is another reason why you should go talk to our friendly young intern out there."

"Now, wait a minute. Last I knew, I wasn't the only one staying at the Celibacy Suites."

"Checked out Wednesday night," I said, and this time the smile won the battle for my lips.

Andy wasn't the sort to pry for gooey personal details, not when they weren't meant for publication, so he stood and rubbed his legs to get the blood flowing again. "Is it serious?"

"Too soon to tell."

He made a show of looking around the room at the floral displays. "These from her?"

"Dunno," I said. "Haven't had a chance to read the cards."

"Hmph," he said, and glanced out toward the corridor, wondering if he'd see Dr. Brenner, then at his watch. "I've got to get back to the newsroom, but I'll be in touch. I have questions, but they can wait. Glad to see you're okay."

He stood there awkwardly before coming close and planting a hug that was short on squeeze. "I'm not Charmin, you know."

"Yeah, well," he mumbled, his head still resting on my shoulder. I guess he reconsidered, because we embraced again, and that time I could tell he meant it. As he pulled back, he asked, "Anything I can do?"

"You can see about getting my phone hooked up. I feel like a potted plant just sitting here, hoping somebody will come by and talk to me."

"Sure. Anything else?"

"Could you call someone for me and let her know where I am? Unless you planted that somewhere in your copy."

He smacked his chest as if mortally offended. "Please," he said. "I would never. Can't say the same for some of the other hacks. What's the number?"

As I gave him Jeannie's name and number, I was suddenly grateful for the spotlight I'd been thrust into. If she'd picked up a newspaper or turned on the television, she might have heard that there'd been an incident at The Bottom Line, but no casualties. Otherwise, she might be worrying about where I was, and if I was okay. She was my special someone, a woman who cared what happened to me above all others, and more healing than anything Dr. Brenner could pre-scribe.

CHAPTER 29

▼

By 4:00, the phone had been hooked up, Jeannie had arrived and we'd fallen into a sort of domestic routine: I was the slug, and Jeannie made sure that none of the hospital personnel came by with salt.

Despite my protests, the little lady had decided that she wasn't going to that night's concert without me, and Dr. Brenner was quite clear that I wouldn't be returning to the scene of the crime. At least, not for another 24 hours. She'd retrieved my ticket from my apartment and brought it, along with her own, to St. Vincent's. We'd decided that we'd give the tickets to Randy and Diane, and let them invite who they may. That was part of my second phone call. The rest was back to sticking my nose where it didn't belong, asking my partner to sniff around for any details about Gordon that came across the wire.

"I've got a buddy down in Durst's precinct, and he filled me in," Randy had told me. "The blood that they retrieved from Sixth Avenue came back with a DNA match. Guy's name is Gordon Spiro. He's an electrician from Indianapolis. Seems a few years ago, he got busted after a bar fight. Judge sentenced him to get anger management counseling. Now here's the ironic part: Seems the group that ol' Gordo attended was big on tapping into your creative side. Leader would have members paint, do things with clay..."

"Write songs?" I hazarded.

"Yeah. When they searched his apartment, the Indy cops found dozens of notebooks with staff paper and musical scribblings. Must've known he could never be the next Mitch Black while the first one was still alive, so he sets out to destroy the original."

"Doesn't matter whether Mitch is dead or just retired. Once he drops off the map, Gordon's got an entrance."

"Exactly."

"So where is he now?"

"That they're not sure of. He took a flight into LaGuardia from Indy on Tuesday, and left himself with an open return. Business being what it is, I'm sure the airlines were more than happy to cooperate."

That's when Jeannie arrived, with Dr. Brenner on her heels, so I had to go back to being a model patient.

"That reporter friend of yours just asked me out," the good doctor said, her perturbation tempered by romanticism. "And somehow I get the feeling that you're not an innocent bystander."

I hadn't had the opportunity to fill Jeannie in on my adventure in matchmaking, so her scoff-filled gaze made an amusing counterpoint to Dr. Brenner's disbelief. "I had to do *something* to pass the time. All this bed rest is making me antsy. Besides, Andy's better than anything you could get in the hospital pharmacy. Fewer side effects, too."

Maybe it was much ado about nothing—it wasn't as if they'd been on a date yet—but there she stood, hands on hips in true sitcom style, fumbling for a response. "Come on," I said. "He's smart, he's funny, he's kinda cute. And judging by the hours you put in here, you probably don't have time to cultivate anything on the outside."

"Who says I'm even looking?"

"If you weren't, you'd have told him no and we wouldn't be having this conversation."

I thought that might put an end to her dodges, but she had one more in her lab coat. "If he's so great, why haven't *you* taken him off the market?"

Jeannie answered for me, taking my hand and kissing it gently. "Oh," said Dr. Brenner. Then, a split-second after the sledgehammer hit home, "Oh!"

I smiled, running my hand along Jeannie's face, stroking it, and hooking around the back of her neck that I might hold her close. Dr. Calamari hadn't gone quite so far as to forbid sex, but with Dr. Brenner, it might be a few months before she let my pulse race. She even broke up our mini-clench under the guise of taking my blood pressure, but my libido knew better.

While the lady in white pumped up the cuff on my arm, my gal in the green sweater went around to the various bouquets and examined the cards, calling out the names of the senders. There was one from Mitch, one from Randy and Diane, one from Pete and the Renzos, one from Janet Seeber, my racquetball partner at the 11th Precinct, and a batch of asters with no card. It wasn't from my parents. If they knew about my condition, they'd bring themselves and send food. Besides, they know I'm not really a flowers kind of girl. Never have been. Not since I was forced to wear them in my hair for an uncle's wedding when I was 6, and proceeded to be besieged by bees.

Of course, when you're stuck in a hospital bed, the thought of visitors is generally what keeps you going through the tedium of doing nothing. Still, it's somewhat disconcerting when someone comes to see you, and you don't know who that person is. The young woman who arrived shortly after Dr. Brenner's departure was such a question mark, but she was sure she was in the right place.

"This is so cool!" she exclaimed, pointing at me as if I were some ancient relic in a museum. Then again, to her, I probably was. She couldn't have been more than 23, tall and thin, with pale blond hair that puffed around her head and cascaded down to her shoulders. She was nicely dressed in a light-blue blouse and navy slacks, but the shoes and purse gave her away: not that I'm an expert at brands, but together they looked like they cost more than my monthly rent.

"Can I help you?" Jeannie asked, taking a step toward the interloper.

"Oh, yeah. Um, hi," she said. "I'm Gloria." She shook Jeannie's hand and waved at me. "I'm like, the *biggest* Mitch Black fan, and, like, after shelling out 500 bucks for a ticket to tonight's show, it'd totally suck, y'know, like, if he'd gotten killed or anything."

Gag me with a spoon.

"Would have been a bummer for him, that's for sure," I said.

"Totally. So I just wanted to, like, thank the person who saved his life. 'Cause now maybe he'll go back to recording and stuff."

I couldn't imagine what "stuff" she was referring to, because there didn't seem to be much of it between her ears. "Yeah," I said. "That'd be nice."

"So, um, Gloria," Jeannie interjected, trying to shoo this pest out the door with her body English, "what brings you by? I mean, it's really sweet of you to want to show your gratitude and all, but Amanda's really got to rest."

"Oh, sure," she said, suddenly sidestepping Jeannie to look me in the eye, "but, like, what I really came for is to deliver a message. You know, for her ears only."

Jeannie looked back at me with concern, but I gave her a Samantha nose-twitch of reassurance, sure that Gloria in all her ditziness was harmless. Or at least, mostly harmless. Still, my personal protector wasn't quite convinced. "Who's the message from?"

"My father."

I'd run into another father-daughter tandem recently, but this wasn't Merlin's little girl. And there weren't many middle-aged men I could think of who'd have something to say to me. But after flipping through the dusty old record collection in my brain, I came across a recent hit. And if I was right, I understood why Gloria had been doing her own song and dance. "It's okay, hon," I said. "Just give us a few minutes, would you?"

Jeannie slid her hands into her pockets, mildly annoyed that I'd undercut her authority. "You want anything from the gift shop or the vending machines?"

"Nah. Hopefully my parents will be coming by with lemon squares. Or cowboy cookies. Either of those trumps anything you can get here."

"Yeah, okay," she said and skulked out.

What surprised me is that the Valley Girl I'd been speaking to went with her, leaving a cool professional in her place. "You asked my father to find someone for you."

That pretty much confirmed my suspicions, but I couldn't be too careful. "You're Sam Pelillo's daughter."

She pulled the chair up close to the bed and sat. "He'd prefer to keep his name out of this transaction."

I tried to picture the capo I'd lunched with just the day before, looking for a family resemblance. Maybe something in her nose, or her dark eyes, but otherwise she took after her mother. "What transaction is that?"

"I asked him to cancel your debt. Your account is cleared."

"What?!" I could hardly have hoped for anything better, but my skeptical nature wanted to know what was in the fine print. "I mean, I thought we had an arrangement."

"Understand something, Miss Ross. That little act I put on when I came in here is the public persona I've adopted to protect my father and myself. As long I can keep the feds thinking that I'm just this dippy blonde, I can keep them from applying the thumbscrews. Not that I'd ever give them anything on my father, but I don't want to be put in that position if I can help it. But there was one scrap of truth in all the Broadway I dished out for your friend: I am a huge Mitch Black fan. Have been since I was, I don't know, 11 or 12. And when I read in the paper that there was this cop who'd saved his life, how could I not do something to show my gratitude?"

Made sense, I guess, but then again, I couldn't imagine what it was like to be the child of a mob boss. The only lie I've ever had to perpetuate for the sake of my father was that I was watching my cholesterol. "But how'd you find out that I was indebted to your father?"

"Dumb luck," she said with a shrug. "I called my father and asked him what would be a good way to say 'thank you' to a cop. He said, 'Is this cop on the payroll?' I said, 'I don't think so.' So he asked, 'What's his name?' I told him, and he came up with the idea. He was about to dispatch someone to your place anyhow."

"Why?"

She pulled a folded envelope out of her purse. "Here's the information you were looking for. I haven't opened it, so I don't know anything more about what went on between you two."

"Three," I said. "We had company."

"Oh, Frankie," she said with a laugh. "That sounds about right. These days, Daddy seldom goes anywhere without him."

"I don't like him," I said, as if there were anything more to say about a killer for hire.

"The ice in his veins has spread to his heart. Makes it impossible for him to care about anyone, really, and just as hard for anyone to care about him."

"Sounds like you know him pretty well."

"As well as anybody, I guess. He's been working with Daddy for 10 years or so…" She trailed off, as if deciding whether to let fly with a piece of personal information. "And he's been trying to get into my pants since I'm about 15."

"You just playing hard to get, or what?" Even as the words dribbled out of my mouth, I could hear how ludicrous they were. What business did I have prying into the sex life of a mob princess? For that matter, why did I care? But at the same time, I thought about Gloria, and how lonely it must be.

"Not that I'd ever sleep with a snake like Frankie Dean, but my father has had a hard and fast rule, which he espouses to every man that comes knocking at my door: 'Fuck with me, I might still respect you. Fuck with my daughter, and I'll be sure to bury you.'"

"Must make it hard to get a date."

Hey, if I can find someone for Andy, how hard can this matchmaking stuff be? What single guys do I know?

"First dates, no. Second dates, yes. Sure, I get offers at work on occasion, but not anything I'd ever follow up on."

"What kind of work do you do?"

"I teach second grade at P.S. 74 in Queens."

"Sounds rewarding."

"To a degree. But there's so much bullshit that teachers have to deal with. I mean, the kids are great, but the regulations, the parents, the budget cuts, the pressure...I don't know how most people stand it."

"You stand it, obviously."

"Yeah," she said, smoothing out her slacks, "but it's not like I *have* to work. I could just sit on my ass watching soap operas and game shows all day, and never have to worry about paying the bills. That's maybe the one real benefit of being who I am."

Just like everyone else, she was a woman who could use a friend. An outside ear to bend. "Have you always known about your father's line of work?"

"My father," she said curtly, "is a contractor."

"Oh, cut the crap, Gloria."

Did I just say that?

"Look. You've been a straight shooter with me, and I've been one with you. I'm not asking about your father's business dealings, or details about who he does business with. We're just talking, and I was just curious. You seem pretty up front about the whole arrangement, and I was simply asking if it'd always been that way."

"Cops and their questions," she mumbled, reminding me that she was the one in charge of this conversation. "My father was arrested the day of my sweet sixteen. Seeing him hauled off in handcuffs, in front of all my friends, that may have been the worst thing I could possibly have imagined. Especially since, up until that point, he was just an ordinary guy who had dealings with cement companies and plumbers and electricians. Not some larger-than-life figure who's in every national crime database, not some name that gets mentioned every time someone with an Italian-sounding name gets killed. But after that day, after his lawyer got him out that very night, he sat me and my brother down and explained most of it. He said he couldn't tell us everything, for our own protection, but he didn't like lying to us. In his words, 'This family comes before that family.'"

Somewhere, in another chapter of my life, I might have been able to feel sorry for a woman like Gloria Pelillo. Sure, I'd made a deal with the devil, but I didn't have to live with him. Nor did I have to grow up wondering whether my father might get whacked. But this was one broad suited to the life she'd been dealt. There was no question in my mind, not as she stood up and strode across the room. Not as she froze me with a cold-blooded stare.

"Be aware, Detective Ross, that this conversation is off the record, on the Q-T and *very* hush-hush," she said, my mind vainly struggling to come up with the movie she was quoting. "And that includes your little chickie at the coffee machines. Because I'm not about to have my personal life added to any O.C.U. dossier. And besides, the one thing I do know about your meeting with my father and Frankie Dean is that we've got pictures. And I'm sure Lt. Donald Dingman of the Internal Affairs Bureau would be very curious to know why you were having lunch with two of the most infamous men in New York. Do you, like, get my drift?"

The charade was back on, and I would be forever caught in its sticky strands. Still, I'd come through the scuffle without a scratch, and that's how it always seems to be: Men blow things up, and leave it to us girls to put it all back together.

CHAPTER 30

▼

The envelope was my box of Cracker Jack, and I could hardly wait until Gloria left, that I might claim the prize inside. After all, the Microwave Bomber had taken one life and nearly destroyed two more. The power of police persuasion might be the only way to ever know why.

The name was unfamiliar to me, as well it should be. In my mind, bombing is an act of cowardice, a reckless disregard for life, limb and property—and in this case, the culprit didn't even have the balls to push the button himself. He merely set the stage and let Charlotte sign her own death warrant. For that reason alone, I was more than happy to turn him over to the 20ᵗʰ Precinct.

"Perelli."

He sounded like he was packing it in for the day, heading home to yet another family who lived in the dark cloud—a cloud that could rip open with a single gunshot or other on-the-job peril—leaving them to molder in the rainstorm of Those Left Behind. "Jason, it's Amanda Ross."

"Hey there, kid. Nice work at The Bottom Line."

That again. "Yeah, thanks, but er, that's not why I called."

"No, of course not. I should be the one calling you. Just that a triple homicide came across this morning and I've been out canvassing all day."

"Gang related?"

"Maybe. 'Til we get somebody to say that they saw something, all we've got is what the lab boys can dig up."

"Same old, same old," I said, "but it turns out this is your lucky day."

"Ooh, don't tell me...Cy Sperling is offering free hair transplants for cops."

"No."

"The IRS picked me for its Pay No Taxes program."

"Jason."

"What, did Kate Winslet ask for my phone number *again*?"

The guy was, as the old folks say, *meshuggah*. "Are you done?"

There was a pause, and I could hear him rifling through the papers on his desk, searching for more nonsense to hurl at me. "Come on, this is A-list material."

I'd hate to hear the B-list stuff.

"No, Jason, what I've got in my hand is A-list material. The name and address of the guy who blew up Charlotte Kilmer's apartment."

Another pause. "You're kidding."

"Nope. No kidding. Doctor's orders."

"Jesus."

"Not exactly. Carlos Ruiz."

"And did Mr. Ruiz just happen to show up by your hospital bed with flowers and a sincere apology for making things go boom?"

"No," I said, hitching myself in the bed. "And before you ask, the answer to your next question is: You don't want to know. The NYPD doghouse isn't big enough for the both of us."

More paper rustling. He was uneasy about it, and that was understandable. "Amanda, I don't want you to get burned for this."

"Already been burned for it. I don't think my eyebrows will ever be the same." The laughter came slowly, but it came, and I knew that Perelli was in for the pound. I gave him the little bit I had on Ruiz, and followed it up with, "What I want to know is who he's working for. Somebody had a reason for wanting Charlotte dead. Not me, not Pete. Just her."

"The ex is always a good bet."

"It doesn't look good with him still among the missing, but that's a little too convenient, if you ask me."

"Hey, convenient would be nice once in a while."

"True that. Now go. Mr. Ruiz is waiting."

I hung up the phone to find Jeannie standing in the doorway, arms folded, face in full glower. She'd heard part if not all of my conversation, and her voice was scolding. "What do you think you're doing?"

"Impersonating a police officer," I said. And when that failed to crack a smile, "If I do it again, you have my permission to cuff me."

"Don't think I won't," she replied with a mix of hurt and circumspection. I wasn't taking the situation all that seriously, and by extension, I wasn't taking her seriously. In her diffidence, she pulled the chair away and sat, sullenly. "You can't expect me to just stay on the sidelines and watch you kill yourself."

Five days into this relationship—or was it six?—and we were about to have The Talk. A bit early, perhaps, with far too dramatic an intro, but she'd called the question. I exhaled. "When you're with a cop, you need to be made of sterner stuff. Because for me, every day is a suicide attempt. And the good days are those I make it through to try again tomorrow. It's a life into which thousands of husbands and wives, boyfriends and girlfriends, entwine themselves every year—but the ties that bind never give any slack. If you can stand being at the end of that rope, day after day, year after year, then you've got someone to hold the other end. If not, walk away now, before you've got enough to hang yourself with."

She pulled her legs up and sat quietly, my speech hanging on the wall like the Hippocratic Oath. Only if she left, harm would be done—the kind that doctors can't fix.

After a long time of John Cage silence—crepe and squeaky soles on the linoleum, equipment and custodial carts wheeled back and forth, the rhythmic beep of my heart monitor, the mouse roared. "Can't I be just a little selfish?"

"Come here," I said, my arms open wide, a giant baby wanting to be picked up. My eyes never left hers as she crossed to my side, interlacing her fingers with mine. "I wouldn't be in this thing if you weren't."

She kissed me then, and rested her head on my chest. A waking dream that turned into a real one as I drifted back to sleep.

The phone woke me some time later, and I opened my eyes to see Jeannie lunge for the receiver, leaving my parents in the dust.

"Hello?" she whispered. "Oh, hi. Yes, she's here, but she's sleeping right now."

"I'm awake!" I protested.

"Oh," she said, continuing in hushed tones. "Sorry. It's Mitch."

I waved to my folks before taking the handset. Their conversation, positioned as they were on the opposite side of the room, got lost somewhere in Morpheus' fog. "Mitch Black Fan Club."

"I was about to ask how you were doing, but I think I just got my answer."

"I'm doing all right for someone who's been shot at, checked into the boards and had her head spring a leak. How about you?"

"I'm over the scared part, but that's just because today's been totally insane. Seems like every news outlet in the country has jumped on this story."

"Really."

"You're the one they should be talking to."

"I've already got a reporter on my case 24/7, and he's all I can handle about now."

"Still," he said. "I owe you a lot…and if there's ever an Amanda Ross fan club, make sure I get the newsletter."

It was sad to hang up with him, not because I'd never hear from him again, but because the years between phone calls were too many, and the chances to spend time with him—like Wednesday night at my apartment—too few, if another one would ever come again. Missing the concert was minor; missing the man was something else entirely.

"You okay?" Jeannie asked, noticing the brimming tears in my eyes.

"Sure," I said. "Fine."

Liar.

"And I hope you two didn't come all the way down here on my account," I added with a smile that was pure bluff.

My mother and father came over, dragging the lone chair. Mom took it while Dad perched gently on the edge of the bed. "They taking care of you all right, sweetheart?" he asked.

"Absolutely, Daddy." I hadn't called him that in years, but I felt like a little girl, safe from the beasts under the bed, in the closet and in my head. And my recent confab with Gloria had left me wanting for a father's protection. He must have spent part of the day at work, for he was wearing a suit and tie, his usual uniform for when he saw patients. He wasn't affiliated with St. Vincent's, but it was a safe assumption he had colleagues who were.

"Why didn't you call us on Monday?" Mom asked. "Jeannie here tells us that you were hurt in some kind of explosion in your building."

"I didn't think much of it. You know me. Hard-headed."

"Don't be ridiculous, Amanda. A hematoma is no laughing matter."

"Please, Daddy, I've already got a doctor here to lecture me on all the things I'm doing wrong. Please, just stay here with me, all of you."

None of them had a problem with doing just that, and in short order they had rounded up another two chairs and broken out the vittles. My father, no stranger to hospital food, had insisted on bringing in deli sandwiches, along with red potato salad and coleslaw. They'd brought four sandwiches, just in case there was another mouth to feed, and Jeannie seemed genuinely thrilled to be included as part of the family.

"This one's for you, honey," Mom had said, handing me a wrapped package. I was so famished that I'd torn off the paper and taken a bite before realizing what it was I was eating. Something disgusting and wonderful from my childhood, something I'd never order myself, for fear of the disapproving looks from behind the deli counter: tuna fish and Genoa salami, with American cheese, on white bread. The only one I'd ever found who could stomach this particular concoction of mine was a neighbor's golden retriever, who'd raided a sidewalk picnic and stolen half.

There in my hospital room we talked, we ate and I formally introduced Jeannie to Cal and Emily Ross. She looked over at them and smiled a secret smile, and I wondered just how long they'd been alone together while I slept. Long enough for at least one embarrassing tale from my youth to be shared.

About halfway through our repast, Jeannie remembered something she had to tell me, and we waited patiently for her to finish a mouthful of roast beef. "I almost forgot," she said. She took another moment to sip some ginger ale, then added, "Randy stopped by to pick up the tickets. Said he was disappointed we couldn't be there."

"I think we're all a little disappointed on that score. Did he say who he'd gotten to take them?"

"Somebody named Janet." My racquetball partner. The one who'd sent flowers. Last I'd spoken to her, she had a new beau. Name had something to do with ducks. Drake. Maybe Donald.

Once we'd cleaned our paper plates and tossed the plastic cutlery, we caught each other up on things that were happening. Personally, I was waiting for another Melody Rapp update, but I suspect my mother wanted to wait a little while before letting Jeannie in on *that* aspect of Ross family humor. Instead, my father told us of the pranks that had gotten played on the new chief of surgery, while Mom filled us in on the latest celebrity wedding she'd been asked to prepare pastries for. I let Jeannie tell them about how we'd met, and our first date at Fairway. It was like a miniature slumber party; all we needed was pajamas and sleeping bags. Well, I was already in a flimsy hospital nightgown, so at least one of us was dressed for the occasion.

Yes, they were spoiling me silly, and if that's what a hero's welcome is like, then I highly recommend it. But underneath all the frivolity and the food—Mom had brought cowboy cookies *and* lemon squares—I could see how deeply concerned they were for my well-being. They had every right to be, and I made a promise then and there—to myself, that is—that I would be more careful and take better care of myself.

We finished off the night with a few rounds of Nothing, a card game I hadn't played in two decades, but for which I hadn't lost my touch. Mom had taught it to me, along with Cribbage, Backgammon, Casino and Chess, helping to fill many a rainy day. True to form, she still carried a deck of cards in her purse, and Jeannie was more than willing to play along. Dad sat out the game, choosing to seek out one of his med school chums in Urology. Besides, Nothing—where each player tries to accumulate as few points as possible—can't be played with more than three people; there just aren't enough low cards in the deck. Even though she swore up and down that she'd never played the game before, Jeannie managed to come up with a perfect hand—all four aces and all four queens—something neither my mother nor I had ever accomplished.

"Cheater," I said, sticking out my tongue.

"Poor loser, poor loser," she retorted, sticking her tongue out as well.

The insults quickly got more elaborate and less mature, and by the time the word "boogers" escaped somebody's lips, Mom had had enough. "You can both knock it off right now."

Apparently Jeannie and I had the same mischievous thought at the same time, because I caught the glint of complicity. And even after years of disuse, Mom's radar remained a finely tuned instrument. "No jumping on the bed!" she exclaimed, before either one of us could get in a single bounce. We just looked at each other, and laughed at how silly we could still be. It was the laughter of children, the kind so infectious that even a sourpuss grown-up like my mother was not immune to its charms. Soon, the tickling began.

Once upon a time, when we were 6.

At 10:30 or so, Dad returned, with news that the staff wanted everybody out so I could get the rest I needed. We dillied and dallied with our goodbyes, Mom whispering in my ear, "She's lovely, honey." It's not like I regularly brought girlfriends home for approval, but it made me feel good knowing that she fit. In fact, they even offered to accompany her back uptown.

"Um, no thanks," she said, looking back at me. "I think I'm going to stay if they let me."

"Are you sure that's the smart thing, dear?" Mom asked. "She really should get a good night's sleep."

"So should I," Jeannie replied, staying her ground. "And my best chance for getting one is right here. Besides, I left her alone last night and look what happened."

"She's got a point, Emily," Dad said with a laugh.

There were more hugs and kisses and promises to come by for brunch before the older generation took its leave. Even then I could hear Mom say to Dad, "It's about time she took an interest in computers, don't you think?"

Jeannie closed the door behind them and retrieved another gown from the closet. I got out of bed for the first time in too long, to brush my teeth and pee. By the time I got back, Jeannie had stripped off her street clothes and donned hospital attire. Fashion-less twins we were, as we both climbed into bed. We didn't say much as we lay there watching the news; I held her and she nestled in my arms. There were more reports about the progress at Ground Zero and retaliatory action against Afghanistan, and even as I watched the clips and saw the towers fall for the 900th time, I was no longer overcome. I was able to look at the images with clear eyes, and reflect upon them with the indignation that America was beginning to feel—and which Mitch had so eloquently put into song.

My emotional straitjacket had fallen away, leaving me naked in the here and now. And with Jeannie sleeping softly beside me, feeling her breath against my hand, the tickle of her skin against my bare legs and feet, I finally felt like I belonged there. As one of the living.

The past had done its job, serving as prologue to the something else I'd been looking for. Something special. Something beautiful. And maybe, just maybe, something perfect.

CHAPTER 31

▼

I awoke to find someone staring at me—or rather, at us. Jeannie had been asleep, but stirred as I pulled up the sheet in a fit of modesty.

"Which one o' you is the patient?" he asked, his voice garbled by remnants of a Southern drawl and a terrible set of teeth. The man was African-American and linebacker huge, but with soft, expressive eyes and a gentle face. "I only got meds for one.".

I waved my braceleted arm at him and he brought over a pill with a glass of water. I was tempted to say that Jeannie and I had been forced to double up due to hospital budget cuts, but I didn't think he'd find that funny. So I took my medicine and angled the bed so I could sit up—making myself more comfortable and cheating Jeannie out of extra winks at the same time.

"Next time you get yourself hospitalized," she mumbled, "ask for a queen."

Much of the morning was spent waiting; I got the impression that I'd be discharged soon, but Dr. Brenner would want to see me before she gave the okay. As much as I longed for the comforts of home, I'd already done the AMA thing.

And look where that got you.

For breakfast, Jeannie and I split a bagel that had had all the New York siphoned out of it, and a cup of orange juice with more pulp than a saw mill. After the previous night's feast, this was cruel and inedible punishment, but a few leftover lemon squares—properly congealed—prevented outright mutiny.

Dr. Brenner came by at around 11:30, by which time Jeannie had gotten herself dressed, spoken to her housemates and brushed my hair; I'd played with all of the buttons on my adjustable bed and counted ceiling tiles.

"How'd things go last night?" Dr. Brenner asked. "Any problems?"

"Nope."

"How about this morning? Any headache or nausea?"

"No."

"Dizziness?"

"No."

"Blurry vision?"

"Strike three."

Still, she checked my pupils, pulse and blood pressure, and had me walk around the room so she could monitor my balance. My legs took a minute to rise and shine, but I didn't stumble over any furniture.

"You know, you're very lucky, Amanda," she said as she watched my progress. "What happened Friday night may have been a false alarm, but don't think for a second that you're clear of a possible recurrence. One more incident like that and you could be down for the count."

So tell me, how long have you been a motivational speaker?

I acquiesced, not only agreeing to serious R-and-R, but also promising to check in with my regular doctor in two weeks. She drove a hard bargain, but it was worth it; I was sprung by 12:30. While I got dressed—my clothes had been washed, folded and stacked in the closet—a wheelchair was corralled for the trip out. Once I was mobile, Jeannie went ahead to flag down a cab, leaving me and Dr. B alone.

"I pulled an early shift today," she said as she pushed me toward the lobby, "so I agreed to let your friend take me to dinner."

"Good for you. But I do have to warn you about something."

"What?" she asked with concern, as if I were about to tell her that he wore a hairpiece, or chewed with his mouth open.

"If he's home before 11," I said with my sweetest smile, "he turns into a pumpkin." I was casting light into a dark place, hoping to generate a spark—or at least chase away the shadows that had blackened Andy's soul.

Jeannie and I took the taxi ride uptown, but she had the cab leave me off at my building. "I have some things to take care of," she said. "I'll stop by this evening."

"Maybe I'll invite James down and we can order in a pizza," I replied. "It's about time the two of you met. I think you geeks would have a lot to talk about."

"Oh, you haven't begun to feel the extent of my geekdom, missy. Just wait until you get to class tomorrow."

With everything that had happened over the previous six days, I'd forgotten about how this whole thing with Jeannie had started. In the end, I couldn't have asked for a better birthday present.

I had been out of my apartment for less than 48 hours, but I found myself exploring it like a child in a toy store. Everything was wonderful and magical and mine—and Carlos Ruiz had failed to take it all away from me. In that regard, living—simply breathing, thinking and walking the Earth—was truly the best revenge.

Having him hauled away in handcuffs feels pretty good, too.

My answering machine was nearly full, mostly with interview requests, partially with well wishes from friends, relatives and people at both the 11th and 20th Precincts; Mimsy chewed up more tape than any of them. There were also a couple of messages from Jeannie early on, before Andy had gotten in touch. That got me to thinking, and what might have happened had I not been able to ask for her. How would she have known where to find me? Who would know to call her? It would be both presumptuous and optimistic to make her my In-Case-Of-Emergency person, but I felt a little long in the tooth to still have my parents listed on all of my contact information.

Where and when does one draw that line in the sand? What is the boundary between a fling and something full-flung? She'd met my parents, my partner, some of my friends. We'd slept together, broken bread together, spent the night in a hospital together. We'd had a week of adventure, instruction and tears. Does that make us a couple? Is it time to raise the stakes?

Fortunately, I didn't have to give myself—or her—an answer right away, for my cogitation was interrupted by the arrival of yet another supporting player in my life story: J.T.

"How ya doin', kid?" he asked as I let him in.

"Better than the dodo, but not quite ready to commit to an adjective."

"Oooookay," he said, and I realized it was the first time it'd ever been just the two of us. No Mitch, no band, no bar patrons. There was something else missing, too: The attitude. The womanizing swagger. J.T. looked almost lost as he kept his gaze flicking about, barely making eye contact. Without the fanfare, and with no skirt or spandex to chase, he was just a guy. So used to having people around him, but lonely just the same. Perhaps even lonelier than I had been.

"So, what brings you by?" I asked, leading him into the living room. "I was just about to make some lunch, if you're interested."

"No, thanks. I don't wanna interrupt anything. I just, um, Mitch wanted me to give you this." He handed me a plastic Tower Records bag. "He'd have brought it over himself, but he didn't want to point the press corps in your direction. Me, I can still travel under the radar."

I looked in the bag and found two cassettes, each labeled with the words "Bottom Line," but no other marks. "He tell you what these are?"

"Bootlegs of a sort," he said with pride. "Made from the sound board at last night's show."

"Tell him thanks, but that wasn't necessary. I mean, I'm sorry I missed the concert and all, but he didn't have to—"

"Have a listen, Amanda. Some things can't be said with flowers." He flashed me the smile, the one that had charmed off so many pairs of panties, and I knew why his routine worked so well. In that moment, I felt special, as if no one else in the world mattered. Yet instead of a perfectly rehearsed line, or a well-placed caress, J.T. gave me a platonic buss on the cheek. "Thanks for being there."

"My pleasure," I said, hugging him in return. I let him out to ply his testosterone elsewhere, happy to have seen a gentility that he hid from public view. If I could find someone, anyone could—even J.T. He just needed to try more groupies on for size. One of them was bound to fit.

I put two eggs in a small pot of water and placed it on the stove to boil. While waiting for that, did a quick survey of the apartment for any screaming-Mimi chores that wouldn't go away or couldn't be ignored. I'd shopped on Tuesday and done a thorough cleaning on Wednesday, so I was all right on those fronts. However, clean socks and underwear were on the verge of becoming endangered species, so laundry would be tomorrow's order of the day. When my eggs were ready, I ran them under cold water, peeled off the shells and mashed them up with some mayo, paprika and black pepper, and slathered the salad on rye bread. I poured myself a glass of ginger ale, popped the first of Mitch's tapes in the stereo and sat back for lunch and my own private performance.

The audio was great, with a minimum of crowd noise, and the event started just as it had on Friday night, only with a different deejay coming out to sing Mitch's praises. Once again, the band kicked off with "Sometime, Anywhere," and with my mouth full of egg salad, I closed my eyes and pictured myself back at The Bottom Line—sitting down this time—grooving to the music and enjoying every minute of it, rather than having it serve as background to my ongoing search for Gordon.

It was when Mitch took to the mike to say a few words that the Friday and Saturday programs began to differ. "Thanks to word of mouth and the Internet," he began, "we no longer have the element of surprise, and I'm sure a bunch of you know what's coming next. But last night, that wasn't the case. None of us saw what was coming, and chances are, I wouldn't be here right now if it wasn't for someone looking out for me. She, uh, saved my life, and so the band and I just wanted to say…"

There was a brief hesitation before the group joined together to play and sing, "I'm gonna take you by surprise, and make you realize, Amanda." I nearly fell off the couch when I heard that, not wanting to believe my ears. "I wanna tell you right away, I can't wait another day, Amanda."

I sat up and stared at the stereo, prepared for the worst, but after a moment, Mitch redeemed himself. "No, that's not what we want to say…especially since I know how much she hates that song." And he was right; that Boston ditty had plagued me all through high school. "Truth is, my friend Amanda, a detective with the NYPD, mind you…"

Mitch paused once again, and I felt a flush of embarrassment as the audience broke into raucous cheers; the concert was a benefit for, and tribute to, my comrades who had given all on 9/11 and in the days after. To even be considered in that company was the highest compliment he could have given me. After the applause, he continued, "Amanda was one of my first fans, someone who came to see me when nobody knew who I was, and nobody would pay five bucks to hear me, much less five hundred." The crowd laughed. "And the best way I know of to say thanks is to just keep playing. To keep making music. So I think she'll be happy to know that I've been on the phone with my agent and the people over at Vertical Records, and that we'll soon be heading into the studio to make another album."

More ecstatic cheers, and I found myself clapping along. "And now," Mitch said, "back to the regularly scheduled concert. This next number is our little tribute to New York, and to all our fans, I promise you, it *won't* be on the new album."

They launched into "New York City Rhythm," followed by the still-untitled 9/11 song, and the medley of hits I'd previously heard. When it came time for "Lonely Hours," Mitch explained that Amy would not be joining them onstage, and he had bought a new acoustic guitar for the occasion. The song, which he'd written in the aftermath of his broken relationship with Beth, was just as poignant and touching—maybe even more so in the intimate setting of The Bottom Line—as when I'd first heard it.

Subsequently, the band smoked through Mitch's catalog of hits, including "Brigade," "Face in the Mirror," "Temptation" and "So Much More," before leaving to a deafening chorus of chants, claps and cheers. After the requisite cooldown, the group came back on and the crowed quieted down.

"Anyone who's ever been to one of our shows knows that this is the point in the set list where we do that drippy love song that everybody's sick of." The crowd fired back a "Nooooooooo," and I could just picture J.T., Tommy and Gil with their "Not this song again!" faces. "But before we do that, I'd like to introduce someone. I only met Randy a few days ago, but sometimes you just get a feeling about someone. And as my mother would say, 'He's good people.' So, Randy, why don't you come on up here?"

This couldn't be _my_ *Randy, could it?*

There was a smattering of polite applause before he spoke. "First of all, Diane and I would like to send our best to Amanda Ross. She's the detective Mitch was talking about earlier, and she's been my partner for two years. She was supposed to be with us here tonight; in fact, she's the one who gave us the tickets. But she had a close call last night, and now she's recuperating in the hospital. The doctors say she'll be fine, and partner, I just wanted to say thanks for being my mentor, my protector and most of all, my friend."

It was hard to tell if Randy knew he was being recorded, or if he knew I'd hear his sentiment, but I found myself mouthing the words, "You're welcome."

"But there's someone else I have to thank tonight. Someone I haven't known as long, but with whom I'm hoping to make up for lost time. Diane, the beautiful young woman sitting right there, you've come to mean so much to me in the short time we've been together, and right now I can't imagine spending another minute without you—much less the rest of my life. You warm my winter nights, and keep the sunshine in my days when clouds roll in. And that's something that I need...now and forever. So I ask you in front of all these people, will you marry me?"

I never heard Diane's response, but I assumed she said yes, for a few seconds later, the volume spiked with exuberant cheers and applause. I was in tears, and wondered how many others were moved by the proposal. Mitch, reclaiming the microphone, said simply, "This one's for Diane and Randy," and dulcet piano tones gave the moment wings. "Just Short of Paradise," Mitch's first #1 hit, became a group sing-a-long and turned the joint into an early reception. Even when the song ended, people still called for kisses.

Mitch closed the show, as he usually did, with "Parting Shot," a blitzkrieg bopper with a killer drum and guitar solos. But by that time, it was nearly 4:00 and I was worn out. I faded out before the music did.

The apartment was dark when I woke, suddenly. I wasn't sure what time it was, or how long I'd been asleep, or even, for a moment, what room I was in. As my eyes adjusted to the blackness, my ears picked up on something, a noise, a creak, a sound that shouldn't have been, and that made me completely sure of one thing.

I wasn't alone.

CHAPTER 32

▼

In that flash of an instant, I nearly forgot everything I'd learned in the police academy and on the streets. I almost called out—before screwing my head back on and covering my mouth. Anyone I knew would identify himself (or herself) soon enough; anyone else, I wasn't about to let know where I was. So I waited.

And waited.

And then panicked.

Where is my gun?!

The horrible realization hit home; I hadn't seen it since firing it on Sixth Avenue. In the best of situations, it had been tagged and bagged and was waiting for me at the hospital security office. More likely, and more frightening, was that someone had swiped it before the paramedics got to me.

I tried to get adjusted to the darkness, but there was just too much of it; even the LEDs and other indicators on the stereo had gone black. The power was out—no, it wasn't, for I could hear the echoes of a football game rising from a television set below. It was just me; I'd blown a fuse. Or had it been blown for me?

Silently, I rolled onto the floor, working to get my best vantage point. There wasn't enough clearance for me to squeeze under the couch, and the bedroom was probably where the intruder was lurking, rummaging through my things—or making a plan to kill me in my sleep. Lucky for me he missed me—dozing in the living room—on his initial entrance.

I heard the noise again, definitely from the bedroom, and I began to have notions of surprising him, ambushing him like some crazed jungle cat. Beat up and bruised as I was, though, I didn't feel like a jungle cat. More like a water buffalo. Or one of those poor, defenseless gnus that always get eaten on Animal Planet. And in a savannah as small as my one-bedroom apartment, there weren't enough places to hide. Part of me wanted to yell for help, or whatever it is that gnus do, but it seemed premature until I could size up my predator.

Quietly, I crept in the direction of the kitchen—the only "room" in the place with two ways in and out. If I could get my hands on a carving knife, or even my serving fork, I might be able to defend myself against a sudden attack.

As I reached the tile floor, I heard the bathroom door swing, followed by a loud "swish" as he swiped open the shower curtain. I straightened up and slowly fingered my way across the counter in search of something sharp; given how I packed my kitchen drawers, opening one was far too risky. I encountered the stovetop and bare counter before coming to the sink and drain rack. Jeannie and I had been too thorough in tidying up after Wednesday night's dinner party; nothing there except my lunch dishes, and an egg slicer wasn't much in the way of protection.

I stepped back, trying to decide whether the broom closet or refrigerator held more promise. Neither contained anything particularly deadly, as far as I could remember—unless I could get him to decimate his taste buds with jalapeño peppers.

The bathroom door banged into the adjacent wall; frustrated by elusive prey, he must have given up on stealth altogether. The question was, would he cut into the kitchen directly, or swing back around through the living room? In just my socks, I wasn't much prepared to maneuver apace, so I needed every advantage I could glom.

I got one when I heard his footstep on the hard floor. I gave myself half a beat, then whipped open the freezer door as hard as I could. Stainless steel met bone and cartilage, and I could hear the crunch as his face got flattened on impact. I don't know if he reeled, but I couldn't chance going in his direction. I darted into the living room and swung around, yelling out "Help!" as I rushed into the bathroom and locked the door.

I'd bought myself a little bit of time to regroup, come up with a plan and listen. In response to his unusual case of freezer burn, my pursuer let out a string of obscenities that made me realize I'd heard the voice before: Gordon. I'd stopped him in his tracks, and he was seeking payback.

The bathroom door wouldn't hold him long. With the hall closet behind him, there wasn't enough room for him to get up to ramming speed, but a solid kick or two would likely split the wood around the knob. I grabbed the box of matches on top of the toilet and struck one, giving myself enough light to check for munitions. Under the sink I found some scented candles from a long-ago romantic evening, and lit them.

The first kick came just as I was reaching for the can of Aqua Net. I heard the door start to splinter, so I popped the top off and stepped back into the bathub and waited, candle and hairspray at the ready.

Even though I expected it, Gordon's second kick—successful in breaking through the hollow door—gave me a fright. He had with him a hunting knife, his silent-but-deadly weapon of choice. Had he brought the shotgun he'd used on Sondra, I'd have been splattered all over the bathroom tile. But this time, he had to get up close and face to face, and that was my out.

"Nowhere to run," he said, he voice shrouded in shadow. He was dressed entirely in black, save for white adhesive tape wrapped around his left arm, just above the elbow. "And I'm going to have my eye for an eye."

"That the chorus of one of your songs, Gordo?" I said, keeping my finger on the aerosol top but the can out of sight. "Another lame-ass lyric from a no-talent hack?"

"Black's the hack," he spat. "Needed you to save his punk ass. But there's nobody here to save yours."

He took aim and stabbed, but I sidestepped the thrust and unleashed hell. One spritz of hairspray turned my flickering light into a flame thrower—and I burned the monster down.

"Aiighhh! You cunt! You bitch!" he screamed as he fell to his knees, pawing at his scorched flesh and smoldering clothes. For Mitch, I took a parting shot, punching him right where the bullet wound should be, and he howled as I rushed past him and into the hallway.

"Help!" I yelled again as I ran for the front door. Just before I got there, I collided with something. Something hard. Something that said "Ow, shit."

There's somebody else here!

I tried desperately to get away, my feet skittering in the entryway, but there in the dark, I felt something grab my arm and whisper softly, "Shh. I'm here to help."

Under the circumstances, I found that somewhat hard to believe, but what choice did I have? Gordon was down but not out, and since he knew where I lived, I could never be sure that I was rid of him until the nails were driven into his coffin. Mitch had lived five years in fear from this man, and me and my invisible accomplice were going to put an end to the reign of terror.

We could hear Gordon stirring in the bathroom, incoherent mumbling mixed with yelps of pain as he discovered the extent of the damage. Yet as he staggered out into the hall, there was no question he planned on finishing the job. His words were perverted by the seared flesh on his lips and tongue, but his rage came through loud and clear: "You fucking twat, you're going to regret the day you were born."

Standing by the door, the blackness had eased somewhat, light from the hall creeping in like spiders on a fan-shaped web. I could make out enough of an outline of my new compatriot to know that he was shorter than me, but not much more. In Gordon's jerky motion, I caught the briefest glint of steel.

"Get by the door," said the voice softly, "and on my cue, jerk it open as fast as you can."

As I slinked over to the door, I thought I knew what he had in mind: Blind Gordon long enough so that we could escape. It was a plan that would have worked, only my comrade in arms had a different agenda.

"Now!" he called, and I pulled the door open.

Light flooded into the room, chasing away the darkness and virtually scalding Gordon's retinas. Who knows how long we had been in the dark, but he recoiled…as a vampire should. He'd been battered and burned, relegated to the ranks of the undead, yet still he kept coming.

Until a shot was fired.

The torn and melted flesh of Gordon's hand clutched at his throat, and the ghostly white of the sudden lightstorm turned to crimson. He was gasping for air, one arm flailing wildly, struggling to take out as many enemies as he could. I stared in horror as the blood flowed, the eyes emptying of feeling, of thought. Unable to do anything for him, I raced to the phone, and found it dead. Gordon had cut the line, and in so doing stripped away his only chance at survival.

I threw myself out into the corridor and began banging on my neighbors' doors, screaming that someone should call 911. I may not have wanted Gordon to live, but I couldn't watch him die.

It was over by the time I returned to my apartment. The man who had fired the fatal shot, he had never moved. Short but sinewy, he had dark hair pulled back into a ponytail, and a beard that could use a manicure. In his hand was a .22 pistol.

"Who are you?" I asked, averting my eyes from the corpse before us. "And what are you doing here?"

"I was in the neighborhood," he said with a nervous laugh. "I had planned to come by to say thank you. Thank you for saving my life. Somehow, I think I just did."

He took me by the elbow and led me out, but stopped beside the door to Charlotte's apartment. Together, we sat, waiting for the police to come. I saw the lines of hardship that had worn into his face; he looked to be about 40, but could easily have been younger. His Dio T-shirt just confused matters, as did the large plush penguin he was toting.

"Allow me to introduce myself," he finally said with an exhale. He offered his hand. "Vic Renzo."

CHAPTER 33

▼

Within about 45 minutes, my apartment had turned into something I was all too familiar with: a crime scene, with detectives and photographers and forensics personnel. I could deal with having all these people traipse in and out of my personal space. I could even deal with the blood stain that might never quite come out of my carpet. What I was having problems with was my role in the whole affair: "victim." Or rather, "intended victim." For some reason, I found that a lot more disturbing than "blood stain," which I'd almost become on Monday.

Once the power was back on, Vic Renzo had a lot of explaining to do. Fortunately, he had no problems laying it out for the crew from the 20th Precinct. He had dropped by his ex-wife's apartment, mainly to see if there was anything he felt Pete should have. The one thing he discovered was the penguin, the first toy Vic remembered buying for his son. He would try to return it to the boy, and if Pete was too old for stuffed animals, it was something Vic himself would treasure.

It was as he had said to me; he literally was in the neighborhood when he heard me cry for help. He retrieved the gun—which he knew Charlotte had kept, even though he never approved of it—from the hidden storage compartment in her nightstand, and crossed to my door, which he'd found open. He had just entered, and was about to make himself known, when he and I went bump in the night.

The detective from the 20th, an older, grayer sort named Baker, took everything down and asked Renzo to come by the station to give a full statement.

"Am I going to jail for this?" he asked.

"Doubt it," Baker replied. "Guy had a knife, so self-defense'll prob'ly stick. There may be some jam on the weapon itself, but you say it ain't yours. We find it's registered to your ex, you should skate. Not for nothin', but the D.A. ain't likely to prosecute no one who saved a cop. You did the right thing."

Vic Renzo had used necessary force. Excessive? Maybe, but I'm glad he was on my side.

Eventually, the medical examiner took away the body of Gordon Spiro and the various suits and uniforms took their leave. Vic and I sat in my living room, waiting for Jeannie, and I asked him about his whispers in the dark, about how I'd saved his life.

"You know anything about chaos theory?"

"Um, no, not really."

"The books give an example of how a butterfly on the other side of the earth could flap its wings, and that little change in air current could have a devastating effect on the weather, some 10,000 miles away. Sometimes, you're the one who gets caught in the storm. Other times, you're the butterfly."

I wasn't sure what this had to do with anything, but I let the man talk. "The butterfly is the one responsible for the damage, more or less. And that's where I come in. Charlotte died because of me."

Renzo went on to explain that he had a severe gambling problem, one that initially cost him his marriage, but ultimately a lot more. "I made the mistake of telling someone I was on the verge of discovering something totally new, a radically different way of encrypting computer files. The kind of protection that no one could get through, not even the best hackers. And that was my entry into the underworld, for this one guy, Dominick, started fronting me cash. He said he'd bankroll me; he just wanted a piece of my technology. Deep as I was in the hole, it seemed like the only way out.

"But you can't get something for nothing, and ultimately Dominick wanted the software. And if I'd been able to do what I thought I could, I'd have given it to him and that would've been that. But it didn't work. And no matter how many times I went over the code, how many times I ran the program, I couldn't find the bug. I tried to explain to Dominick that these things take time, and that eventually I'd get it going. He wouldn't have any of it. He had me dragged out of my apartment, and he set me up in a basement somewhere, with a bed, a computer and a thug watching the door. He expected me to sit in front of the terminal and figure the damn thing out. And when I couldn't, he decided to turn up the flame."

I was beginning to understand. "He said he'd hurt somebody close to you if you didn't deliver."

"Yes. And I begged him, pleaded with him not to do it. It tore me apart to hear it was Charlotte."

"Seems to me, if they really wanted to hurt you, they'd have gone after Pete."

"They take away my boy, they take away my reason to live. As crappy a father as I might have been to that kid, he's the only thing I ever did right."

The rest was pretty simple. Once I'd given Perelli the bomber's name, they'd picked him up lickety-split. Carlos Ruiz was an explosives geek, one who liked to play with fire and C4. But he wasn't any kind of master criminal, and when Perelli squeezed—told Ruiz he could get the death penalty for attempted murder of a cop—he squawked. Sold out the man who'd hired him: Dominick. To hear Vic tell it, Dominick had gotten so enraged by all the delays that he was ready to pull the plug—not just on the program, but on the programmer, too. When the police arrived, early Sunday morning, the party was over.

"I'm sure somebody down the line is going to show up, expecting me to settle my debt," Vic said, standing up and stretching. "But until that time comes, I'm trying to do right by the people I meet. Starting with you."

I stood with him. "So, now what?"

"After I go down to the police station, I'll get in touch with my parents, let them know I'm okay. And if Pete wants me in his life, then maybe I'll give the daddy thing a second go-round. See ya, Amanda, and thanks again."

"Ditto," I said, to yet another person disappearing through the revolving door in my mind. Then, realizing there was something I hadn't done, I grabbed the phone and dialed.

"Hi, this is Randy. Sorry I can't take your call right now, but please leave your name and number and I'll get back to you."

"Congratulations, kid," I said after the beep. "Sorry I couldn't be there to share in the moment, but the doctors had other plans. I think she's wonderful, partner, and I wish you a lifetime of happiness. In the meantime, next time I see you two together, I'm going to shower you with champagne. Savor the sweetness, Randy. Savor the sweetness."

I hung up, and for a brief instant, I was there at The Bottom Line, awash in the joy that the future and all its possibilities bring. Mitch was performing; Randy, Diane and Jeannie were singing along; and all of New York was smiling, sharing and celebrating. Just short of paradise, indeed.

My own sweetness arrived shortly thereafter, but she turned sour upon seeing the blood and catching a whiff of flame-roasted flesh, the odor that hadn't even begun to fade.

"This is what you call taking it easy?" she asked sarcastically.

"No, this is what I call staying alive. Gordon was here."

"What?" The tartness slipped into sympathy as she threw her arms around me. "Oh, dear God, I'm sorry. What happened?"

"Come sit down," I said. "You miss a few hours with me, you miss a lot."

"I'm beginning to see that."

James came by around 7:00, by which point Jeannie and I had lit candles, opened the windows and sprayed plenty of air freshener. The odor wasn't gone, but it had dulled some to resemble a failed cooking experiment rather than, well, a successful one. Besides, once James and Jeannie sized up each other's computer knowledge, they were off and running, talking about RAM and ROM and gigs—with nothing more said about Gordon. I was able to interrupt just enough to ascertain that Jeannie wanted sausage on the pizza and James wanted mushrooms. Once the 'za arrived, mouthfuls of crust and cheese were enough to bring that conversation to a close.

"Do you have a good hair stylist?" James asked suddenly, as he mopped a blot of sauce off his chin.

"I haven't found someone here in the city, if that's what you mean," Jeannie said. "Why, you do hair on the side?"

"No. Just that Psycho Kitty over here will turn your hair gray. You'll need a colorist inside of a few months."

I threw a piece of crust at him. "I don't care if she goes bald. She'll still be beautiful to me."

"*I* care if I go bald!"

The chit-chat didn't get nearly as puerile as it had the night before, but we had a good time just the same. James gave us a little more detail about his disastrous trip to Boston, and Jeannie talked about things she wanted to do around the city—only her pronouns were leaning heavily on "we" and "us," rather than "I" and "me," and that made me smile.

For the most part, I kept quiet for the rest of the night, listening to two of the dearest people in the world to me. Even when Jeannie talked about going down to Ground Zero, even when I went into the bathroom—where the charred smell was still overwhelming—I didn't fall apart and my world didn't collapse. Wacky Jacky might have a thing or two to say about it, but from my perspective, I was mentally ready, willing and able to return to active duty. And with any luck, the physical stuff would soon catch up.

After all, if I'm going to keep doing the kind of crazy nonsense I'd done all week, I might as well get paid.

Epilogue

▼

The next morning, after Jeannie and I spent another chaste evening in bed, we went down to Ground Zero. For some things, there are no words to describe them, save for the emotions they stir. We were both overcome by horror and sadness, disbelief and anger, staring in shock at the falling of something so mighty. There were tears in my eyes for the people who had paid the ultimate price, but I found an inner strength that had long been missing. Even though I had brought my camera, the images were permanently burned into my brain, and I needed no other record. Anyone else who might care to see them could catch the continuous loop on CNN.

For spiritual uplift after that, we decided to do an abbreviated version of my planned tourist trek. We goofed around at Madame Tussaud's, rode on a double-decker bus and tried to get into the Empire State Building, only to find that the observation deck was still closed to the public. We both snapped lots of pictures, and had the occasional stranger take one of the both of us. When she had to get up to New York Tech for a 3:00 class, I sneaked off to my neighborhood one-hour photo place and had the rolls developed, so I had something to bring to class that night.

Over the next few weeks, I did my regular check-ins with Wacky Jacky, eventually obtaining a clean bill of health. In consultation with Dr. Brenner, I got the same from my GP, and just after Thanksgiving, I was back on the force full-time. To celebrate, Randy and Diane came by with a cake. I didn't shower them with champagne, as I'd promised, but there were plenty of hugs and tears. They're planning a September wedding, and they're registered at Macy's, in case you're invited.

Now that I've got an e-mail account, I'm able to keep in touch with Pete, and he's doing fine upstate with his grandparents. His dad is renting an apartment nearby and is working for a software development company in the Executive Park outside Albany. Vic still hasn't conquered his encryption program problems, but he hasn't given up, either. Meanwhile, Pete is making lots of friends at his new school and his grandparents have shown him how to ride a horse. He's adjusting pretty well to "country life," although he misses some aspects of city living. The Renzos have promised to bring him to a Mets game sometime next season, but it's not quite the same as having the ballpark just a subway ride away. And yes, he took the stuffed penguin; he keeps it on his desk, next to his Mike Piazza baseball.

Country living has been something of a regular topic these days, and it began shortly after Jeannie moved in with me in early December. Seems she's been putting out resumes, looking to get a teaching job, and many of her best prospects are upstate a ways. Not as far north as Albany, but still a good hour and change outside of the city. It's given me a lot to think about, since I've forever felt that Manhattan was in my blood, and it's where I would always stay. But my city had been damaged, and I with it, so maybe it's time to move on. I'll keep you posted.

Meanwhile, Jeannie still hasn't shown me the pretzel thing. She says she's saving it for a special occasion, like our anniversary. The tease.

Finally, right around Valentine's Day, record stores and Amazon.com were flooded with requests for *Five Years of Solitude*, the new album by Mitch Black. It contained the post-9/11 song he'd unveiled at The Bottom Line, now titled "From the Ashes." Strangely, the day I bought myself a copy, one arrived in the mail. I didn't quite understand the significance until I looked at the track listing and saw the title of the last song: "Protect Me." I quickly pulled out the CD and popped it in the player, skipping to the final track.

> "In a time when the signs
> Are flashing 'Danger'
> And we can no longer count on
> The kindness of strangers
> We must fall back on friends,
> The kind who don't pretend,
> Who see us through to the end
> And help wounded hearts to mend.

Protect me.
Deliver me from evil
And the terror deep inside.
Protect me.
Shine a guiding light
So I no longer have to hide.

When duty called one and all,
You were more than I could be
To slay the dragon breathing lightning
And set the whole world free.
I'm just a shooting star
With acoustic guitar,
But word will travel far
How wonderful you are.

Protect me.
Deliver me from evil.
And the terror deep inside.
Protect me.
Shine a guiding light
So I no longer have to hide.

In a time and place where no one knew,
Somehow you found the thing to do.
I think you know just what I'm saying:
It's 'cause of you that I'm still playing."

After a high-voltage (no pun intended) guitar solo, the chorus repeated, so I
ripped out the liner notes to read the lyrics over again. In small type, just below
the title, were the words "For Amanda."

Mitch had said thank-you in the way he knew best: through his music, but he
had an encore that even I couldn't have imagined. I turned to the last page of the
CD booklet and found a white piece of paper taped there. Carefully, I undid the
tape and unfolded the paper. It was a signed and notarized contract, giving me
one percent of the royalties from *Five Years of Solitude* and every subsequent

album Mitch recorded, plus 50 percent of the royalties from the single "Protect Me." It was a grand and outrageous gesture on Mitch's part, and I responded in familiar fashion.

I fainted.

0-595-30665-9